I0556481

The Many Universes of Mickie Dalton

The Third Volume in the Mickie Dalton Trilogy

Michael Davies

The Many Universes of Mickie Dalton

First Printing June, 2008 in the USA
Second Printing November, 2008 in Australia

ISBN: 978-0-9818087-2-7

Published by The Mickie Dalton Foundation
Kempsey, NSW
Australia

Acknowledgements

As before, my sincere thanks for the support of the Principal of St Joseph's, Mr Peter McGovern and the Head of English, Mr Andrew Rout, to Leanne Whittall who ran the classes and to Jennifer Rush for setting up the contact with Andrew Rout.

To the young people who made this project such an exhilarating experience, my admiration and affection.

James Arblaster
Paul Foster
James Goddard
Evan Hayes
Vincent Muller
Alicia Quinn
Samuel Troutman
Sebastian Wattam

Catherine Fitzpatrick
Melissa Foye
Michael Guinery
Gabrielle McCann
Adam Piovarchy
Michael Robson
Tarryn (TJ) Viney

And once more, to Callum in Australia and Linda in the USA.

To Judy Casey

For everything

Chapter 1 – Conflicts of Interest

"Hey, this is just like playing Loopies in Hangar Ten, but in the open!" Melkana leaped off the ramp of the shuttle and soared three metres into the air, landing with a skilled knee-bend action developed from years of playing their favourite game in the vast hangars of the Ship.

"Well, the gravity is just about the ten percent we set for Loopies," Fencris retorted and followed her dreamlike, slow-motion path to the ground. "Wow, it feels weird having the wind blowing during this," he said with a delighted laugh as he turned back to the shuttle.

"Okay, Drellion, show us how it's done," Mickie said with a wide grin.

"Watch and weep," the youngest of the four said and calmly launched himself off the ramp, turned head over heels four times and landed perfectly on his toes to the applause of his friends.

"Too good for me," Mickie said and tried just a single loop in his path to the ground, but a small gust of wind threw him off his line and he stumbled sideways as he landed, emitting a small gasp of pain as he felt something crack in his ankle.

"Mickie, what happened?" Melkana was the first to get to him where he sat on the grass clutching his joint.

"I think it broke. I just never expected a wind gust! In two years, it's never happened aboard the Ship!"

"Of course not, dummy!" she said. "How bad is it?"

"Just give me two minutes," he said as the others arrived and sat down on the grass with him. The ground was soft enough, but the grass had a slight blue tinge to it, just as the sun of the planet Loomara did. Around them, the trees had a weird look to them, hugely tall and slim, almost like wheat stalks rather than trees, but fifty metres high.

"Ah, the Pfafth thing," Fencris said with a knowing grin. "I must say, that ability to control your own cells is pretty nifty. I wish I could do it." Amusement sparkled in his red eyes, sharply evident in the blue skin of his face that had taken a darker shade under the sun of this planet.

Mickie didn't hear him. His mind was deep inside his own ankle, seeing every cell of each bone, identifying the small crack and instructing new cells to grow, bond and heal the break.

"That should do it," he said, refocusing his vision to the world around him. With a small push down of his hand he rose to a standing position, easy when gravity on this world was less than ten percent of what he had known as a younger boy on Earth.

"So what's all this lazing around by you lot?" The amused voice was Allie's, walking up in the weird, slow-motion style that low gravity caused in those who moved by the use of legs. Alongside her, Grant was less successful, even in the low gravity affected by the cast on his knee resulting from a break during a spirited game of Gravity Ball a few days earlier.

"Your very peculiar son just cracked his ankle trying to outspin Drellion," Melkana said with a grin. "But he's already done that weird Pfafth thing and mended it."

"You're okay then, kid?" Grant asked. "Fully healed?"

"For sure. I'm really glad I remembered how to do that. The memories of life as Markel keep coming up with some wild stuff!"

"No chance you can teach me how to do it, is there?" Grant asked. "This bust knee is a real nasty one."

"Sorry, Dad, wish I could."

It had been a strange few months since Mickie had woken from the half hour in a coma in which he had lived nearly a century as a Pfafth in a time a million years before. At odd moments, new memories suddenly thrust themselves into his mind, and the extraordinary talents of what had once been the most powerful race in the Universe, the rulers of forty galaxies were gradually returning to him. The ability to heal his own body by direct control of his cells had returned only three weeks before when he had cut his hand while working with Fencris on building a small anti-gravity unit and he had found himself mentally entering the wound and directing the cells to heal.

"Okay, panic over then! Allie and I have business to attend to with the city managers. You and all the other kids are free to blow off steam and get some sun. We'll see you for lunch at noon, okay? The computer will remind you."

"None of the locals will come near us?" Melkana seemed disappointed.

"Unlikely," Allie replied. "Alien contact is a very new experience for them and they seem a bit shy. It took us a long time to persuade the Loomaran leaders to have a meeting. I know we want some of the plants from this place, they produce a lovely aromatic oil that works wonders on muscles and joint pains, but so far, we can't work out what they might want in exchange!"

"Okay, see you at noon!" Mickie leaped with every ounce of effort and flew dizzily to the frail branches of one of the elongated trees, at least four metres above the ground. The others did the same and for a while they sat like birds, high above the surface, revelling in the low gravity and giddy sense of height. It was a major effort of will to jump off the branch and let himself float to the ground, but Mickie remembered to bend his knees and prevent the shock of the landing.

"You may not have weight, but you still have mass!" the teacher had warned them the previous day. "Just as in Loopies, there's a lot of kinetic energy, and two of you colliding with each other or with a tree will still hurt, so be very careful!"

"I have to try this outdoors Loopies thing," Drellion said as he landed just a short distance away. "Something about the wind in your hair is a real buzz!"

So for an hour, the group worked at mastering the unusual effects of wind gusts and the distracting condition of having the surrounding scenery move in the wind while they tried to control their leaps and spins. As always, Drellion mastered the new techniques first and claimed a massive victory when he caught Mickie at the apex of a six-metre jump after a quadruple spin that was perfectly timed.

"Bow to the master!" he said with an imperious wave at the group, and was quite undisturbed or surprised to receive a loud chorus of derisive raspberries in reply.

"I haven't even *seen* a local yet," Fencris complained as they sat on the grass for a break. "Does anyone have any idea of what they look like?"

"A bit like the Kaloti, but smaller and thinner," Melkana replied. "I had a squiz on the computer last night, and it's a bit freaky. Their houses are like them, very high and thin."

"They've got a problem if they ever want to go travelling," Mickie said thoughtfully. "This has to be the lowest gravity world anywhere. In fact, I can't understand how it keeps an atmosphere. But it means they couldn't even feel comfortable on the Ship, never mind normal planets, unless they always wore gravity belts."

"It would be difficult even then," Fencris added. "They'd be terribly fragile and they could get horribly hurt by any sort of collision. It would be like us trying to live on Kamotar."

"I suppose." Mickie said, recalling the huge, boisterous race of three-armed beings of a planet where gemstones were as common as gravel. He was about to continue, but the Ship's computer interrupted him as it did all for of the group.

"Fifteen minutes to noon," said the computer, known specifically to Mickie as Albert, and to everyone else by individual names so that direct and private communications could be maintained by each of the crew. By unanimous consent, all four of them turned to head back to the collection of tall, narrow buildings that formed the town. They moved to their meeting with Allie and Grant in a series of high, exhilarating waves that they had never done before with so much space and with the feeling of the wind in their faces. When they reached the agreed meeting place, Drellion was able to stop neatly, having beautifully judged the height and angle of his last take off so that he could stop with a supple knee bend. The others failed to remember that they still had kinetic energy, despite the low gravity and sprawled ungracefully on the ground, coming to a stop by the feet of the astonished and amused adults who were coming to meet them.

"Well, so much for all that training you kids were supposed to be getting with Loopies," Grant said with a partially-suppressed chuckle. "Back to the drawing boards for three of you, I suggest."

In some embarrassment, the children pushed themselves to their feet but then couldn't help laughing at the ridiculous sight they had presented.

"So how did it go?" Drellion asked as they took their places at a table and chairs that seemed to be part of an outdoor restaurant area. The chairs were just benches, though they and the tables were higher than was comfortable for human-sized individuals.

"I think it was successful," Grant replied. "They will be happy for us to take limited quantities of the plants we identified as sources of the oil, and they'd love some of our computers in exchange. I showed them our latest little gadget here, and it blew them away!" He touched the small case he had slung round his neck, lifted it free and placed it on the table. "It's still the only one in existence and it will be until the factory on Kalamos gets geared up to produce more. I brought it along, hoping they'd like it."

"Okay, grub's up!" announced Allie, opening a larger case she'd been carrying. "We can't eat their food and they can't eat ours, so I brought lunch along." She began laying out small covered trays that began heating as they touched the table and the delicious smells of some of their favourite dishes floated around the group.

"So what are they like to deal with?" Melkana asked, lifting the lid off one of the trays and reaching for a fork.

"It was weird," Allie replied. "We've had some difficulties building up a vocabulary and grammar structure from the telepathic exchanges they've had with the Speakers, so this was not an easy negotiation session. The language boxes were only a little help, and we had to sweat out quite a few points using the Speakers, the devices, even some drawings to get ourselves understood, and I'm still not sure we've done it. But if I have it correct, we'll gather about twenty ship-standard kilos of the two plant types we want, check them for quality and of it's okay, we'll leave them the computer until we come back for the next trip on a bigger scale."

For the next few minutes, conversation lagged as they concentrated on lunch, and Mickie realised how hungry he was from the lengthy session of outdoor Loopies. But movement caught his eye off to one side, and he forgot about food.

"Look!" he said. "Loomarans!"

About fifty metres away, a small group of the strangest creatures Mickie had ever seen had gathered. There were about twenty of them, he counted, and they were almost like stick figures he used to draw as a child. They were about two metres tall, he estimated, they had two legs and two arms and a head that seemed greatly out of proportion, being spherical, but about twice the size of a basketball. The limbs looked the thickness of one of his fingers, and not even at the chest were any of them wider than his upper arm.

"I think those are children," Allie murmured. "The ones we've been meeting seemed a bit taller than these."

The Loomarans had arranged themselves in two lines and they began a dance of extraordinary grace. It looked to Mickie like waves of wheat bending in a breeze that varied in speed, so that the waves began at one end of the lines, moved beautifully to the other end and back again, varying in the degree of the depth of the wave as it moved. From somewhere unseen, a musical note began, reminding Mickie of the plaintive, beautiful tones of Fencris' Cangrar pipes. It was entrancing and hypnotic.

"Have they come just to entertain us, do you think, or is this some other form of communication?" Melkana whispered, clearly delighted with the spectacle.

"I really don't know," Allie replied softly. "I'll see if I can get the Speaker to inquire about it."

All of them were becoming increasingly hypnotised by the spectacle, but Mickie caught a tiny movement out of the corner of his eye. Another of the Loomarans had slowly moved up behind them, its thinness being lost in the background of the trees, but Mickie saw the movement when the creature's long arm suddenly moved across the table and seized the tiny case containing the newest and most advanced computer from Kalamos.

With the case in its possession, the Loomaran bolted across the field and the dance before the group stopped abruptly as the dancers joined the rapid flight.

"Oh hell!" Grant stood up furiously then staggered a little as his knee cast hindered his movement. "It was just a distraction for someone to steal the computer! We need that for the final negotiations!"

Mickie and the other kids immediately gave chase. Ahead of them, an excited, triumphant chattering seemed to falter as the pack looked back and saw that the kids were gaining ground. It occurred to Mickie that perhaps they had expected the visitors to be incapable of handling low gravity and were astounded by the speed of the pursuit. But it was Drellion who handled the situation best. Leaping at slightly lower angles of take-off, he rapidly left the other three behind and caught up with the Loomarans. Then he changed the angle, leaped higher, straight at the one carrying the computer and caught it, wrapping his arms firmly round the Loomaran's whole body, pinning the stick-like arms to make it impossible for the computer to be thrown to another of the gang.

In dream-like motion, the two landed and Drellion grabbed the computer case, prising it from the Loomaran's hands and stood away, letting the creature rejoin its friends. He returned to the group of watchers in a series of long, graceful strides, stopped neatly before Grant and handed him the case with a small bow as applause broke out.

"Little bro, that was astonishing!" Melkana said with a delighted laugh and gave him a hug, making Mickie realise with a start that Drellion seemed to have grown in recent weeks and was now taller than his sister.

"Drellion, you cannot imagine what grief you saved us," Grant said and shook the boy's hand.

Drellion laughed with pleasure. "Whoever would have thought that Loopies would pay off so well?" he said.

"Mickie, your attention is required," came the unexpected voice of a Speaker in his mind. It was not the familiar tones of Speaker 356 with whom he had always communicated, and it was a cause for sudden thought about just what mechanism translated a telepathic voice in his mind into a perceived spoken sound. One day he'd discuss it with the Speakers, he decided then returned to the matter.

"Please explain," he said.

"I am Speaker 1241," the voice replied. "And I am about to facilitate communication if you approve."

"Go ahead," said Mickie.

"Mickie, my name is Sendagon," said a new voice, transmitted by the Speaker. "I am about a hundred metres away to your right. I really must talk to you."

Mickie looked to his right and saw a man standing alone, about the distance he had said. "Who are you and why do you want to speak to me?"

"I am Pfafth and your people need you," came the reply that kicked Mickie as if he'd been thumped in the belly. The sounds of celebration around him seemed to fade as the shock ran through his body.

"Mickie? You okay?" It was Melkana who noticed Mickie's mental withdrawal from the group. She touched him lightly on the shoulder. "Not jealous that my little brother got the bad guy for a change, instead of you?"

"That man over there. He's Pfafth and he wants to talk to me."

"Oh-oh! Allie, Grant, get over here," she said softly and waited till the others had turned their attention. "Mickie's had a call from a Pfafth. That guy over by the trees."

"Has he said any more?" asked Grant.

"He said my people need me. He's obviously from inside the Blocked Galaxy."

"What do you want to do?" his mother asked.

"I have to talk to him. But if he wants me to be part of that stupid revenge war stuff, he can go and kick himself."

"I agree. You should do as you said," Grant said. "At least you may learn more about what the situation is. Get him to come this way and meet you half way. And I'll tell Speaker 356 to monitor the conversation so that we can hear it, if that's okay by you."

"Thanks, dad. I wouldn't be surprised if he was also monitoring it for his own people. Speaker 1241, link me to Sendagon."

"Done, Mickie."

"Sendagon, meet me half way between your current position and mine."

"Certainly, Mickie."

Mickie set off, moving slowly in order to get time to force calm upon himself. In a few seconds, he received support from Speaker 356.

"I am now monitoring the conversation, Mickie," said the voice of the entity speaking from many millions of light years away. "And my colleague, Speaker 1241 has no instructions to monitor it for the Pfafth's use."

"Thank you, Speaker." Mickie was close enough now to see that the other man looked perfectly normal, like any Human or Kalamosian, but that was expected, knowing from Markel's memories that the two species were in fact one, physically identical to the Pfafth.

They stopped about two metres apart.

"So what do you want?" said Mickie, not caring about common courtesies.

"We know that you have learned of your origins and your destiny, Mickie. The time is now right for you to come home and do what is necessary for us."

"And just what is that?" Mickie could feel his anger rising (or was it Markel's anger he was feeling? he wondered).

"If you experienced the life of your ancestor Markel, then you know very well what your destiny is," Sendagon replied.

"So it was you who placed that sculpture there for me on Kamotar?"

"Yes, we had it made on Shuramee many thousands of years ago for just that purpose."

"Then you screwed up, Sendagon. Because it turned me right off the whole idea of whatever it is you want to do."

The other Pfafth began to look angry. "That's impossible! The entire message was constructed to give you the real, true story of the Pfafth history and your destiny. Surely you are now ready to take the place history has built for you?"

"The only place I want, Sendagon, is with my family and friends. Take that message back to your Managing Committee. They blew it."

Sendagon's anger was clearly building and Mickie sensed massive frustration and probably fear in the other man.

"Markel, you don't understand," Sendagon said loudly. "It is time now for you to return with me to our home planet. You must meet the people and their leaders and prepare to take us back to mastery of our old Empire."

"And how am I supposed to do that? I'm a fourteen-year-old boy and you expect me to lead the Pfafth?"

"You are not a fourteen-year-old, and you know it. You lived a century as the greatest Pfafth who ever was, you have his memories, his leadership and you also have his powers. In fact, you have far more power than even he did, because you have been subjected to the most intensive breeding program we could devise. Don't you understand, Markel, you will be the greatest individual in the Universe? You will be controller of forty galaxies."

The words shook Mickie to the core, but then he began to laugh, despite the disturbing way the other man was calling him Markel. This was sillier than any second-grade science fiction comic from his childhood. Master of the Universe? He struggled to control the trembles of laughter in his voice.

"So tell me, Sendagon, how many of you can pass through the time gate from your galaxy? And how do you think you will cope with the Sillaron's suppressors that diminish the Pfafth powers? And how will you fight those Sillaron? Like Markel asked you a million years ago, do you know who and where your enemies are?"

"The time gate will not matter. Yes, only about fifty of us can pass through it now, but you will bring the galaxy back into the same time as the rest of the universe. You may not realise it yet, but you do have that power. Just as you have the power to know where the Sillaron are. And somewhere, there must be a solution to the Sillaron's suppressor. We believe you can find it."

Mickie fought to stop his face revealing that he already had found the suppressor and the mechanism to counter it. He had paid for both with a huge diamond given to the women of Korrobodor, the inventors and builders of both devices. *He had the power to move a galaxy in time?* His mind rejected the claim as nonsense.

"Come back with me, Markel," Sendagon said urgently. "The Management Committee is waiting for you, all the Pfafth are waiting for you. We will have a huge state reception, a parade, you will formally take your seat as the Chairman and then we will assign all the teachers and scientists we have to helping you find the powers within you. We will seek out the Sillaron and destroy them and we will be where we were before, the greatest power in the Universe. And you will be the most powerful of all of us."

Mickie stared at the man. Sendagon's face was alight with almost religious ecstasy, his fervour making his eyes shine and he shook his fists aloft like a triumphant boxer over the body of his fallen opponent. Mickie felt sickened.

"No," he said. "I want no part of being a master of the universe. Damn your Management Committee. Damn the Pfafth who want to rule. Damn your war of revenge and damn you for trying to make me care about these things. Leave me alone."

The man seemed to be about to attack Mickie as if he could force him to do his will. Seeing the movement and the rage in the man's face, Mickie held up his hand.

"Are you that stupid, Sendagon? If I have the powers you say, then I can kill you without raising a sweat. Is this what you want?"

Sendagon took a step back, his face displaying his frustration.

"Markel, they sent me to fetch you back. We are trapped and horribly imprisoned forever if you do not come with me. How can we keep on living as a forgotten people when we were once the greatest power in the Universe? Please, Markel, you *must* come back!"

"I may have Markel's cells within me, Sendagon, but I am not Markel. I am Mickie Dalton. I may be Pfafth, but I have no sympathy with your dreams of restoring rule over forty galaxies. Remember what Markel told you a million years ago. *You cannot go home again.* You have a whole Galaxy to claim as your own. What more could you possibly want?"

He turned and repeated the slow, languorous, bounding trip back to his friends and family. Allie folded her arms round him and he could feel her tears in his hair.

"Well said, kid," said Grant. "We're very proud of you."

"Hey," said Fencris and slapped him on his back. His eyes flashed his admiration.

"And you can't be a master of the universe," Drellion said with his wide, glowing smile. "Not till you've beaten me at Loopies, anyway!"

Mickie felt exhausted, but happy. In his sudden confidence, he turned to Melkana. "I think that merits another hug," he said.

She seemed to consider it for a moment, her head on one side. "Well, okay, seeing as you've turned down being the Lord of The Entire Universe," she said with a smile and put her arms round his neck. She kissed his cheek and whispered more privately. "That was pretty damned good, Mickie. You really told that horrible man." Then she pulled away and the magic faded a little. But he still felt as if he had just conquered worlds, though without the complications.

Chapter 2 - Crossing the Time Barrier

"Well, at least we all know we're really safe on this planet, after it used to be the most dangerous of all calls!" Fencris seemed in cheerful mood as the Ship broke out of hyperspace and the world of Zlan appeared in focus in the viewing screens. "I'm looking forward to visiting with you this time and having a brotherly chat with our buddies!"

"Yuck, no!" Melkana said with an exaggerated shudder. "They may be our pals and all that, and I know they've saved our lives several times, but the idea of cavorting around with a bunch of spiders the size of a house, frankly, does *not* appeal!"

"Well, *I'm* coming," Drellion said. "I wouldn't miss this for anything. Those things were utterly awesome, the way they just crash-dived on the Korrobi and wiped them out! Hey, we might even see some of the little yerkels still alive, all wrapped up in silk and being eaten by the Zlan kids!"

"What a revolting idea!" Fencris said. "Not that I don't wish the very worst possible on those things, but I decided I never wanted to see one again, ever."

"Me too," Mickie agreed. "Drellion, nix the blood-lust and just come for the trip, okay?"

"You're no fun, you guys! No fun at all!" Drellion had gained hugely in maturity and confidence since the episode on Loomara. Having saved the trading process completely had made him realise he was more than just somebody else's little brother and was instead a fully functioning member of the crew, as well as a superb athlete. Mickie felt that Drellion had grown five years in the last two weeks.

Leaving Melkana in the coffee lounge, the three boys made their way to the hangar where a large shuttle was filling up with crewmembers who would descend to harvest the invaluable plants that grew so richly on Zlan. This time, there were no armed guards and no sense of fear in the shuttle. While many of the crew still felt great unease in the presence of the huge spiders, everybody knew for certain that these beasts were their close allies and no danger. Another difference existed. This time, the crew had communicated with the Zlan before arrival and had already gained consent for harvesting in an area where there was no risk of environmental damage or causing difficulties for any of the residents.

The shuttle doors opened, reminding Mickie of the last time he had descended alone to meet the Council of the Zlan. It was just a few months ago, but so much had happened since then that it felt like a lifetime, almost as long as Markel's. With Fencris and Drellion, he waited until the harvesting crew had left then they walked out onto the ramp into the scented, humid air.

"I love this smell," Fencris said. "I've never had the guts to come down here before, but I'm realising what I've been missing. *Holy Cow!*"

He was brought up short, the shock exploding into words as he saw that there were hundreds of the Zlan crowded in front of them.

"That is not exactly a pretty sight," Drellion said. He too had stopped, and Mickie could see his hand was clenched tightly on the rail down the ramp. But both boys were staying in position, controlling their natural fear instead of bolting back into the shuttle.

"Stick with me, guys," Mickie said and led the way down to the ground. "We are happy to see you, my friends," he said loudly to the mass of black spiders.

"And you bring us joy with your arrival, young Pfafth," came the silent voice in his head. *"And you too, Fencris of Cassolea and Drellion of Kalamos."*

"Holy Pooh!" murmured Drellion. "I've just been personally welcomed by a mob of bloody great big spiders. This beats everything."

"Your confusion is understandable. We hope you can overcome the fear we know you are feeling."

Drellion swallowed then released his high-voltage grin. "I think you can count on it! This is just so totally cool!" He walked ahead of Mickie and advanced on the nearest spiders. He raised his hand in a high-five, something the boys had learned from Mickie. "Put it there, man!" he shouted gleefully and laughed out loud as the Zlan raised one limb and touched his hand. With the success of that move, he then walked along the front row of Zlan, repeating the process and laughing with the sheer joy of the experience.

"Good grief, is that little Drellion high-fiving the worst nightmares in the whole Universe?" Fencris said, not hiding his admiration at the sight of the youngest of them breaking down all barriers of fear.

"Hard to believe, eh?" Mickie replied. "C'mon, let's go and join him."

As the other two reached the row of Zlan, one reared upright. *"It is good to see you again, young Fencris of Cassolea. We owe you a great deal for the deeds of that day on Korrobodor that allowed us to serve our Pfafth. I was the one that spoke to you then."*

"Well, you scared the living hell out of me," Fencris said.

"I hope no longer."

"No, no longer. You saved us all then, and you are my friend."

"Would you like to see the remaining Korrobi from that day? We still have many feeding our young."

Fencris' blue skin turned a little pale and he shook his head. "Er... no, I think I'll pass on that. But they have been adequate, have they?"

"More than adequate. The quality of their blood has boosted the strength of this year's brood of young Zlan. It was a great hunt that day."

Fencris turned to look at Mickie. "I think that's as much as I want or need to know," he said. "Can we just walk around and get some fresh air?"

"Is there any area you would wish us not to go?" Mickie asked the Zlan.

"It would be best if you stay in this open area and avoid the trees," the Zlan voice replied. *"The forest is where our incubation areas are and many of the hatchlings are about to leave their hosts."*

Mickie shivered a little, realising that the hosts were the possibly still living bodies of the Korrobi who had planned to kill the Ship's children and drink their blood.

"When they leave the hosts, they are not yet capable of communication or comprehension," continued the Zlan. *"They could be harmful. We have directed your harvesting crews into safe areas."*

"Okay!" Mickie waved and set off to tramp around the several square kilometres of open land. Even after only two weeks in flight from Loomara, the fresh air and scented atmosphere was still a great delight and he and the two other boys intended to make full use of the experience.

The exercise was a joy. Although humid, the scents and strange odours were captivating and the boys ignored the heavy sweat they were building up. For all the delights of intergalactic travel on the Ship, the atmosphere aboard was pure, sterile and safe, and the opportunity to breathe planet-bound air was always eagerly taken.

"Wow, look at that thing!" Drellion exclaimed as a butterfly passed a few metres ahead. The wingspan was over a metre and the wings were gold and black, a startling and beautiful sight.

"I don't think I want to see the caterpillar that it comes from," replied Fencris. "Hey, are the Zlan following us? They seem to be everywhere in the trees and way back behind us."

"I expect so," Mickie said, quite unconcerned. "Remember, their whole reason for living is to protect me, and now probably you two as well."

"And the other Pfafth, wherever he or she is," Fencris added.

"That too," agreed Mickie. "I wonder why they can't locate the other one now?"

"Actually, I used to wonder why the Zlan didn't leap to Earth to protect you from your father before they did that first time," Drellion said. "He was certainly beating you up enough."

"Yes, I've been thinking about that, also," Fencris said.

"And did either of you come up with an answer?"

"Yes, I think the trouble was that the Zlan had been conditioned over a million years before, and then the Pfafth disappeared." Drellion spoke thoughtfully. "They had absolutely no idea about it and had forgotten the entire thing. And you hadn't been in a genuine life-threatening situation till that time when the mob attacked you on Earth. Then it triggered off the programmed instincts, but only in one of them. Maybe he had the conditioning nearer the surface than the rest."

"And then once they'd realised it was there, more and more of them rediscovered their own programming until now all of them have it," Fencris said.

"I think that's it," Drellion agreed.

"You know, I think the kid has nailed it," Fencris said. "But now that they know what a Pfafth pongs like, wouldn't they know where the other one is?"

"Probably not," Drellion said. "I think that they need the trigger of being in serious danger. Somehow, they'll sense that, though I'm damned if I can understand how, and leap to the rescue. So it means that the other one hasn't been in a life-threatening mess so far."

"Hah! That's probably right, too!" Fencris said with a laugh. "And let's face it, this little Pfafth buddy of ours has kept them busy enough since his first visit here!"

"You two are just too clever for your own boots," Mickie said, privately impressed by the analysis by his friends. It made complete sense to him. "So we won't probably find the other one until something happens to threaten her."

"You're sure it's a girl?" Fencris looked intrigued.

"I think it has to be," Mickie replied. "I think the whole idea is that we're supposed..." He stopped, feeling embarrassed.

"To start a family and be the parents of a new race of Pfafth?" Drellion finished for him.

"Yeah, that," Mickie mumbled. "And it's a rotten idea. I just want to live normally."

"What, with us lot? Don't be daft!" And with that, Drellion threw a pile of grass he had quietly picked while falling a little behind all over Mickie, who let out a yell and tackled Drellion, wrestling him to the ground. All three began a general battle, releasing all the energy that had been stored while on Ship, rolling in the sweet-smelling grass of the meadow until they stopped, covered in sweat, and lay back to gather their breath.

But after twenty minutes or so, Mickie opened his eyes from the comfortable siesta and realised that a crowd had gathered. He sat up to see that a number of Zlan had approached to within a few metres. In some amusement, he realised that such a sight would have caused heart failure from fear a few months ago, and still could frighten his friends. He looked down and saw they were both lying as he had been, eyes closed enjoying the fresh air. He spoke softly.

"Hey, guys, our spider buddies have gathered around. Remember that they're friends, don't panic."

He watched as the two boys opened their eyes. Both flinched, but showed great self-control.

"Whoa!" said Fencris. "I'm glad you warned us. I think my blood pressure is still up a bit. What's going on?"

"I don't know. Let's ask them."

He got to his feet as the others did the same. Drellion still looked a little white-faced but was recovering fast.

"Is there something you want to tell me, friend Zlan?" Mickie asked.

"There is someone here who arrived a few moments ago," said the Zlan. *"He is Pfafth, so we honour him. But he wants to meet you and we cannot allow it until you consent. Will you meet this Pfafth?"*

"Oh bummer, don't say it's that twit who spoke to me last time," Mickie said. "Doesn't he understand the word 'no'? Anyway, okay, let's see this mysterious Pfafth."

The crowd of spiders parted slowly, opening a channel that lengthened until it was about thirty metres long. As the last spider moved away, a man was revealed, standing motionless, looking straight at Mickie. It was not the man who had accosted him on Loomara. He and Mickie walked to meet each other and stopped a few metres apart. Drellion and Fencris had followed and were standing just behind Mickie. The stranger gave them a quick glance and looked back at Mickie.

"You are Pfafth?" Mickie asked curiously.

"Do you think I could have got here without a ship and stood among these nightmares without being chewed to pieces if I was anything else?" The man seemed amused, and Mickie couldn't help a grin. He noted that the man spoke in the same Kalamosian dialect as his parents.

"No, I suppose your qualifications are pretty good," he said. "So, have you also come to persuade me to lead the Pfafth back to times of glory and mastery of the Universe?"

"Absolutely not. Obviously Sendagon has got to you already. I assume he failed to convince you with offers of leading the Management Committee, state processions, infinite wealth and assorted stuff like that?"

"He failed miserably."

The man took his eyes off Mickie for a few moments and looked at the other two who were staring at him in fascination. "Do you want to continue this conversation alone or do you trust these two?"

"These are my dearest friends and I trust them with my life. Whatever you say to me, I would repeat it to them anyway, so let's not waste time. Why have you come to see me?"

"Primarily to persuade you not to follow the Sendagon path, but it looks like you've already made that decision."

"Yes, I made that after waking up from my life as Markel. Do you have a name?"

"Brandon."

"Okay, Brandon, so if persuading me not to become master of forty galaxies was your goal, is there anything else you want of me?"

"Yes, I want you to come back to our home planet, but not the way Sendagon wanted. This is just for a visit, not to stay. And no publicity, just a tour of the place as an ordinary citizen with nobody knowing who you are."

"Why?"

"Then you would fully appreciate why the dreams of restoring the Pfafth to universal supremacy are so much garbage."

"Why do you want to persuade me of that? Don't you want to be the most powerful race in the universe? And do more of you think the same way you think?"

"Mickie, I think I need to tell you just what's going on among the Pfafth."

"Jeez, it's about time!" Fencris couldn't keep himself from chiming into the conversation. "We're a bit sick of you guys fighting over Mickie all the time! Don't you have anything better to do?"

Brandon's laugh was relaxed and genuine. "You Cassoleans always were very direct," he said. "We're all delighted that the species is rediscovering its old talents. We've missed you!"

He turned serious again and his gaze took in all three boys. "We are definitely split, back on home world. Most Pfafth have grown up and spent their lives in a state of rage and hatred against all things Sillaron. They believe they have been deprived of their right to rule the galaxies again and they live for the day when you will return and lead them there."

"That's insane!" Mickie was shocked by the blunt words from Brandon.

"Yes, that's exactly what it is. Those of us who travel Outside know that time has passed by the Pfafth. But we cannot persuade the others that they have no hope and no right to their old position. Just a few of us have been waiting for you to grow up enough to try and prevent your corruption to that madness. And it's been a long battle. We even sabotaged the Maragos sculpture so that you'd get a true history of Markel's life and what happened."

"You *sabotaged* it? How did you do that?"

"Not just how, but when!" Brandon grinned again and Mickie decided he liked this Pfafth a lot more than he had liked

Sendagon. "The original sculpture was commissioned over forty thousand years ago, before the Shurameen world died and it was Maragos himself who made it. But our people had already decided you had to know the truth and we persuaded Maragos to build in the real history, not the heavily censored history that the Management Committee wanted you to learn."

"Mickie, that's nuts!" Drellion said. "How could they have done something for you forty thousand years before you were born?"

"Not that crazy, young man," Brandon replied. "It was not specifically Mickie here that we were planning for, but whoever finally was selected as the best result of the breeding program to take Markel's place. The candidates that the Management Committee thought might be suitable the last few hundred years have always been called Markel, by the way." He looked firmly into Mickie's eyes. "As were you, a year after you were born. That's why you were named Michael when a Committee agent placed you on Earth and arranged for your adoption. It was the nearest approximation."

Mickie's pulse was pounding. At last he was hearing some definitive facts about his origins. "I was born in that Blocked Galaxy?"

"You were."

"But there were other Markels before me, who turned out not good enough?"

"Oh yes, more than twenty possible candidates were eventually found inadequate. But at the age of twelve months, the standard tests we had developed for the future Markel showed that you were it. You had it all, all the powers, all the abilities, everything was there waiting to be developed as you grew up. That's when you were taken Outside to Earth, the Committee arranged the financial backing to ensure you were adopted and brought up properly."

"Hah!" Fencris laughed in derision. "If that's a sample of the Management Committee's brilliance, then you're right! There's no way those whackoes are ready to rule the Universe!"

Brandon grimaced. "Not good parents, eh?"

"You might say that," Mickie said. "So what do you want to do?"

"Like I said, come back with me, have a look at what the Pfafth have become, make up your mind and then I'll bring you back here."

"I need to check you out," Mickie said.

"How do you plan to do that?"

"Will you agree to a scan of your mind by a Speaker?"

"Of course."

"Speaker 356, are you monitoring this conversation?"

"Yes Mickie, I am."

"The man named Brandon consents to a scan of his mind by you. Is his story true in all respects?"

"It is."

"You've already run the scan?"

"It takes very little time, Mickie."

"I'll say!" Mickie was startled. He switched his attention to the Ship's computer. "Albert, put me in touch with my parents."

"Hey, kid, what's up?" Grant's voice came through immediately. "How are you guys coping being surrounded by nightmares?"

"The Zlan are fine, dad. Another Pfafth has arrived."

"Another...?" Allie joined the conversation. "Is he trying to get you to go back and become lord of all you survey, like the last one?"

"He wants me to go for a visit, but not for that reason. You were right, Allie, there are factions within the Pfafth. This guy is one of the dissenters."

"Have you had the Speaker check his story?"

"I have, Allie. He checks out."

"There's certainly no way anyone can hide the truth from a Speaker scan," Grant said. "What do you want to do, son?"

"I think I have to go with him. He said it would be a private visit, no publicity, nobody will know who I am. He wants me to see what has happened to the Pfafth."

"But can you get there?" Even through the computer's communications link, Mickie could hear his mother's anxiety.

"There and back, Allie. This guy here, his name is Brandon, he'll show me the way through the Time Barrier, though I think I already know how to cross it. And believe me, I have no wish to stay there."

"I hope so, Mickie." Allie's voice sounded forlorn.

"Hey, both of you, I've already said the only thing I want is to be able to be your son and travel with you and my friends. Nothing's going to change that."

"But we'll be out of contact while you're away," Grant said. He too, was showing stress in his voice.

"That's the worst part," Mickie agreed. "But I don't think there's anything can hurt me. I promise I'll be back."

"Mickie, are you sure about this thing?" Fencris was showing serious concerns and similar anxiety reflected in Drellion's face.

"I need to know," Mickie replied and grasped Fencris' hand and shook it, did the same with Drellion, then stepped back. "Hey, tell Melkana what I'm doing, won't you? I don't have the time now to explain."

As the two boys nodded, Mickie turned back to the older Pfafth. "So how do we go?" he asked. "I have no visual point for the galaxy and no clear idea of how to cross the Barrier."

"Something we learned from the Cassoleans," Brandon replied. "I can transmit to you the view of where we go first. It's a loose solar system just outside the Pfafth Galaxy and it's in regular Universal time. Okay?"

"Okay," Mickie said and closed his eyes.

Brandon's voice spoke audibly at first. "Let's see the view from space, first."

Startling in its clarity, the memory surfaced in Mickie's mind of the first time he had teleported from the old Pfafth home world when, with Kerrala he had left under the guidance of a Cassolean girl. He felt himself swoop upward into dark space, so that the world of Zlan hung below his feet. Somehow sensing the mental presence of Brandon, he continued away from the planet, accelerating ever faster until the entire Galaxy was spread below his feet. It was so like the experience of his Markel youth that he felt emotional, almost tearful as he recalled how it was to travel with Kerrala.

"To that galaxy there," came the soft, unspoken voice of Brandon as a huge spiral galaxy appeared, brighter than the others as Brandon somehow highlighted it for Mickie's grasp. He reached out and pulled himself to the beautiful whirlpool of stars, aware that Brandon was with him the whole time.

"Now that one," and another galaxy was seized and used to pull him another few million light years. "And now that one."

They paused above the starry sea of the next galaxy, but Mickie could tell that the Galaxy next along the path was the Pfafth hiding place. He recognised it from the time when the Ship had stalled in its flight there. A moment later they had crossed the millions of light years and were in the region of the Blocked Galaxy.

"Now watch as we move round the galaxy," came Brandon's silent words, and Mickie swooped round the mass of golden light that held no sign of individual stars. Then in front of them, he saw the single star of a small solar system that contained twelve planets.

"The third one," said Brandon as they flew towards it. "That southern continent... the eastern shore... there, that river... that building..."

Mickie opened his eyes to find himself sitting comfortably in an armchair in a beautiful room with picture windows looking out over a river with mountains in the background. This had been his first conscious inter-galactic teleportation... and yet it hadn't ... he could also recall the many times he had teleported during his life as Markel. And now he recalled the fatigue that hit him every time he had performed this titanic exercise of travel, but to his surprise, he felt only tired, not drained of every ounce of energy as he had in the past.

But it had hit Brandon. "This is our safe house," Brandon said, the dead weariness evident in the way his body slumped in another armchair. "There is nothing on this planet but animal life, none of it dangerous. We'll sleep here and cross to the galaxy tomorrow. Going through the gate doesn't need anything like as much energy as the trip here did, but we could have a full day once we get there. Your room's there." He pointed at a door to Mickie's right. "See you in twelve hours." He hauled himself to his feet with difficulty and walked to the other side of the room where another door opened for him. Mickie stood, remembering how he had felt the first trip with Kerrala, wondered if the breeding program that had produced him had increased his teleportation strengths as well, and decided to stay awake for a while longer as he thought about the extraordinary events that were occurring. But two hours later he walked into his own room and was soundly asleep within minutes.

* * * *

Mickie felt like he was standing on the edge of the deepest ravine imaginable. Behind him, all of existence glowed in sparkling gold, stretching for infinity backward and to both sides. Ahead of him, the golden landscape gleamed again, but in between was a jet black gap, utterly without colour, form or depth. Existence and Time stopped at his feet. Beyond was Nothing. But beyond the Nothing, Time and Existence started again. Mickie had no idea of how to measure the width of the blackness.

"It's a gap in Time."

Brandon was standing beside him, looking across the Nothing.

"Just one second, but it's a barrier that almost nobody can cross," Brandon continued. "I've been here many times and it never fails to terrify me."

"What would happen to something dropped into that gap?" Mickie was struggling to control his fear. Somehow he had to cross that void and he was no longer as sure that he could as he had been a few hours before.

"I don't know," Brandon replied. "I've thought about bringing a stone or something and dropping it down there, but something tells me that would be catastrophic. I sense that perhaps it would damage the entire fabric of the universe, maybe disturb Time in some way."

"And we're supposed to cross that?"

"We are. You do know how, it's in your mind. That was one thing that we established when we copied Markel's memories and imprinted them in the Maragos sculpture. I can help you find it."

"What you did, showing me how to get to the Blocked Galaxy and how to reach this portal, that was never a Pfafth talent. We had to use the Cassolean telepaths for that sort of visual assistance."

"Many Cassoleans came with us when the Pfafth retreated to the new home world. Just a tiny handful of us have been able to develop enough telepathic transmission skills to learn that talent from them. There are now fifty of us and we all work for the Management Committee as Agents for Outside. Most of the agents still believe in the destiny of the Pfafth and support the Management Committee's goals. Only twelve of us refused that path."

"Do they know?"

"No, we keep it secret. If they knew of our dissent, we'd be killed. We use our freedom to go Outside to learn what the rest of the Universe is doing and eventually choose a place to live. We look for Sillaron, also."

"So we might have run into one of the other agents when we stopped off at the safe house?"

Brandon shrugged. "There are no more than five or six crossings a year in either direction. The chances were infinitely small."

"But if we had?"

"Then I would have had no choice but to kill him. Your visit must be secret."

Mickie shivered. "Show me how to make the jump," he said.

"Close your eyes."

Mickie obeyed and suddenly got an image much like had got when being shown Fencris' memories of exploring his mind to locate his telepathic skills. He felt as if he were in a strange, yet familiar building, sensing every brain cell and thought that raced through his head. Somehow he was being drawn to a particular location... there was a door to be opened.... he was through it and there he saw a mechanism. It was odd, not a machine, but a way to twist the mind... to drive energy down a particular path... to turn suddenly at just the right millisecond...

"That was it," Brandon said.

Mickie opened his eyes. He was no longer at the edge of Time on a golden landscape. He was in a field. Just a plain, grassy field with a wire fence off to one side, and a breeze blowing waves in the short grass. A hundred metres or so to his left, a small house stood alone in the rural scene.

"Welcome home, Mickie. It's been twelve years since you were last here."

"This is Pfafth home world? Where's the town?"

"A little way off. We always come to this spot when leaving or returning, it saves causing any excitement with the people."

"Why would it cause excitement?"

"Because going Outside is always believed to be the Trip To Recall Markel. You've no idea the religious overtones your name causes. Each time one of us went, if they knew it was happening, there would be mass excitement, prayer vigils, all sort of silliness as the mobs would await Markel's Return to Lead Them Against the Enemy."

"That's insane!"

"You said that before, and you were right both times. The Pfafth are insane. Let's go into that house. There's clothing there, and you have to get out of the Ship's uniform. There's a gravity car to get us into the town."

They set off across the field, walking over perfectly ordinary grass. It could have been any field in England, Mickie thought. Even the house seemed ordinary, just a small, two-storey building of brick, with windows and curtains. Only the remote key that Brandon carried in some concealed place showed the difference, as a door swung open as they reached it.

"Completely impenetrable for anyone without that key," Brandon said with a smile. "And to get the key, they'd have to cut my chest open, and it still wouldn't work without my brain signature. There's a wardrobe in each of the bedrooms, find something that fits you. The styles are all suitable for normal wear."

Ten minutes later, Mickie was looking at himself in the mirror, wearing simple grey trousers, a tee shirt and a ski-jacket, looking like any teenager on Earth. "Not exactly what I expected of a two million year-old civilisation," he muttered aloud. He turned and walked back into the main living area to see Brandon dressed much as he was.

"This is weird," Mickie said. "I could wear this back on Earth."

"You mean, where are the shimmering jump-suits, the brilliant colours, the hi-tech gear? Welcome to the mid-industrial era style of today's Pfafth. You should feel quite comfortable and you fit in well like that. Let's go."

At least the gravity car was a technological advance on Earth, Mickie thought, realising it was exactly the same as he had ridden in as Markel, a million years ago. "These things haven't changed much," he commented as they flew a metre above the ground over the rural landscape.

Brandon didn't reply, but pointed ahead. "Markel City," he said. "Capital of home world."

It didn't look like a global capital city. It didn't seem to have even the scale and grandeur of Mickie's home town of Manchester on Earth, never mind something like New York or London, as he had been expecting. It was just a city, with some tall buildings, nothing exceptional.

"Home world doesn't have a name?"

"It's always been just 'home world.' The original one was called the same. Somehow it never got any sort of name but that. We kept the tradition. The thing now is that this is the *only* world we live on."

"The only...? You mean in this whole Galaxy, the Pfafth are living on just one world? They haven't explored, colonised, expanded?"

"Strange for a race that once colonised forty galaxies and several thousand worlds, isn't it?" Brandon's smile was sad.

"But why? How could you just stick around and do nothing?"

"Because for a million years, everybody just assumed that you'd be showing up soon and leading them back to the old glories, so why bother to colonise this backwater galaxy?"

"It's *insane!*"

"You keep saying that. And I keep telling you you're right."

"So what are we going to do here now? It's called Markel City?"

"It is most certainly called Markel City. Just as the continent is called Markel. At least we didn't call the planet Markel. And we're just going to wonder around, listen to people, read the news and just see what the Pfafth are doing these days."

"And nobody will recognise me?"

"Not a chance. You don't look at all like the original Markel and anyway, there's been such nonsense spouted about him that pictures of him tend to be highly idealised. You're just a kid from the country having a look around Markel City."

"Okay! Where to first?"

"Just a quick tour of the city, I think. It's not that glamorous, but you might as well see it."

Brandon was right, Markel City was nothing glamorous. It was just a commercial city, as far as Mickie could tell. It certainly did not seem to have the historical or cultural points of interest that Manchester had in his rapidly declining memory of his one-time home town. It had few attractive buildings, no major parks and no river ran through it.

"Pretty ordinary, huh?" Brandon said after an hour of traversing the streets.

"That's high praise," Mickie said. "There's nothing outstanding about it at all. What's the population?"

"About two million. Nothing massive."

"No, it seems very small for a world government centre. And what's the total Pfafth population?"

"Are you sure you want to know?"

"Of course!"

"Mickie, the entire population of this planet is just eighteen million."

"Eighteen...? Brandon, a million years ago when you came here, there were eight million. Surely you've grown more than that?"

"We did, at first. Then we were full of excitement and anger and lust for revenge, and the population grew to over three hundred million over the next few thousand years. But things sort of went quiet as we learned that the program to breed you was planned for a million years, and no wild army of reclamation of our old empire was going to happen for thousands of generations. I think the life went out of us about then, and the population has slowly declined."

"That's awfully sad," Mickie murmured, feeling a wave of depression run over him at the way the once proud species had decayed.

"That's the Headquarters of the Management Committee," Brandon said as they pulled into a large city square. The building he was pointing out filled one side of the square, but displayed nothing to suggest it was anything but a dull office block.

"Can we go in?"

"Later, we will. They have the public debates in the afternoon. We'll take a seat in the public gallery. Very few people bother, so we'll have no difficulty."

He steered the vehicle into a parking area and stopped, climbing out as it settled the short distance to the ground. "Let's walk around," he said.

Mickie followed him and the walked over the square to the office building. The front had a large, impressive entrance, and there was a statue some ten metres away. It was of a man, holding his right arm up in what looked horribly like a salute given by the old Nazis of Earth's World War II.

"Oh no, it's surely not?" Mickie said.

"It surely is," Brandon said with a laugh. "That's you!"

Mickie walked up close. He had learned how to read Pfafth script during his hallucination as Markel and now he read the plaque on the stand.

"Markel," it said. *"The greatest of all the Pfafth. He saved us by bringing us here and he will lead us back again one day."*

"Yuck," he said and looked at the statue. The face was noble, the expression one of seeing far into the distance, with concern and strength written all over the face. It certainly resembled nobody Mickie knew and he could not recall how Markel had actually looked.

"Can we move on?" he asked.

"There's a coffee shop over there," Brandon said, nodding at the end of the building and they strolled along the short distance to enter and take seats by the window. The dozen or so other occupants gave them no more than a passing glance. So far, Mickie had not seen anything like the throngs of people he had assumed he would see in the world's capital city, and those he had seen appeared very ordinary. Most had been dressed as he and Brandon were, in every-day working clothes, and he had seen nobody with flair, or great style, no beautiful women, no luxury vehicles, nothing at all to suggest the possible centre of the Universe's greatest civilisation.

"Why is everybody so *dull?"* he finally had to ask.

Brandon grinned. "The last few hundred years, it's been this way. Our sociologists have explained it as a reaction to the impending arrival of Markel. News of your presence Outside has filtered through to here, so we've been gearing up for your return any day. We've been told that you were adopted by ordinary working-class people, so the whole culture of home world now is to be like you. Mickie Dalton chic, you might call it!"

"So they do know my age and that I was on Earth?"

"Not specifically Earth. The Committee didn't want your location known so precisely for fear of Sillaron interference, though how the Sillaron could learn anything happening on home world beats me. But from the start, we've known that only Earth and Kalamos could be your adopted home, having Pfafth-standard beings. Our agents had evaluated both planets over the last century or so and realised that civilisation on both was sufficiently advanced to place the Markel child there, once we had him."

"And what about the second Pfafth? Do you know anything about her? It is a her, I assume?"

"Not a lot. You're right, it's a female, but I don't know much. I don't even know if she's already been born, or was born well before you, nothing. Of course, she has Kerrala's cells, what you would know as DNA, but whether a fully developed Kerrala has been identified, I really have no idea. And I don't believe that she will have been given a Maragos sculpture to teach her who she was. The emphasis has always been on you, the Markel leader being set up to take the Pfafth home again."

"Honestly, Brandon, it all sounds pretty sick!"

Brandon said nothing as a young woman approached and asked for their orders and he ordered two coffees and some cakes. Mickie realised Brandon had spoken in Pfafth, the first time he had heard the language, and though he understood fully, he felt uncertain that he could produce the same accent, given the changes that had occurred over so many millennia. He said so to Brandon.

"Not a problem," the other replied. "Regional accents have developed. You'll be understood and nobody will be concerned. The Pfafth capacity for curiosity has diminished almost to zero, anyway."

Mickie heard the bitterness and sadness in Brandon's tones. "This is very depressing," he said. "And frankly, it's one hell of a let down. Here I am, back on my home planet, and it's one bloody boring place. I think I should go home right away."

"Stick around a bit," Brandon said calmly. "There's much to see. Here, let me read you something from the papers." He reached over to a rack against the wall and pulled a very ordinary-looking newspaper to the table. "Here's a typical item," he said and began reading.

"As tensions rise with the expected imminent return of the new Markel to home world, clashes have broken out between rival sects around the continent."

"Rival *sects?* What the hell are they talking about?"

Brandon smiled a slow, sad smile. "You've become a religion, Mickie. There are some who believe you will raise everybody on the planet to the same level of power as you have, return the galaxy to the same time as the rest of the Universe and lead the rampaging armies Outside to seek out and destroy the Sillaron and take control of the old forty galaxies. That's the orthodox viewpoint, taught in our schools and believed to be the "correct" one."

Mickie was feeling almost breathless with dismay at what he was hearing. He could only shake his head in disbelief. Brandon repeated his sad smile.

"The less-orthodox view, discouraged by the Committee, is that you will return, destroy the Committee for its disobedience to your wishes expressed when you resigned a million years ago, chastise the people for their evil and teach us how to live in peace in our single Galaxy. The two variations in this philosophy are that some think you will restore the Galaxy to the same time as the outside, while others think you will increase the time barrier to lock us in some sort of Purgatory for all Eternity."

The waitress returned with two large mugs of coffee and a plate of small cakes and Brandon didn't speak until she was out of earshot again.

"And these groups fight each other?" Mickie felt cold. "What, they fire mind bolts at each other?"

"Dream on, kid! Less than one hundredth of one percent of the population can still fire a mind bolt," Brandon replied. "About the same number can move objects by the power of the mind, or read another person empathically. I think the number of people who still possess the standard set of Pfafth talents such as we used to have in your time as Markel would be fewer than two or three thousand. Again, the different sects have different views. Some think you will teach everybody so that they get back all the powers, like I said before, the orthodox view. The others think those powers are heretical, and you alone will cleanse the universe of the Sillaron."

He gestured out of the window. "I think you're going to see something."

In the square outside, a parade was marching, entering from one side and filing round to take up three sides, leaving empty the one occupied by the Committee building. Several thousand people were now standing were just a few had previously scurried around on their private businesses. Many carried banners and Mickie looked hard to read those he could see. Finally, he was able to see one full-on to him. *"Markel will Lead Us to Greatness Again,"* it said.

"This is just awful," he murmured.

"Wait a while. It gets worse, if experience is anything to go by."

It did get worse. A man advanced to the front of the office building as several others pushed a small platform to the same point. He ascended and began a speech. His voice was loud, and some form of speaker system was in operation to carry his words over the whole square. The coffee shop was well insulated, so Mickie could only hear odd words and phrases, but what he heard was bad enough.

"Markel, our Leader, our Lord... return our Empire... death to the Sillaron... Markel will return soon... the Pfafth will rule again...."

The speech was frequently interrupted by huge outbreaks of cheers and much waving of banners. Mickie saw another one. *"Markel, please come home and lead us."* After one particularly voluminous roar of applause, the crowd began singing something that sounded suspiciously like a hymn. He looked over at Brandon who was watching the display without expression.

"It's called the Markel Hymn," he said. "Honest! You don't want to know the words, I guarantee. Every schoolkid on home world learns it before he or she is five."

Mickie was beginning to feel physically sick. But things got even worse.

From another side of the square, another group had advanced and they filed into the centre of the area. They too were carrying banners. One said, *"You can't go home again."*

"The opposition has arrived," murmured Brandon. Meanwhile, the coffee shop had cleared as the other occupants had left, whether to join one or other of the sides outside or to get away from potential violence was unknown.

Mickie began to extend his empathic senses outward and into the crowd. What he found appalled him. Mostly the sensation was of rage, of frustration and plain, simple hate. The last was the most variable. Mickie found that some of the hate was directed at the opposite crowd. But much of it was also directed at the Management Committee inside the building. It seemed to stem from frustration, from envy... but as Mickie tuned his senses to read more deeply, he was shocked to discover the main focus of deep, bitter hate was against... themselves. He realised that the mass of people outside were deeply ashamed for the state of the Pfafth race, their fall from supreme power and now their realisation of their imprisonment, blocked away from the rest of the universe but also from their greatest terror, the Sillaron.

The noise level was mounting and Mickie knew that soon

the violence would break out. He saw the first forays by one group against the other side and rapidly the scene became a pitched battle. Again, Mickie extended his sense, looking for mind bolts, but didn't detect a single one. He looked across at Brandon who seemed undisturbed by the scene.

"I read your confusion," Brandon said. "But this scene is common just about every year, this date, the accepted date of the Great Flight, when Markel brought the Pfafth here and raised the Time Barrier. It's a world-wide national holiday and it's why I brought you here on this day, to see this."

"Thanks a lot," Mickie said ironically. "How long does this go on?"

"Any moment, the police will arrive," Brandon said. "Ah! Spot-on timing."

It could have been any riot back on Earth, Mickie decided. He had seen similar sights in Manchester during some spirited anti-war demonstrations, vans full of riot cops, many of them leading charges against massed demonstrators, water cannon, large numbers of arrests and finally a huge crowd of milling, confused people slowly drifting away.

"The greatest species of all time, the rulers of forty galaxies in all their splendour," said Brandon. "See your people, Mickie. You want to lead *them* back to glory?"

"Nobody could lead them anywhere," Mickie said, almost weeping at what he had seen. "They're no longer a super-race. They're just like people back on Earth."

"Exactly. Earth, Kalamos, Pfafth home world, just three identical races, and now the Kalamosians are the most advanced and the Pfafth the least. Finish your coffee and let's get out of here. Not a lot more to see, but I want you to see it, anyway."

He left some notes on the table, picked up a cake from the small plate and downed it in one bite, took a last gulp of the coffee and stood up. Mickie had drunk half his, but had left the rest, aware that it didn't taste anything nearly as good as the

Mayoowani coffee that was standard on the Ship. He stood up and followed Brandon outside.

The place was a mess. Broken banners littered the square, the whole area looked like a heavy rainstorm had passed through, the result of the police water cannons, and here and there, a few bloodstains remained, not yet washed away. Following Brandon as he crossed the square, Mickie deliberately walked over a banner that said, *"Markel, Lead us back to Glory,"* and was pleased to see muddy water seep through and mess up the cloth.

Brandon had entered a small park. It looked quite normal, not unlike the park in Manchester where Mickie's adventures had begun. Pathways meandered through grassy areas, a small pond was visible a hundred metres away and a little woodland stretch followed one of the paths. Most of the people walking down the paths bore the marks of the recent confrontation, and conversations seemed rather limited.

Brandon took a seat on one of the park benches and Mickie's mood stayed bleak, remembering how he had sat like this on Earth when the mob attacked him.. It seemed several lifetimes ago.

"But there's something I don't understand," Mickie said, remembering what was niggling at his mind. "When the Ship tried to get here, all hell broke loose. The computers went crazy, the engines failed, we had voices telling us we had to leave, all sorts of stuff. It was pretty advanced technology. I can't see anything here to suggest that this planet could have produced it."

"It did, but it was a long time ago. Those machines that did that, they were built within a century of Markel's death and placed in a few million robot satellites spread out a few light years from the borders of this galaxy. It's pretty amazing they're still functioning after a million years, but then, the Pfafth were pretty amazing a million years ago."

Brandon's attention seemed to be fading, and Mickie looked curiously at him. "Something worrying you, Brandon?" he asked.

"They always take a walk along here about this time," Brandon said.

"Who?"

"You'll see." He closed his eyes and leaned back, looking quite relaxed, but Mickie reached out with his empathic sense and realised that the man was tense, not afraid, but not looking forward to some coming event. He wondered what was about to happen.

An elderly couple walked slowly towards them. They looked tired, unhealthy and sour expressions on both made them a most unattractive pair.

"Brandon, I didn't know you were back! Why haven't you been to visit us?" The woman's voice reminded Mickie of his adoptive mother on Earth, a whine of discontent in the tone and hoarse, as if from too many cigarettes.

"Hello mother. And you, father. I got back just this morning, no time yet to call."

Mickie heard the tension in Brandon's voice. This was not a happy meeting with his parents.

"Well, you never do. After all we've done for you, it's very inconsiderate of you. Who's this?"

"It's Markel, mother. I've just been Outside and brought him back to lead the Pfafth back to Glory."

Mickie was stunned. Had he just been betrayed? Huge rage began to build up inside.

"What a disgraceful thing to say, Brandon. You know you mustn't joke about such things. You always did have these stupid dreams about being an Agent for the Committee and going Outside."

"If you were younger, I'd give you a good hiding for that," the man said angrily. He had the same croak in his voice and

Mickie wandered if the Pfafth had discovered tobacco. He realised that Brandon was playing games for his own fun.

"Yes, father, I'm sure you'd enjoy that, just like you always did. Anyway, of course this isn't Markel. I've just been on another sales trip down south and this is my girlfriend's son."

"Well, it's a disgrace for you to be going out with a divorced woman," the woman whined. "After the way we brought you up, really it's disgusting."

The two people sat down on the bench and both Brandon and Mickie instinctively moved away from them. They didn't smell all that clean and there was an odour of staleness about them. The woman reached into her bag and extracted a small packet, opened it and took out a tablet, which she popped into her mouth. Her husband snatched the packet from her and took a tablet himself.

"You take too many of those damn things," Brandon said with contempt. "They're killing you."

"They're my only pleasure," the woman whined. "You're always complaining."

Horrified, Mickie watched this scene, remembering almost identical scenes from his long ago life as a boy on Earth. Brandon's parents were obviously the same cold, uncaring, selfish parents as his own had been, and similarly addicted to some sort of drug. He got up and moved away from the bench, incapable of staying near such awful reminders of his old life.

Luckily, it was only a few minutes before Brandon's parents left, not looking at Mickie at all. He walked back to the bench.

"That was horrible," he said. "You have my sympathies. They're just like the terrible people who adopted me on Earth. He used to beat you up as a kid?"

"Only until I punched his nose and made him bleed all over the carpet," Brandon said with a lazy grin. "So your parents on Earth were like that?"

"Just about."

"Interesting," said Brandon. "You got taken away from one set of hideous parents, only to be stuck with a second lot. What are the odds against that?"

Mickie felt his insides tremble. "You don't mean...?"

"Yes, I do. They're your parents also. I'm your brother."

* * * *

"They were the first signs that perhaps the entire breeding program might have faults," Brandon said.

It had taken ten minutes for Mickie to calm down after that explosive information had been given to him. A few trembles still shook him, but he had drawn on his extraordinary powers of control to force calm on himself.

"Twenty-five years ago, they seemed an ideal couple. Both had been produced from the program, though neither had shown enough Markel or Kerrala qualities to be considered candidates. But they had passed all sorts of tests and had agreed to have their first child with more of the Markel DNA, and the boy initially was thought to have all the attributes they'd been looking for. That was me of course, but it turned out I'd got lower abilities in a couple of talents, for which I'm eternally grateful. I would not, under any circumstances, want to face what you're facing. But I still had a very high score on the Markel rating, so the Committee took me off to be trained as an agent. I was happy with that, because it gave me a chance to get Outside and see what the real Universe was doing. And it also let me get away from those two, which was even more important. Then ten years later, they tried again, and this time, along came you!"

He grinned in a friendly manner. "And this time, my little brother is the real, live Markel they'd been aiming to produce for a million years. Of course, that meant you were taken Outside when you were just over a year old and placed on Earth until you were big enough to develop all the powers."

"I've never understood why that happened. Why not raise me here?"

"A lot of minds worked on that, and they eventually decided that the risks were too great if you stayed with the Pfafth. The expectations would be too high, the pressures on you would be terrible and they thought you'd probably burn out before you were ready for your job. They decided you'd be better off growing up a normal child until you were ready to see the Maragos sculpture."

"But wasn't somebody watching me? Didn't they realise I'd gone off with the Kalamosian ship?"

"You sort of slipped through the system. Very sloppy work by a couple of agents who have since paid for their crimes. Much panic in the Management Committee, I can assure you. And looking for you was an immense problem. If we'd been able to ask the Speakers, it would have been easy, but if one of us had asked them, all the Speakers would know immediately, 'cos they all know what every single one of them is working on. And we had no idea if the Sillaron were still around and if they dealt with the Speakers, because if they did, they'd know about us at once. So we didn't dare."

"So how did you find out about me?"

"Rumours started flying around the Universe about this amazing kid in a Kalamosian trading vessel, and finally a couple of agents picked them up. That's when the Committee called all of us to start looking for you and bring you in."

"So how did it work out this way?"

"We were lucky. Sendagon found that you'd visited Kamotar where the original messages had been engraved on the cliffs, so he went and added the new lines knowing you'd eventually see them on the next visit. Then, when the Ship arrived, he timed the job of placing the sculpture so that the locals would see it and you'd get to hear about it also. Of course, he didn't know that the message had been sabotaged forty thousand years ago and you got the full story, not the propaganda version they wanted you to see. I was on the search team of course, being your brother, so as soon as Sendagon reported his horrible mess-up on Loomara, I went in to get you next, took a fairly safe chance with the Speakers and found you on Zlan."

"So what are you going to do now? They're bound to find out soon that you've been working against them all these years. What would they do?"

"They'd execute me for treason."

"Then you'd better come with me, right now! Let's get off this sorry mess of a world and get back to the Ship. I'm sure they'd love to have you in the crew!"

"No, I'm done with travelling, little brother. What I'm going to do is move over to Kalamos with my lovely lady and settle there. I've already talked with a Speaker, and he says they can put a block in my mind so that nobody can ever read my history and find out what I am. I'll just be an ordinary Kalamosian, and I have enough wealth to live a very pleasant life indeed."

"Then let's get going, now!"

"In a short while. How about one last adventure on your home world?"

"What?" Mickie was intrigued by the smile on his brother's lips. He had something interesting in mind, obviously.

"Remember I said the Management Committee has a public debate this afternoon? It starts in about thirty minutes. How about we go in, and at some point, you announce yourself and tell the idiots what's what? Then we leap."

"But wouldn't the Committee have all the best minds among the Pfafth? They'd have enough power to destroy us both, or capture us somehow, surely? "

"Not a chance, kid! The original Committees used to be selected according to their powers, but it got awfully corrupt.

It's been a hereditary position for generations now, and the present bunch is quite useless. I'm completely certain of that, because I *do* have most of Markel's powers, remember, and I've been able to get into all their minds and find out what they've got. And it's not a lot! They couldn't capture a dead rabbit!"

For a few moments, Mickie resisted. He really wanted to get off this pathetic world with its insane ideas and rejoin his family and friends. But the idea of telling the Management Committee some home truths was a great attraction.

"Let's go!" he said, and the two brothers walked back across the square and entered the Management Committee Headquarters.

As part of a school project, Mickie had once attended a meeting of the city council in Manchester. This setting reminded him of the event. A long, polished table sat in the middle of the huge room under soaring cathedral ceilings. Thirteen chairs sat round the table, one massively ornate at the head, six, less ornate but still impressive, down each side.

Around the room were a dozen rows of wooden benches each row higher than the one in front. A quick glance round the room showed that two rows at each side were perhaps half full of people, an audience of about a hundred citizens of Markel City.

"Quite a good turnout," Brandon said softly and led the way to the row at the bottom of the meeting table, sitting in the middle so that they would face the Chairman when the Committee members took their places.

"A good turnout? You could fit a thousand people in this place!"

"Mickie, usually you get more Committee members than citizens at meetings here. There's very little of anything interesting that ever takes place, usually just silly speeches about how we will one day run the Universe again after Markel has returned. Now that it's known that you're out there, interest is picking up and as I said, today is the national holiday for the Great Flight."

A door slammed open somewhere in the back of the room and the sound echoed into the ceiling. A line of people filed in and took their seats at the table. There were nine men and four women, Mickie noted. All the group seemed about the same age, somewhere in their forties he estimated, and only one was dressed in anything other than conventional clothing. This one exception wore black robes and a gold chain with a medallion hanging on his chest. The man was short, of stocky build, with a full head of jet-black hair.

"Chairman Vemanor Markel," murmured Brandon. "The chairman is always given the courtesy of the Markel name added to his or her own. While the Committee members are now all miserable shmucks who inherited the position from their equally miserable shmuck parents, the chairmanship is rotated every four years. He's been in the job for six months and he's very full of himself."

"This is all very pukey," Micky said, trying not to laugh at Brandon's words. "What are we going to do?"

"Leave it with me," Brandon said. "But be ready to leap. Here's the location of the Time Barrier portal."

Mickie's mind was filled with the image of the golden landscape and the immense reach of Nothingness that lay between the Pfafth Galaxy and normal time. With the image came the complete understanding of how to get there and the way to cross the barrier back to the safe house on the planet of the small solar system.

Somewhere, a gong rang out. All the visitors stood up, as did the Committee members.

"We ask all the forces that created the Universe to hear our plea," said the chairman. His voice was unimpressive, high-pitched, with no obvious character. "We ask that the re-born Markel return to us soon and lead us back into the mastery we once held, so that we can destroy the treasonous Sillaron and bring peace and prosperity back to the forty galaxies as once we did so long ago."

Everyone sat down again.

"Good grief!" Mickie whispered. "I don't recall any religious elements among the Pfafth before!"

"It's grown in the last few hundred years," Brandon said. "I think it reflects the degree of desperation that's afflicting us."

"I declare the meeting open," the chairman said. "Manager Hargomet, what news of the agents and their search?"

A tall, skinny man rose to his feet.

"My boss," Brandon said. "He's in charge of all the agents who can go Outside."

"Chairman Markel, all of our forty-three active agents are Outside, seeking the reborn Markel," the man said. "I last heard that Sendagon was about to make contact with him, having tracked him to the next port of call for the trading vessel in which he is travelling. I hope to hear the results in a few days, in fact I can even expect that Sendagon will return with Markel to begin our war against the Sillaron."

"You say all your agents are Outside?" the chairman said.

"Yes, Chairman. That is, apart from the seven who are currently sidelined with ill-health or injury."

"But isn't that one of them? I recognise him from a previous meeting."

All eyes in the room followed the chairman's gesture and turned to where Brandon and Mickie were sitting. Brandon rose to his feet.

"I am Brandon, Chairman, and I returned from Outside just a few hours ago."

A loud buzz of interest ran through the listeners. Mickie wandered if any of them had ever actually seen someone who had been Outside.

"And why did you return?" demanded Hargomet angrily.

"Your orders were to remain Outside and attempt to make contact with Markel!"

"That is quite correct."

"Then why have you returned?" Hargomet seemed to be almost hysterical, spitting with rage. "I can have you court-martialled for this!"

"Why would you have me court-martialled for obeying orders and succeeding in my mission?" Brandon said with a laugh full of contempt.

A complete silence fell over the room. Mickie had extended his empathic sense over the Committee members and he felt the startled realisation of what Brandon had said. And he felt the surge of attention switch to him.

"Your turn, little brother. Give 'em hell," Brandon said softly and sat down.

Mickie stood up, his heart pounding.

"My name is Mickie Dalton. I appear to have the powers of your one-time leader, Markel, and I have many of his memories, but I am not Markel, even though you named me that way when I was born here. I have not come here to lead you back to mastery of forty galaxies. I have not come to lead a war of revenge against the Sillaron."

The silence in the room was like that inside a glacier. People seemed frozen, many not even looking at him. Among the Committee members, expressions varied from open-mouthed incomprehension to white-faced shock. Finally the chairman found his voice.

"And why should we believe the claim of a child that he is the reborn Markel?"

"As I have just denied any such claim, your question is foolish," Mickie said. "I have his powers apparently, so I am Pfafth. I have his memories because one of you placed a Maragos sculpture where I would see it and fall under its influence. But I am not Markel reborn."

"I see no reason to believe you." Chairman Vemanor Markel seemed furious at the situation.

"Chairman," said Brandon, standing up again. "Tell me, who could sleep like a new-born babe surrounded by a hundred of the Spiders of Zlan, the way I found him? Who could follow my lead and teleport himself across a hundred million light years and then through the Time Barrier? Could any of you? What other Pfafth infant is there Outside other than the Kerrala child? And who could quote what Markel told the Management Committee a million years ago? And you already know full well that the Maragos sculpture was tuned only to the mind of a Markel child. This is the kid you've been looking for, believe me."

He sat down again and crossed his legs, looking with interest at the high ceiling.

"You could have briefed this boy with all that history," the chairman snapped. "He could be like yourself, another rejected Markel from the breeding program that you smuggled Outside. I see no reason to believe any of this."

Mickie extended his senses into the man's mind and realised what was happening. Vemanor really did believe that Mickie was the genuine article and he was terrified by the realisation that would now lose his position as chairman if Mickie cared to claim it.

"Chairman Vemanor Markel, do not fear that I will take your job," he said in a conciliatory manner. "I don't plan on staying. I just want to repeat what Markel told your Committee when you first embarked on this insane program. *You can't go home again.* You can't become the rulers of forty galaxies again. You can't dominate other civilisations again. You can't modify the breeding of other species to suit your purposes again. You no longer have those powers. The Sillaron are out there and they still want to eat your souls."

There was a moan of terror through the large hall. Mickie

had not realised how deep was the conditioning of all Pfafth, so deep that even the mention of the great Enemy's name could induce terror.

"And anyway, there's another problem for you." He looked round the room. Every single face was now focused on him. Even Brandon had turned his attention from the ceiling, realising Mickie was about to reveal new information.

"Even if all of you regained your ancient Pfafth powers, even if you escaped the barriers of this Galaxy and destroyed the Sillaron as you have dreamed for a million years, you still could not establish a new empire. There is a power out there that is far superior to you or the Sillaron. I don't know where it lives, I don't know anything about it other than my friends and I have met it, and it is greater than anything you could possibly have dreamed. I don't think it likes the Pfafth. And it doesn't like the Sillaron much, either. I don't think either of you want to attract its attention and starting a whole new war would do just that. I suspect the consequences could be quite nasty for both of you."

Brandon had stood up, staring at Mickie as he imparted this bombshell.

"So you'd better live with this," Mickie continued. "I'm not going to bring the Galaxy back to Universal Time. Fact is, I haven't the faintest idea how to go about it. So you can't get out, other than about fifty of you, and you sure aren't going to take over the Universe with *that* army. So you're stuck here, and that's the best thing, because the Universe has become too dangerous a place for you. Maybe in another million years you'll have re-learned how to do all those Pfafth things and you can try again. But I don't want to have anything to do with your stupid wars and dreams of revenge. Meanwhile, you've got a whole galaxy to play in, so why don't you re-learn how to teleport around it and do something useful with it? Now, if you'll excuse me, my brother and I have other places to be."

Inside his mind he reached out for the jump-off spot for crossing the void in Time and took himself to the golden landscape alongside the black canyon of Nothing. A few seconds later, he and Brandon were in the safe house on an empty planet orbiting a lone sun outside the Blocked Galaxy of the Pfafth.

All Mickie wanted to do for the next few hours before he went to sleep to prepare for the leap home the next day was to talk to his family and friends through the services of the Speaker.

* * * *

Brandon and Mickie were sitting sociably in the living room of the safe house the next morning, preparing for the return home and discussing Brandon's plans to take up residence on Kalamos when the interruption came.

One second, just the two of them were sitting there, the next the furious person of Sendagon was in one of the other chairs. A tiny breeze from the displacement of air reached Mickie's face. It was the first time he had ever witnessed somebody teleport into his immediate presence, other than the Zlan, and the effect was startling. He jumped, then relaxed. Brandon seemed undisturbed.

"Well, hello there, fellow Agent Sendagon," he said with a friendly wave of his coffee mug. "How nice of you to drop by!"

"What the hell are you doing here?" bellowed Sendagon. "I thought you said you wouldn't go back to home world!"

"Are you talking to Mickie or to me?" Brandon asked. He sipped appreciatively at his coffee.

Mickie had his empathic senses at full alert and he saw the furious energy build-up in Sendagon.

"Don't do it, Sendagon!" he said quickly. "Do you seriously believe you can hurt either of us with one of your mind bolts while I'm in the room?"

Sendagon clearly hesitated and Mickie saw the rage replaced by a growing fear.

"Sensible man," Brandon said. "Here you are, totally pooped from a long teleport, facing the returned Markel all his powers increased by several multiples and an almost-Markel who still has a lot more weaponry than you do, and you think you can harm us? Silly fellow, relax and have a cup of coffee. It's the best Mayoowani can offer."

Mickie watched Sendagon slowly control his anger as well as his realisation of how close to calamity he had come.

"Are you on the way to home world or on the way back?" the other agent demanded.

"We've had a very pleasant visit to home world," Brandon said. "Not even a full day, but I think Mickie saw enough to realise he'd made the right decision about helping the Pfafth become the rulers again."

All the air seemed to escape from Sendagon. He slumped back in his seat, seeming completely exhausted, even more than the usual fatigue resulting from teleportation.

"You won't help us, Markel?" he asked, looking at Mickie.

"Sendagon, surely you realise there's nothing to help. That's not the old Pfafth back there," Mickie said, waving generally at the nearby galaxy. "They don't have the old powers, the old talents, not even the old energy. All they have are pathetic dreams. They're less effective than even Humans from Earth could be as Rulers of the Universe."

Sendagon slumped forward, covering his face in his hands. "I know," he mumbled through obvious grief. "I suppose I was stupid to believe it all."

"So what will you do?" Brandon asked in sympathy. "There's nothing to go home to."

"I don't know. All I can think of right now is sleep." With difficulty he stood up and walked across to one of the bedrooms, closed the door behind him and Mickie heard the bed shake as Sendagon seemed to collapse heavily onto it.

The other two stood up also.

"So where to, little brother?" Brandon asked.

"Back to Zlan. The Ship's still in orbit there as they're harvesting another crop of plants. What about you? Kalamos, I suppose?"

"Kalamos it is. I've got a nice house not all that far from yours, so I'll see you when you get back on the next vacation."

"You're sure you won't come back to the Ship? I've never had a big brother and I like the idea."

Brandon grinned. "I think it's pretty cool, too! But no, I'm done travelling. I want to study the works of Maragos. I think I'm beginning to understand how he did it and I might try making something along those lines. But you'd better come and see me when you get home, kid, or I'll give you a big brotherly spanking."

Mickie fought to control the tears rising and wasn't successful. "You can count on it," he said with difficulty, and the two men embraced for a few seconds.

"Go on," said Brandon. "Your friends are waiting for you."

Mickie nodded, closed his eyes and reached out for Zlan. A few seconds later, he was standing in the aromatic, heavy air of the Spiders' world and the sound of harvesting equipment told him where to find his parents.

Chapter 3 – Expansions of the Mind

"You know, I'd almost forgotten about these things!"

Mickie and his friends were sitting in his cabin, studying the contents of the box given hurriedly to him by one of the women of Korrobodor as the crew boarded the shuttle. A comment made during a post-Loopies drink of *Sle'Ach* had reminded him and they had come back to the cabin to study the artefacts.

"Which are the suppressors and which are the counters to them?" Melkana said, looking at the items lying in the box.

"Hard to say," Mickie replied.

There were nine objects sitting in front of them, neatly arranged in three rows, lying in soft paper, looking almost like jewelled duck eggs. Six of them were white, three were dark blue, all of them with a fine network of gold in what looked like random patterns.

"Good lord, I've just realised we've already seen one of these things!" Fencris said in astonishment. "Isn't that what Allie picked up after we killed the Sillaron in the observation room?"

"Damn, but you're right!" Mickie remembered how Allie and Grant had puzzled over the mysterious object and sent it to the engineering section for an analysis. Nothing had ever been learned about the object. It had proved impervious to any X-rays, scanners or any attempt to break it open. Eventually it had been put away and forgotten.

"And just one of those things was able to cover a whole area and suppress the Pfafth powers?" Drellion looked impressed.

"Not just the Pfafth," Mickie said. "It blocked out the Zlan as well as the Speakers and cut out all the Ship's functions also."

"In that case, we don't want to be fiddling around with them," Fencris said seriously. "Imagine what would happen if you activated the suppressor, the Ship stops functioning and we've no idea how to deactivate the thing. The Captain would throw you out of the airlock!"

"Can't imagine that we could," Mickie said. "Look at how they poked around with the other one and nothing happened."

"Well, you know what they say. When all else fails, read the instructions," Drellion said with a smile.

"What instructions? There aren't any instructions." Melkana looked at him with a frown.

"True. But I bet the makers have them."

"Ah!" Both Mickie and Fencris grinned cheerfully. "The lovely ladies of Korrobodor!"

"You men are so obsessed with those women! I really don't get it!" Melkana tried to hide her laugh and failed miserably.

"Speaker 356?"

"Yes, Mickie?"

"Can you make a connection with the Korrobi woman who gave me these devices? I don't know her name."

"I have analysed your memory and identified the mental patterns. She is here."

"Mickie, what a pleasant surprise!" The contralto voice sounded in Mickie's head and he gave a quick mental instruction to the Speaker to open the conversation to his three friends also.

"I'm embarrassed to say I don't know your name," he said, feeling a little silly in the memory of the image of this beautiful woman.

"I am Villandelle. How may I help one of the people who saved us all here on Korrobodor?"

"It's the suppressor I got from you. How do I tell the difference between the two devices and how do I make them work?"

"Ah yes, I remember that you left in quite a hurry and I didn't get a chance to tell you those things. It's quite easy, the blue ones are the suppressors, and they're the very last of those we made."

"And how do they work?"

"Also easy. Just hang one of each round your neck. They will both immediately establish a connection with your mind and you'll know how to work them after that. It's like using any limb or muscle."

"That simple? They look very fragile. Will they stand up to heavy treatment?"

The woman's laugh was strong and genuine. "Mickie, you could put those little eggs under your shuttle as it landed hard on a high gravity world and you wouldn't get a scratch on them. They'll probably outlast the planet!"

"Wow! I'm impressed. But we already had one of these we found after we got rid of the Sillaron some months ago. It never gave any impression of having any abilities."

"It wouldn't, not after establishing mental links with the first wearer's species. Once it's done that, only another mind of the same species can access it and nothing you could do to it would trigger a reaction."

"Okay, I see. How is life on Korrobodor now?"

"Every day is a delight Mickie, thanks to you and your friends, especially those terrifying spiders. Though some of the children still have nightmares about that day."

"Tell them they're not the only ones," Melkana chimed in. "A lot of the children aboard the Ship are still having therapy for the same reasons."

"Villandelle, does anyone know I have these things?" Mickie asked, realising how useful the devices could be.

"Only a few of my partners, those who were at the lunch with you. And none of us would want anyone to know about them, knowing how they nearly killed our saviours. You secret is safe with us, Mickie."

For a few more minutes, the kids chatted with the woman then said their goodbyes.

Mickie picked up one of the blue devices from its insulated bed and found that it had no loop for suspending on a chain. He resolved to acquire a small bag with a chain and hang one white, one blue little egg round his neck from then on. The suppressor had nearly killed him several times and he wanted to make sure he could always counter it in future.

"If you think you could spare one of those things, I'd love to try and work out how and why they function," Fencris said.

"Sounds like a good idea," Mickie replied, extracted another blue egg and handed it over. "One suppressor for the Cassolean telepathic genius. I'll be interested to see if you can even open it up!"

"Probably not," Fencris said with a wide grin and stuffed the little device into a pocket of his tunic. "But I think I'll have fun seeing just what it's transmitting!"

"Talking of transmitting, Fencris, how's the telepathic stuff coming along?" Melkana seemed happy to see the suppressors packed away and the conversation with the woman from Korrobodor completed.

"It's really wild!" Fencris said, and his red eyes almost glowed like flames. "Now that we've discovered that we could do this, the whole Planet of Cassolea has gone nutty over it. Even in just a few days, several hundred of us have discovered how to communicate telepathically and the World University has set up a project to find out how it works."

"Is it causing any problems?" Mickie was intrigued by a world where everybody communicated by mental waves.

"The academics are a bit worried," Fencris said. "They're concerned that we might lose speech capacity once everybody uses telepathy, but it's doubtful that more than a small group will be able to do it. However, that's another problem they're worried about, if it might cause some sort of elite section of the population to develop. But the big one is privacy. Not everybody wants to receive messages from somebody at any time, so the big project now is to develop some sort of blocker for when you don't want to be available."

"So you've really put the cat among the pigeons on Cassolea," Melkana said. "I'm not sure it's such a great idea, even if it did save our lives on Korrobodor."

"It's a fact," Fencris agreed. "I'm a hero for discovering the Old Cassoleans with the help of our Pfafth buddy here, but young Fencris is also the villain for opening up this telepathy thingy. I think I'll stay aboard the Ship for a while until things settle down at home!"

"Good! I think we're all pleased about that!" Melkana looked cheerful. "After all, Mickie's no competition at Loopies, so we need you!"

Mickie blew a loud raspberry at her. "So is there anything new and different about the Cassolean brand of telepathy?" he asked.

"There sure is!" Fencris seemed cheerful about the security of his circle of friends. "We can only have one conversation at a time, a bit like you said the Zlan do. But the main thing is, it seems to be highly visual. We can transmit fantastic pictures and memories."

"Just like the Old Cassoleans did for us when we had to learn how to get to a new location," Mickie said.

"Well, some people have developed a whole new art form with that talent," Fencris said with a grin. "They've worked out how to record their memories so that other people can read them, and they've recorded fantastic adventures that some of them had and selling them! I think I could make a fortune from some of the stuff we've gone through!"

"You've already got a fortune from our discovery on Shuramee," Melkana laughed. "You don't need any more!"

Mickie had gone thoughtful. "You know, it's funny, but Brandon, my brother seemed to have learned that skill. He said there were some Cassoleans who had gone with the Pfafth when Markel took them to the Blocked Galaxy and they were still living back there. I'm sorry, I'd forgotten he told me that, what with everything else going on. It's just come back to me."

The others were staring at him.

"There are Cassoleans on Pfafth home world?" Fencris was stunned. "We have to get them out of there!"

"I can't see how you can do that," Mickie said. "Cassoleans can't teleport, so they can't get out on their own, not even to the time portal. And I don't think the Pfafth have any space ships any more. Even if they did, crossing the Time Barrier would be impossible."

"Yeah, I suppose you're right," Fencris muttered. "I think I'm going to have to work on that. You and I will have to talk about how you do that time jumping stuff and maybe I can work out how to get a shuttle to do it."

"In that case, I expect the problem to be solved in a few weeks," Drellion joined in at last. "You guys are getting boring and there's a whole empty hangar down there just waiting to see me perform my Loopies Miracles. Last one in Hangar Ten is a Big Headed Korrobi yurkel!"

And with that, the four of them raced for the door and the transporter to the shuttle hangars.

Chapter 4 – Under a Flag of Truce

The walk was hard, uphill, sometimes steep and gravity was at least ten percent higher than aboard the Ship. But all four friends were happy to work hard and exercise muscles that didn't always get properly used. They were breathing deeply, but Mickie knew that they needed this break.

The Ship had broken out of Hyperspace that morning and the standard working parties had made planet-fall with a shuttle full of mining equipment.

"Rare Earths," Grant had said. "Extraordinary chemical qualities in astoundingly lavish quantity, especially some stuff called thulium and lutetium, and these are not that common on most planets. Where we mine is well outside populated areas, and anyway, our techniques allow us to siphon off the stuff without damaging the top surfaces. The locals love brandy, the Mayoowani coffee and the leaves from Harliya that make empathic material, so everybody is happy with the trade."

The planet was called Hemetov. The people were human-like at first glance, until one saw the third eye and the second nose at the back of the hairless skull, and they had little, if any artistic or musical culture.

"Yes, quite boring to anyone except somebody whose job is studying alien species," Allie said with a laugh. "Nobody is expecting you to join us for the diplomatic and trading meetings. The planet is dead safe, the whole school is down here, as they always are when we visit this place. Somehow, I don't think we'll be having a repeat of Korrobodor on this trip!"

"Ye gods, I hope not," muttered Melkana. "One meeting with those little yurkels is three too many! Is there anything at all on this planet that might need the Zlan Armies to descend in vast hordes to rescue our accident-prone Pfafth friend?"

"Nothing we've ever met," Grant said, struggling not to laugh at Melkana's words. "No noxious snakes, insects, no carnivorous animals, no Gelkka, nothing interesting at all."

"You're right, dead boring," Fencris said in agreement. "Alright, let's just walk off all the fat we've been accumulating. I feel flabby!"

"Okay, the sea coast is thataway, about eight kilometres," Allie said pointing down the road. "You've got some rations? Good, see you back here for lift-off in seven hours."

With a wave, the two adults climbed into the wheeled buggy that had come down in the shuttle and rode off to join the mining crews that were already setting up their equipment in the bleak surroundings. The ground was not flat, but not scenic either, just rolling hillocks of mostly featureless earth and occasional bushes that were just scrub. The wind was gentle, coming from the direction Allie had indicated the coast lay, and already they could smell the salt air.

Conversation had been sparse. All of them were lost in their own thoughts. Mickie found his mind swinging between the astonishing events of his visit to the Pfafth home world, the horrible discovery of his real parents who were no different from his awful adoptive parents back on Earth and the wonderful fact of an elder brother who had become an instant friend. He looked forward to the next leave back on Kalamos and spending more time with Brandon without the dangers getting in the way. And he frequently found he had switched his thoughts to the increasing effect that Melkana was having on him. He was fourteen and all the girls on the ship were becoming distracting, but Melkana most of all. He sneaked a look at her, just to his right and a little ahead of him, and once again thought that she was really gorgeous. But then, so were several other girls in the school, he thought with smug satisfaction and several of them had been paying considerable attention to him in recent weeks. There was a Kalamosian girl called Nevinandra, she seemed especially interested and had already asked if she could join them on this walk, though had found she was needed to join another group on a school project instead. Mickie felt mixed emotions of regret at not having her along and relief at not having to worry about Melkana and her reaction.

He looked at the others. Fencris was striding out with enjoyment, but his fixed stare into the distance told Mickie that his Cassolean friend was working on some project. Mickie wandered if it was the task of discovering how the time portal worked and how to engineer a shuttle to go through it to get the Cassoleans living on Pfafth home world. Then he wandered how those Cassoleans might react to suddenly finding others of their own species who had been separated from them for a million years, and if they would even want to leave their homes.

Drellion was already a few hundred metres in front, testing out his superb physical condition and eager to see the ocean.

Mickie laughed in sheer happiness at being with these wonderful friends and the decisions he had made that he would abandon the Pfafth and just concentrate on living a normal life as a Kalamosian trader on board the Ship. He decided to ignore the worries about Melkana and work on improving his fitness.

The sea air grew closer. The temperature was too low for swimming, but just having the sea near was always a spirit-lifter, Mickie knew. Soon, they saw the green-blue ocean, heard the tide and the sound of sea birds and they all broke into a run to get to the beach.

Not really a beach, they saw when they arrived. It reminded Mickie of the coast of Lancashire on the few occasions he had been there. More rocky and stony, little sand and what there was had a grey shade to it, not exactly the golden sands of the more exotic countries like Australia or Thailand that he had always wanted to visit. But it was ocean, fresh winds and salt air, and they loved it. They found a small break in the rocks that provided a shelter and settled down to enjoy the food and drink they had brought with them. Later, they spent a hectic hour chasing among the rock pools, paddling in the surf and examining the odd species of marine life they found on the sand or in the pools.

But as Mickie bent over a pool to look at what seemed like a minute sea horse, he realised the others had gone silent. He stood up, looked around and saw that they were staring at a point back in the direction from which they had come.

"Just what the hell is that?" Fencris said loudly, the volume covering up confusion and possibly fear.

The four friends instinctively moved closer together. Mickie shivered. He knew what it was.

"It's a Sillaron," he said.

*   *   *   *

For several frozen moments, they stared at each other, the four children and the strange black shape.

"So what the hell is it doing here?" Fencris finally asked.

"Probably hunting me," Mickie said, struggling to keep his voice calm. "But I've no idea what it can hope to do on its own."

"Mickie, aren't we all getting fed up with strange people just dropping in one you from all corners of the Universe?" Drellion said, the lightness of his words contradicting his obvious nervousness. "I mean, it's all a huge compliment to you and all that, that everybody wants you to help them rule the Universe, but it's getting a bit freaky."

Ahead of them, the Sillaron had started moving closer and the four couldn't help themselves but step backward until Mickie stopped the movement angrily.

"Damn, but I'm fed up of being afraid of these things. Let's see what it wants." He walked forward defiantly and stopped just a few metres away from the Sillaron. To his delight and admiration he realised that the other three had followed him and stood alongside.

"Looking to eat my soul, Sillaron?" Mickie called out. "You'll need some friends to help you."

"On your Earth, they have a ritual called a flag of truce," came a silent, telepathic voice in his head. "I wish to have a discussion under a flag of truce."

Astounded, Mickie looked at the others. "Did you hear that?" he asked. Fencris nodded. The other two shook their heads. He turned back to the Sillaron.

"How are you communicating?" he asked.

"We have some telepathic skills," the creature replied in the same way.

"Speaker 356, can you see a Sillaron a few metres in front of me?"

"I sense an entity, Mickie but I cannot establish communication."

Mickie thought for a few seconds. "Do you speak the language of the Pfafth?" he asked in that tongue.

"Of course," replied the Sillaron in Pfafth. "We all speak the language of our greatest enemy."

"Then do so. Our Ship's computer has been programmed with that tongue and my friends will now understand you. Tell us again why you are here."

"I wish to talk under a flag of truce."

"Why?"

"Perhaps because a million years is too long for a war."

"Or perhaps because you have heard the Pfafth are ready to leave their galaxy and come Sillaron-hunting with new weapons?"

He sensed the shock in the Sillaron.

"That cannot be true," it said.

"Why not?"

"Because nobody can pass the time barrier."

"Foolish Sillaron, do you not know that many Pfafth agents have travelled back and forth over the years of the Pfafth retreat? Do you not know that I did that very same trip just weeks ago and met the Management Committee?"

The tall black shape seemed to rotate, as smoke appeared to billow around it. A white face flashed for a second then vanished again behind the curtain of black. Mickie retained a memory of huge, oval eyes that stared briefly.

"Sillaron, know this. I can bring the Pfafth Galaxy back into normal time. And the Pfafth have had a million years to apply their extraordinary talents to developing weapons for just one purpose, to destroy you, and their anger has not declined since Markel took them there."

Mickie had no compunction in lying to this creature. However little affection he had for his own Pfafth species, the Sillaron had slaughtered them once and they deserved no courtesy from him. Anyway, he sensed some weakness in the entity and wanted to explore it.

"Then it is even more important to discuss the situation," the Sillaron said. "Such a war could destroy many planets and millions of lives, because we too are renewed in our powers. We must talk with you."

"We?"

"The leaders of the Sillaron."

Mickie thought for several moments. He recalled incidents and facts from his life as Markel, especially the information he received after the Pfafth had retreated to the Galaxy they would block from normal time.

"I think you are lying, Sillaron. When Markel took his people to their new home, the Cassoleans took the few spaceships, leaving you marooned on the planets you happened to occupy. The Speakers do not work with your telepathy. How can you be a force that could threaten my Pfafth?"

The shock reverberated from the Sillaron. "How can you know these things, Pfafth? They happened a million years ago!"

"That should prove what I just said, Sillaron, that I have just returned from meeting the Pfafth Management Committee where I learned all the history."

"Then your Pfafth are a little out of date. While they have been hiding like cowards behind a barrier of time, the Universe has marched on. There are other space-going species whose ships we can use."

"Albert, is that true?" Mickie sent a silent message to the computer.

"We know of no Universal telepathic species other than the Speakers and the Zlan," Albert replied. "Though Fencris' achievements on Korrobodor show that there is certainly one other whose identity is unknown. There are five space-going species known to us, other than the Kaloti, only two have hyperspace capability, neither as efficient as the Kaloti. The Sillaron's claims are unlikely but possible."

"Speaker 356, can you do a rapid search and see if there are any space-going species that have carried Sillaron in recent years?"

"Stand by."

"Then perhaps it is so," Mickie said to the Sillaron. "A war between the two most powerful species in the Universe can only harm everyone. What is it you want?"

"We want you to come to Sillaron and meet with the leaders. We believe we can come to an arrangement for peace."

"You have to be joking, Sillaron!   You have tried to exterminate my species and now you want me to come to your planet where you will try and get from me the secret of reaching the Pfafth home world. Don't be a fool!"

"I have no idea of how to convince you, Pfafth. We want you to come to our planet to see that we are really like you. We have families, we have commerce, we have peace. We know that a few of our extremists have tried to kill you, but we hope we can show you that they are exceptions. We can take care of them."

"Mickie, my scans show that no space-going species have knowingly carried any Sillaron, ever." The calm voice of Speaker 356 broke through Mickie's thoughts. "I have set up a telepathic block in all four of you. The Sillaron cannot read you, should you wish to have a private conversation or contact your parents through the Ship's computer."

"Well, thanks, Speaker, that's clever of you! Guys, what do you think?"

"Mickie, that thing is talking through its rear end, if it has one," Fencris said firmly. "You can't trust it further than you can spit into a typhoon."

"Seconded," said Drellion. "Based on what the Speaker just told you, the Sillaron's been lying the whole time."

"Thirded," said Melkana briefly. "That's one lying funnel of smoke. Ugly thing."

"But I tell you what, Mickie, you're handling this thing very well."   Fencris looked amused, despite the worry about the arrival of this strange and frightening creature.

"Thank you!" Mickie was warmed by Fencris' approval. "The trouble is, he *could* be telling the truth. We don't know all the species in the Universe, so there *could* be something that's able to transport them around. Look how you just discovered a whole new species nobody had known about before."

"Mickie, you're not planning on taking him up on that invitation, are you?" Melkana looked horrified. "Just you alone on the Sillaron planet?"

"It's about as horrible as I thought the trip to Zlan would be," Mickie said, sensing his own fear and worry about such a meeting. "Possibly worse, 'cos I've got all of Markel's memories about those things slaughtering millions of Pfafth. But I can't stop thinking that somebody needs to learn more about the Sillaron because we know nothing at all."

"Anyone visiting that lot should go with a huge army," Drellion said. His hostility directed at the Sillaron was obvious.

"And that's a good idea," Fencris said. "Particularly as you have a private army of the worst nightmares in the Universe!"

"This is something I have to talk over with my parents," Mickie said. "I can't decide this on my own, not even with you guys."

"Good!" said Melkana with obvious relief. "Let's hope they persuade you not to go. Do you realise how awful it's been, you hopping off to strange places while we're not sure you'll ever get back?"

Despite his deep anxiety, Mickie felt greatly cheered by her words. Confidently, he turned back to the Sillaron. "I'll talk it over with others," he said. "I'll meet you here tomorrow at this same time."

The Sillaron didn't reply but moved away rapidly before vanishing behind an outcrop of the coastal dunes.

"What a strange thing," Fencris said, echoing everybody's belief. "I wonder how many of them there are on this planet?"

"Can't be too many," Drellion said. "On all the planets where we've had problems, like Merrison or Gelokk, the Sillaron seem to have had huge control over the population, so there must have been quite a lot of them. There's no evidence that they're controlling this place, 'cos it's been considered quite safe for decades. I reckon it's just a few of them and they're declining fast."

"You know, Melkana," Fencris said, his eyes flashing. "Your kid brother is getting just too darn clever. Hit him a few times, will you and keep him under control?"

Drellion looked pleased with himself and Mickie had to agree that the youngest of them was displaying fine analytical skills.

They packed up their food and equipment and set off on the long walk back to the shuttle.

*   *   *   *

"Do I have any alternative?"

Mickie was sitting comfortably in his parents' cabin, cradling a drink of *Sle'Ach* while Allie and Grant had taken something stronger, a glass of their finest single malt scotch that they said they kept for very special occasions.

"This is one of them," Allie had said as she took the bottle out of its storage. "Not exactly what I had thought, but our son has reached a major crisis point."

"Yes, you could walk away and ignore the whole thing," Grant said in reply to Mickie's question.

"But you don't think that's really an option, do you?" Mickie asked.

"No, not really." Grant shook his head and Mickie could sense the sadness in both parents. "Because if you do, you'll never know for sure if the Sillaron are still hunting you, or what their capabilities are."

"I think that's their fear as well," Allie said. "They've had no contact with the Pfafth for a million years. They have absolutely no idea of what's gone on in the Blocked Galaxy. For all they know, you may be right in what you told them. The Pfafth are all ready to come pouring into the Universe, armed with incredible weapons and burning to destroy the Sillaron."

"And what could the Sillaron have been doing in all this time, themselves?" Mickie wondered. "Maybe they've been doing just that, and all they need is the information in my head of how to get through the time barrier."

"Highly unlikely," Grant said. "For a million years, they've had no enemy to hate, and the lust for killing dies off in that sort of time. And remember what you told us from Markel's memories about when the Pfafth first went into hiding. The Sillaron didn't have any spaceships, they couldn't teleport and while it seems they have low-range telepathic skills, they didn't have the universal range of the Speakers."

"We've both been talking to historians, social scientists and others," Allie joined in. "They're all in agreement, the most likely thing to have happened is that the Sillaron have declined as much as the Pfafth have. After all, we've seen no signs of any major developments beyond the control they seem to have on Gelokk and Merrison. If they were all-powerful, they'd have tried to take control of the forty galaxies the Pfafth used to rule, and they haven't."

"So should I go to the Sillaron planet?" Mickie felt a mixture of excitement and fear at the idea of confronting the Great Enemy in its own castle.

"Mickie, you're not the sad, abused little boy we met on Earth three years ago," Allie said gently. "You've lived a complete lifetime as the greatest leader of the most powerful race known, you've faced up to horrible dangers as Mickie Dalton and you've overcome some dreadful enemies. We cannot tell you what to do. There are forces acting on you that are far greater than anything we can handle."

"Then I have to go, don't I?"

"You're the only one who can make things clear, Mickie," Grant said. "But be armed."

"Indeed I will. Like Fencris said, I have the greatest nightmare army in the Universe."

* * * *

Mickie stood alone by the coarse beach and waited. It was exactly the same time of the following day as he had met the disturbing, tenuous shape of the Sillaron in the company of his friends. This time, he was alone, but his expanded senses told him there was... *something* nearby. It was the feeling of danger when walking alone through darkened streets, tiny anxieties as dark, silent wings flew overhead.

"So the Pfafth returns with a decision?"

One moment there had been nothing, but in the space of just a few seconds, the darkness on the ground had become the slowly revolving black smoke of the Sillaron.

"I said I would."

"And your decision?"

"I will come to the world of the Sillaron and talk under a flag of truce with your leaders."

There was a moment of silence as if the Sillaron was absorbing unexpected news, but Mickie sensed a flash of triumph. Was it the satisfaction of achieving a chance at peace, or was it the victory of the next stage in the destruction of the Pfafth? Mickie could not identify the alien mindset.

"And you will come alone."

"No."

This time, the emotion from the dark creature was obvious. It was fury. "You must come alone!"

"No."

"Why, do you not trust the Sillaron?"

"Don't be foolish." Mickie let his contempt show. "You ask me to come alone to your planet when you have already demonstrated so often and so successfully that you can cancel out the Pfafth powers. What sort of leader gives all his strength away like that?"

"You must come alone."

"I will not. I think I shall return to my Ship and tell the

Pfafth it's time to go Sillaron hunting. I can bring the galaxy back into the Universe in the next few hours and release my people and their new weapons. They are eager for the killing to start."

"No! Wait! I must get guidance from my masters."

That's interesting, thought Mickie. *The Sillaron seems frightened by my threat, which means it believes it possible. And how is it going to get guidance from its masters on another world possibly millions of light years away?*

"We came to the same conclusion," said the voice of Grant in his mind. "This might be very informative."

He and Allie were in contact through the Ship's communication computers that were monitoring Mickie's translation device in his shoulder. The other three kids had also asked if they could monitor the conversation and Mickie had agreed, feeling that he needed every bit of support he could get.

"How long will it take to get that guidance?" Mickie asked.

"My masters ask who or what will you bring with you?"

Whoops! The Sillaron seems to have direct telepathic communication with its bosses, Mickie thought with an unpleasant start. "Speaker 356, did you detect any communication from the Sillaron?"

"There was something, Mickie, like a burst of static. But I could not identify it."

"Mickie, I did!" Fencris sounded astounded. "I just heard it quite distinctly! I think it must be using Cassoleans. There must be a colony of my people still on their world, left over from the Pfafth war."

"Okay, stay monitoring, Fencris," said Grant. "But under no circumstances transmit on the Cassolean band. Let's keep your ability secret."

Mickie returned his attention to the Sillaron. "I will bring two Zlan bodyguards."

He sensed the fear and distress in the Sillaron.

"No! There is no way we could have those terrible creatures on our home world!"

So the Sillaron fear the Zlan like almost all other species do, Mickie thought. *Good, that's a plus.* "Those are my terms," he said aloud.

"Mickie, he's communicating with his home again," said Fencris. "He's asking for guidance from somebody. It's definitely being processed by a Cassolean, I can tell. Okay, the message is back ... they agree. They say they can handle the Zlan. That sounds suspicious."

"My masters agree." The Sillaron spoke again.

"Mickie, we just asked the Speaker to see if he could locate any more Sillaron on the planet," said Allie. "He was able to identify a definite entity talking to you and he searched for similar patterns. There are just nineteen of them."

"Good," said Mickie in response to the Sillaron. "Tell me, how many are there of you on this planet?"

"Several thousand."

So now we know. The thing is definitely lying. Mickie couldn't be sure whether to be even more worried about that, or not. *But at least we're forewarned.*

"Then you must give me the coordinates of your world and the location I must come to," Mickie said.

Instantly, images began to fill his mind. They were hauntingly familiar. Not just the images, but the way in which they appeared.... it was so like the way the young Cassolean girl had fed the directions to Markel the very first time he and Kerrala had teleported to start their careers. He felt tears rise behind his eyes as he remembered how beautiful Kerrala had looked, how angry she had been at the flirtation that had taken place with the Cassolean... *yes, definitely Cassolean image telepathy*, he decided.

But then the image itself... it was the galaxy of the original Pfafth home world he saw, taking Markel's memories. So close to the Milky Way of Humanity's Earth, just twelve million light years. *So that's where the Pfafth originated!* And the Sillaron world was also within that galaxy, just four hundred light years away, a mere step on a galactic scale. He printed the pathway to the Sillaron world in his mind, waited for the location of the city, the building, saw them both.... and he returned to the seacoast and the cool, salt-laden wind that sighed in from the ocean.

"I will be there in the morning of that city's time zone," he said. "With my bodyguards."

"I shall advise my masters," replied the Sillaron.

"Do that," said Mickie and turned to walk away. This time, he was certain. The Sillaron radiated triumph. *The meeting may be held under a flag of truce,* he thought, *but the war is still raging.* He couldn't entirely suppress the wave of fear that ran through him.

Chapter 5 – In the Enemy's Camp

He appeared in the middle of a cathedral-sized hall. At exactly the same moment, two of the biggest Zlan appeared, one on either side of him. Mickie was delighted with the timing, exactly what he had asked for when he had contacted the Zlan a few hours earlier. He found that he had no fatigue at all after this teleportation and knew that he had developed immunity to it. Even before he got his bearings and began to look around, he was satisfyingly conscious of the wave of utter terror that swept like a tsunami through the hall.

The place reminded him of Westminster Abbey. It was vast, at least a hundred metres long and half that wide. Lining the walls and rows of balconies were possibly two thousand of the weird, swirling shapes of the Sillaron. They had spilled onto the floor to within a few meters of him, but the frightening appearance of the two spiders had forced the crowd back against the wall, and the writhing smoke and flashes of terrified white faces formed a bizarre pattern around him.

"Let's enhance the effect," Mickie said telepathically to the Zlan and led the way in a slow, deliberate stroll round the perimeter of the floor area. The fear levels rose sharply as he passed within a metre or two of the Sillaron. Completing the circuit, Mickie returned to the middle of the floor, the two massive spiders towering three meters high taking up a position just a short distance behind him. Mickie could have sworn he detected a wave of amusement from them and decided that if he lived through this day he would try telling them human jokes and see what happened.

"So," he said loudly in Pfafth. "Who speaks for the Sillaron?"

The only sound was the continuous shifting and stirring as the mass of frightened Sillaron tried to move further away from the nightmare sight of the two Zlan. But directly in front of him, a pool of darkness began to spread, almost sucking the light from the already gloomy hall. Despite his pleasure in the fear of the massed Sillaron, Mickie felt his own fear rise as the darkness grew, expanded vertically and became a tall, dense shadow. This was the same as the horror that had taken over the Ship and ordered his death as a sacrifice on Drudyenko, but it was more than Sillaron, Mickie knew. This was something considerably more powerful and evil.

"I speak for the Sillaron." The voice was cold, utterly without any human tone and it radiated hatred.

Mickie felt a wave of intense terror. But he had learned that emotions could be caused by external forces and he carefully examined the ripples of horror that ran through him. He detected that he had been the subject of a deliberate telepathic wave that was intended to cause precisely the fear he had experienced. While his unease and worry about this new entity remained, the uncontrollable terror immediately dissipated. And something else became clear, also.

"And why do you speak for the Sillaron when you are not Sillaron yourself?" he said loudly and realised he had struck a chord. An audible gasp ran through the crowd. *Did the Sillaron not know this already, or was the gasp a result of the fact being made so public?* Mickie wondered. There was something very wrong with the Sillaron society.

"Because the Sillaron are *mine,*" the voice said with fury simply blasting from the centre of darkness. "And now, so will be the remaining Pfafth."

Mickie sensed the suppression device go into effect. A nervous shifting by both gigantic Zlan told him that they too had sensed the curtain fall over their telepathic communications and other powers, and he made a brief gesture to them to stay calm. They obeyed and went motionless.

"I'll ask my question again," Mickie said. "Who are you and why are the Sillaron your personal possessions?"

"You are about to die horribly!" the creature screamed, the anger so great that in a human it might have indicated intense madness. "Why do you waste time by questioning *me?*"

"Surely the condemned have a right to know who their killer is, don't you think?" Mickie had realised the intensity of the strange creature's fury and begun to understand that it was not sane. He was deliberately provoking it to see what would happen.

"Then know that I am the Sillaron master! I have owned them for a million years and soon I will own the rest of life! And your pathetic bodyguards are useless against me."

Mickie sent a thought directly at the little device hanging round his neck. The curtain blocking all their telepathic talents fell away, and in the tiniest fraction of a second, Mickie sensed the threat and directed an order to his Zlan guards.

"*GO!*" he said.

Instinctively, they teleported away, just as two bolts of energy from a heavy weapon blasted the marble floor where they had stood.

"So this is the flag of truce I was promised by the Sillaron, is it?" Contempt dripped from Mickie's voice.

From the black shape in front of him, a scream of outraged

fury shook the entire hall. "That is not possible!" the creature howled. "My weapon still functions, your Pfafth powers cannot work!"

"So now it is your turn to fear, Sillaron Master," Mickie said firmly. "My guardians dodged your bolts, despite your silly little suppressor. Now it is time for you to worry about where they are, and if they can teleport, how soon will it be before a thousand Zlan arrive to take their revenge against you and all your kind?"

"They cannot!" screamed the dark shadow. "However they escaped my control, I still have you and soon I will feast on the Pfafth millions when I have pulled the secret of their location from you."

"My armies of Zlan will soon outnumber your Sillaron," Mickie said calmly. "The last time they came to my aid, they took many thousands of your friends, the Korrobi and used them as food for their children. Now they are about to come for the Sillaron."

All around him, fear erupted. Waves of Sillaron began to move to the huge doors at either end of the cathedral-like space, but they found them locked. Howls of panic began to echo round the hall, but a monstrous bellow of rage silenced the frenzy.

"Now what, Pfafth?" came the silent enquiry from a Zlan into his mind.

"Cover the planet," Mickie ordered. "Do no damage, do not start a hunt, but show yourselves everywhere. See how many of these creatures there are."

"A hunt would be valueless," said the Zlan. "There is no food in these things."

"They can be grateful for that, then, even if they have no need to learn it just yet," Mickie said. He turned his attention back to the mysterious shape in front of him. As he did, he felt the suppressor come on again and smiled to himself as he countered it immediately. He knew he could kill that weapon any time he cared to.

"Millions of the Zlan are now covering the planet," he said. "I have but to release them and they will start a slaughter of your people that will make the killing of the millions of Pfafth look like a children's party game." He had no compunctions about telling this lie to one who had betrayed a truce.

Somewhere, somebody had found the way to unlock the doors and a huge flood of black, smoky shapes began moving to the outside. The doors were almost the size of the entire end walls and the building cleared in minutes.

"Your servants seem to be deserting you," Mickie said in the echoing silence. "Perhaps they value their homes and their children's lives more than ancient dreams of slaughtering Pfafth."

"I will reclaim them when I choose," the malevolent voice said. "Just as I will claim the souls of your Pfafth, just as I already control the Gelkka, the Drudya and those primitives on Merrison. Who can stop me?"

"Well, we seem to have done a pretty good job of stopping you so far," Mickie said. "And that's before we bring out our newest ally."

"And just what ally is that?" the dark shadow said with a sneer.

"The one my friend Fencris met when he called the Zlan to Korrobodor. I suspect he regards you as nothing more than a minor irritant."

But the leader of the Sillaron had gone.

Feeling a little shivery, as if walking into a black cave where there might be poisonous snakes, Mickie advanced on the spot where it had been. There was no sign that anything had stood there just seconds ago.

"Damn, I didn't record this for nothing," Mickie murmured and activated his last weapon.

From the set of tiny but powerful speakers he had hung round his waist, the thundering sounds of a cathedral organ began, and Mickie realised he had made a perfect choice of music for the occasion. The Great D Minor *"Toccata and Fugue"* by Johann Sebastian Bach filled the huge vaulted hall and echoed gloriously. Somewhere under the magnificent sounds he heard just one final scream of pain and despair, then nothing.

"So it's not the same one that we killed before," he said aloud. "That one had learned to counter the effect of music. This one didn't know about it. I wonder how many more there are and where?"

"Young Pfafth," said the voice of the Zlan in his head. *"We have covered the planet. There are very few of these things here. Our best estimate is no more than five million and the technology looks limited. Most are in small villages."*

"Just what I had begun to suspect," Mickie replied. "The Sillaron have declined just like the Pfafth and live on nothing but old hatreds. My thanks for your service, friend Zlan. Please feel free to return home."

"But there is one other thing we have found that you must know."

"What is that?"

"We have a colony of about five thousand Cassoleans just a few kilometres from you."

Of course! There had to be Cassoleans somewhere! "How are they responding to your presence?" he asked.

"They were terrified at first. But we have established some basic communication with them and have at least told them that the Sillaron rule is over. It would be advisable to come and meet with them and explain the situation. The idea of a whole modern Cassolean civilisation elsewhere might be overwhelming."

"I agree, but how far did you say it was?"

"About a thousand kilometres."

"I don't know how to get there, then. I can't teleport short distances as you can, and I've seen no sign of mechanised transport. It would take me days to walk there."

"We have the solution. Come outside."

Curiously, Mickie walked out through the massive cathedral doors into the bright sunlight to be met by the sight of one of the largest Zlan he had yet encountered, even larger than his two bodyguards who had accompanied him to the Sillaron world.

Then he understood the solution being offered and his first reaction was horrified denial.

"Yes, we thought you might not like the idea at first."

Mickie was certain, the Spider had an echo of amused irony in its tones and with that realisation he laughed out loud and lost the reaction. He walked up to the beast, examined the legs like pillars in front of him and realised that the stiff hairs on the limbs made climbing quite easy. Moments later, grinning widely, he sat where he was quite certain no member of any of the species he had so far encountered had ever sat before, on the back of a monstrous spider. He gripped some of the hairs standing in front of him and felt a small tremble as the scene before him flickered out of existence for a fraction of a second to be replaced by another.

A small crowd of Cassoleans stood in front of him. Behind them, the buildings of a small town looked attractive, with low, elegant structures painted mainly in black and white, reminding him of the historic towns in England's west Midlands. From his elevated position he saw the crowd's first frightened reaction as the enormous Spider materialised in front of them. Then they steadied, as they consciously recalled that the Zlan were their allies. But as they saw Mickie sitting atop the monster, a sigh of awe ran through them.

Mickie stood up and somehow lowered himself down the front leg of the beast, turned and walked towards the front row of people.

"Hello," he said. "My name is Mickie Dalton."

* * * *

Establishing full communications was a strange, complex business. While Mickie's shoulder communicator could handle standard Cassolean languages, the people of the Sillaron planet had been separated from their civilisation for a million years and the dialect had diverted well away from anything his translator could understand.

The Zlan communication band was sufficiently like the Cassolean for them to get some standard concepts through, but it was enough to get them to work with Speaker 356 who scanned several minds, worked out the new waveband and was able to get sufficient data to set up free communications. Once he had returned to the Ship, Mickie knew, the Speaker's data would be fed into the computers and the new dialect added to the range of languages managed. But for now, they were finally able to speak through the telepathic links of Speaker 356.

"We have legends of former times," the Cassolean leader said. He gave his name as Velkazim. "We have legends that tell us that once we were an enormous race that numbered millions and we served the greatest powers in the Universe. But we fell from grace many millennia ago and we have lived on this planet, ruled by the Sillaron and forced to serve them as punishment for our crimes."

"The crimes were not yours," Mickie replied. "But your legends are true, and the Cassoleans are still a wonderful, beautiful race that number in the billions and they are ready to welcome you home to Cassolea."

A sigh ran through the crowd. Mickie saw tears in Velkazim's eyes.

"That's what the legends say also, that one day we could return to our former home. You say that our people are *billions* in numbers?"

"They are. And while they have much to show you, you have even more to teach them, for they lost many of the Cassolean powers when those events occurred that separated you. They are only just now recovering them, but they need your wisdom in how to control them."

Velkazim looked stunned, and turned to face his people for a moment. Then he turned back. "How do we go about this reunion?" he asked.

"Speaker 356, will you establish contact between Velkazim and the leaders of the Cassolean government?"

"Leave it with us, Mickie," said the Speaker.

Mickie took the hand of the Cassolean. "I think both of your groups have a lot to learn from each other," he said. "Good luck."

He turned back to the Zlan. "Your work today was even greater than on Korrobodor," he said. "Now it's time for both of us to go home."

Mickie closed his eyes, found the image of the dull mining world where his Ship waited in orbit and took himself back to his friends and family.

Chapter 6 – Contacts With the Past

"I'm really not sure I can handle any more of this!"

Mickie was sitting with Grant and Allie in their cabin and the effects of the last few weeks were showing. He had started trembling with shock, his throat had dried up and he had begun feeling acute sickness. One of the Ship's medical crew had examined him and reported severe reaction to stress, given him a strong sedative and left him to the best therapy he could have, time alone with his parents.

He sat on the front of his seat, elbows on his knees, staring down at the floor. He felt acutely depressed.

"It's hardly surprising," Allie said gently. "You've had more to deal with than anyone could possibly have anticipated, discovered more about yourself than you could have dreamed and faced up to some horrible dangers. Just look at what's happened in the two years you've been with us and how far you've come."

"Dangers I got the whole crew into," Mickie said, feeling appalled at the threats the Ship and its crew had faced since he first came aboard.

"Mickie, we're a trading ship covering several galaxies and exploring others. That's what we do and we've made ourselves rich by doing it. But life-threatening risks come with the job. Everybody who signs on knows that."

"You wouldn't have faced being killed by the Korrobi if it wasn't for the fact I'm Pfafth," Mickie persisted, stubbornly. His depression was forcing him to see the worst side of everything.

"They wanted the blood of all our kids, regardless of your being Pfafth," Grant said firmly. "And remember, you got us out of there by knowing that the Cassoleans used to be telepaths. Now sure, Fencris is one astonishing genius and he worked out how to recover that talent and that saved us, but we'd have been sucked dry by those little horrors if you hadn't been around. The Zlan came to rescue you, not us."

"I suppose so," Mickie grumbled, almost clinging to his depression.

"And never forget that this is the richest trading ship in history because of your find on Shuramee," Allie chimed in. "So, enough of the blues, kid. You have a trombone lesson in a few minutes and you're behind on some schoolwork, the teachers tell me. Get to it."

"So you don't mind that the Sillaron are still a problem and whatever it was that was controlling them is still out there and still a danger?"

"I think we can handle the Sillaron now," Grant replied. "And whatever that thing was, I doubt it's much of a threat any more, now that you have the anti-suppressor gadgets. And the greatest weapon of all, you always have! Remember, music is a killer to it. At the worst, you can *sing* it to death! Even with *your* dreadful singing voice!"

Finally, that broke Mickie's black mood. He jumped up and went to Allie. She stood up and they exchanged hugs. Mickie realised that he was as tall as she was now.

"Just remember," she murmured. "You're our son and we love you. The best thing Grant and I ever did was finding you on Earth."

He smiled and moved to Grant who gave him the same hug. Mickie still had a little way to grow to match his father.

"What Allie said," Grant said. He left his arm on Mickie's shoulder and began leading him to the door.

"So you don't mind that I turned down the job of Master of All the Universe?" Mickie said, keeping a straight face.

"Not at all," Grant replied. "Lousy pay, awful hours and Allie and I sure didn't want to go on our knees any time we wanted to talk to you."

"I can see that," Mickie said. "It's very hard for aged people like you going to your knees."

Grant laughed, released him and lightly smacked him on the head. "Show respect for your elders and betters," he said. "And work at that trombone. It's too horrible having to listen to you practice still."

Feeling a lot happier than he had an hour ago, Mickie headed for the school's music room.

* * * *

The four friends sat before the main screens in the Observation Room and watched the planet of X'Katcxo explode into being from the featureless blackness of hyperspace.

"I really don't think I'll ever get tired of that sight," Melkana said with a sigh.

Murmurs of agreement came from the other three.

"It feels years since were last here," Fencris said. "I really look forward to staying at the house with the swimming pools again. We are staying there, aren't we?"

"So Grant said," Mickie replied. "And you know what? It *has* been over a year since the last visit."

"It was quite a party," Drellion joined in. "I must say, I could look forward to wearing that green and white uniform again. Heck, even Mickie looked moderately acceptable in it!"

Mickie grinned. "And remember that sad little kid that got thrown out of his family at the soul-reading? He's done pretty well as a crewmember with us. I heard he's been promoted to the engineering section and studying hard for his engine maintenance licence."

"We should probably go and get our bags," Melkana said. "The shuttle leaves in half an hour."

Chatting excitedly about the visit, the four went to the transporter to get to the residential deck, and twenty minutes later, met up again in the hangar bay to take their seats in one of the shuttles heading to the planet's surface.

"It's a big team going down this time, Allie," Mickie commented as he saw three large shuttles filling up with crewmembers. "What's happening?"

"Lots of stuff," she answered. "We're setting up a major university section to start recruiting flight crews to replace Kaloti. The X'Kasxi have been the best species so far in their aptitude and several ships are already manned entirely by them. But it takes some years, so we've started a full-scale push to recruit and train new people."

"The Kaloti advised us that we only have another twenty years of their presence and then they'll be gone," Grant added, a sombre look on his face. "They still won't tell us how they know so precisely, or why they're vanishing."

"But they don't seem worried," Melkana said, some of her distress showing. "Why won't they tell us anything?"

"Maybe they will, in their own time," Allie said. "It's just another of those great mysteries of our universe. Anyway, we also have some geological teams spreading out over the planet. The last trip showed massive veins of some very useful minerals at both poles and in a few other areas, and with the X'Kasxi's consent, we're looking to extract some. So it's going to be a busy week here."

"And what will you be doing?" Mickie asked his mother.

"I'm hoping really, *really* hard to get some more time with the Guide, X'Kaa Tz'Horzash whom we met last time and whose house will be our residence again. Some of the hints he gave about spiritual life, a possible after-life, the nature of the soul, all these are on my list and I hope he'll be a bit more forthcoming this time."

"I think I'd like to talk to him, also," Mickie said. He felt his hands start to tremble lightly. "I think...." His voice tailed off as memories began to flood back into his mind.

"Mickie? Mickie, what's happening?" Allie's voice was sharp. "Those reactions coming back?"

"I've just remembered..." Mickie could hardly speak, so strong were the floods of emotion shaking him.

"More from the life as Markel?" Allie had her hand on his shoulder and was looking firmly intro his eyes.

"It was the trip I made with Kerrala. We met an old Guide in a little village outside the main city."

"You mentioned that before, some months ago, after you'd woken up from the hallucination. You said then that the X'Kasxi seemed to know more than they were letting on."

"Yes, I remember. It's just that the memory is so much stronger this time, and..." He broke off again, sensing something different in his mind.

"And...?" prompted Allie.

"And this time the Guide wants to talk to me about that."

"How do you know?"

"I've no idea," Mickie said. "I just do."

For the trip down to the surface and the half-hour land journey to the mansion house of their host, Mickie was totally withdrawn from the group as he relived the memory of the strange trip Markel and Kerrala had made over a million years ago to this same planet and been told such frightening facts by a spiritual leader of the X'Kasxi.

The very young pair of Pfafth had been sitting on a bench in the square of the small village. Their mission had been to try and sense the attitude of the X'Kasxi using their superlative empathic talents, because the local management of the Pfafth Empire believed something subversive was going on.

"I am X'Kaa Gaishaxan," the ancient X'Kasxi Guide had said.

"My name is Markel and my colleague is called Kerrala," Markel responded. "We are honoured that you chose to greet us."

"We must always show respect for the Masters of the Universe," the old man replied.

The answer was disturbing, not in the words, but in the tone of them.

"And yet we detect something other than respect," Kerrala said. "Amusement, perhaps? Possibly contempt?"

"Presumption of absolute superiority and mastery of the Universe is invariably amusing to us," the Guide answered. "It always precedes a downfall."

There! That was the moment at which Markel had realised this was no ordinary conversation. Mickie felt the same ripple of fear run through him as Markel had experienced so long ago.

"This meeting was not accidental, was it?" Markel asked. "You were sent to deliver a message to all of the Pfafth."

"Neither the meeting nor your choice of today's travels," the old man agreed.

"But I chose this village at random!" Mickie could clearly remember the utterly outraged and bewildered tone in Kerrala's voice.

"That is your belief," the Guide said. "But you are wrong. Your visit was determined by others."

"But nobody told me which place to choose! I just picked it from several villages within a day's travel."

"I knew of your visit six days ago," the Guide said with a small smile.

"Six days ago? We were still on Tracomal at Sector Government Headquarters six days ago and we hadn't even been told of our trip to X'Katcxo."

"So who told you we were coming?" Markel demanded.

"Those higher souls." The Guide smiled gently. "My friends, nothing is ever as it seems. Infinite power is not infinite power. Mastery is not mastery. And as you have already seen, young Master Markel, benign rule is not always benign rule."

Mickie remembered his shock that somehow the Guide knew what was deep inside Markel's mind, his growing doubts about the nature of the Pfafth rule over its colonies.

"And is it the X'Kasxi who will lead the uprising against us?" he asked.

"The X'Kasxi, Master Markel? How could we possibly lead an uprising against you? You could destroy us in seconds."

"Then who?" But the old man walked away without replying, leaving Markel and Kerrala staring at each other in bewilderment and distress.

Even after a thousand millennia, Mickie could remember Markel's fear of what was to happen. He wondered if he would get any answers to that million year-old confusion on this visit.

* * * *

The first two days of the visit were much like the trip of over a year ago. The boys shared one vast room with its own, equally vast swimming pool, while Melkana had her own, smaller suite, also equipped with a pool. It was a feature of X'Kasxi life that they all decided was something they should adopt back home. They resolved to ask the Ship's Captain if a pool could be fitted out on board.

The dinner session was the same highly formal event they had previously experienced. Again, they were issued the smart green and white tunics in the colours of the House of Tz'Horzash and enjoyed a lavish feast in the main hall.

On the third day, Mickie asked if he could borrow a gravity car to seek out the little village where Markel and Kerrala had met the old Guide who had warned them of the Empire's collapse. But as he tried to give directions based on his memories, the young X'Kasxi who had offered his services as a driver shook his head. He had introduced himself as D'Zhi of the House of Tz'Horzash.

"The City has expanded many kilometres beyond the area you mention. Instead, I can take you to our records and see if we can find references."

"You have records going back a million years?"

"Even beyond," D'Zhi replied.

Mickie sat silently in his seat, the implications of the man's words causing some disturbance in his mind. If the X'Kasxi were sufficiently civilised over a million years ago that they had continuous records, that surely put them ahead of any known civilisation, he thought. While the Cassoleans and Pfafth, even the Sillaron went that far back, none of them had managed to maintain a continuous line of their civilisations. And a million years ago, his memories of Markel told him that the X'Kasxi were even then a highly cultured and sophisticated species.

The car had stopped outside a massive building that covered several hundred metres along one side and towered at least sixty floors above them.

"Our Hall of History," said D'Zhi, obvious pride in his voice.

"I'm impressed!"

They climbed out of the vehicle, which moved away automatically to find a parking spot. The two young men entered the building and Mickie was led along an enormous tiled corridor, into a transporter that took them silently to some location at the telepathic instruction of the X'Kasxi and they exited into a large, circular hall lined with doors.

"This way," said D'Zhi, leading them to one of the doors, opened it and entered. "I reserved a research room as we travelled."

The room was a pleasantly furnished study about the size of a large office. Several lounge chairs sat around the walls, leaving the centre empty. The X'Kasxi took a seat against one wall and indicated Mickie should do the same.

"Show the city of Brx'Jashcha as it is today," he said.

Much like the Ship's computer did in Mickie's education sessions, an image of the city appeared, as if viewed from many thousands of metres above.

"Show the scale in kilometres, with numbers in Earth-standard format," D'Zhi instructed, and a line appeared beneath the map. Mickie peered at the markers.

"The city is over a hundred kilometres across?" he exclaimed.

"With a population of just over forty million. It is seven times the size of any other city on X'Katcxo."

"This is wild! I can't imagine how you manage a city that size!"

"We are proud of the fact that it works so well," D'Zhi smiled. "Now, let us see the city as it was a million years ago."

Soundlessly, the map imploded and a small town appeared in its place. But the original outlines of the present city remained in faint lines, a long way from the centre. The main highways and roads of the modern city also showed as faint lines.

"The centre is just like it was then!" Mickie said with interest. He could see that the main roads meeting in the middle of the little town were firmly on the outlines of the earlier map. The scale showed that the ancient town was just three kilometres across and a new legend was displayed showing the population as just two hundred thousand.

"Can I ask questions of the computer?" Mickie enquired.

D'Zhi nodded. "Go ahead, anything you want."

"Are there any records of a Guide named X'Kaa Gaishaxan from the same time as this map was taken?"

"X'Kaa Gaishaxan of the House of Hj'Bjarnesh lived from 812 to 934 Modus 5."

Mickie's heart pounded. He was about to make a connection with the million-year-old history that he had experienced in his coma. But there was a problem.

"What do those numbers mean?" Mickie was baffled.

"We have several historical eras," D'Zhi replied. "I can't remember the details of that one, so let's check. Computer, give that era in years based on today's date."

"X'Kaa Gaishaxan of the House of Hj'Bjarnesh was born six hundred and nine thousand years ago and lived one hundred and twenty-two years."

Excitement ran through Mickie. So this *was* the same Guide Markel and Kerrala had met. With the length of the X'Katcxo year being what it was, that meant the Guide had lived to an age of over a hundred and eighty years of Earth time and in a period about a million Earth years ago.

"Where did X'Kaa Gaishaxan live?" he asked.

On the projected map, a small circle appeared, some twenty kilometres north west of the town centre.

"Do you have a map of the place as it was then?"

The projection was immediately replaced by one of a small village and Mickie drew in his breath sharply. There was one central square and that could only have been the location where Markel and Kerrala had sat and met the old Guide. He felt tears rise at the memory. He decided to try a wild card.

"Is there any record of the Guide meeting representatives of the Pfafth?"

He sensed the sharp look thrown at him by D'Zhi.

"There is no such record," the computer replied.

"Then are there any records of Pfafth rule over the planet of X'Katcxo?"

"Records of the era of Pfafth rule are restricted."

Oh wow! Mickie thought. *So they really do know all about the Pfafth and they've never said a word.* He felt his heart thumping even harder.

"Who may access them?"

But there was no reply from the computer. Instead, D'Zhi rose to his feet.

"Mickie, it is now time for you to meet with X'Kaa Tz'Horzash of my House. We must go."

Aware that very strange things were happening, Mickie followed the young man out of the Hall of History.

"We will take a detour on the way home," D'Zhi said as they stood outside the massive building waiting for the car to bring itself from the parking spot.

"A detour? Where?"

"I think you will know it when we get there."

As they drove, Mickie tried to read the man's state of mind, but found himself unable to. Just the faintest traces of excitement and pride could be detected. But after fifteen minutes or so, Mickie realised where he was.

Although large, modern buildings ringed it, the square was still obviously the location where Markel and Kerrala had met the Guide a million years ago. There was even a park bench located where the two young Pfafth had been sitting, though its construction of modern materials made it very different in appearance. D'Zhi stopped alongside the seat and said nothing, obviously expecting Mickie to step out. He did and slowly walked to the bench, trembling as the memories of that extraordinary meeting rose up in his mind like a gusher of oil released from the deep earth.

The image of Kerrala was perfectly clear. Her calm, clear eyes, perfect skin and dark hair that fell down her shoulders,

Mickie remembered how her eyes had reflected bewilderment and distress as the Guide told them the days of the Pfafth Empire were running down. It had been on this very spot.

He touched the seat with trembling fingers and wondered if the Kerrala child bred with her DNA would ever appear and what she was like.

Then he firmly walked back to the gravity car and they drove back to the House of Tz'Horzash for Mickie to meet their host who might have some answers for him.

Chapter 7 – Revelations of Infinity

"I see you, Mickie Dalton of Kalamos."

"I see you, X'Kaa Tz'Horzash."

The ritual greeting completed, Mickie tried to relax, sitting cross-legged on a cushion. About three metres away, the Guide who was also their host while on X'Katcxo sat in the same manner. They were alone in the room where Mickie had once watched the soul reading of the young X'Kasxi when he was deemed unfit for entry to the House of Tz'Horzash and instead, sent to join the Ship as a new recruit.

The Guide reached down for the small cup of mint tea and took a sip, which Mickie knew was a signal that he could do the same. His throat was dry and he was as nervous as any X'Kasxi pup reaching the time of his Ten Year Reading when his soul was read and his future determined in just such a meeting as this. But Mickie's nervousness was helped by knowing that his parents were watching the scene from behind the mirrors.

"We met a year ago when you last visited us," the Guide said.

"That was my great honour, X'Kaa Tz'Horzash." Mickie had spent over an hour with Allie and Grant reviewing the standards and styles of courtesy with the X'Kasxi.

The Guide bowed his head slightly. "You and your colleagues had brought great wealth and prestige on this House, so the honour was mine. I remember then that you caused me great surprise."

"Surprise, Guide?" Mickie remembered clearly the shock displayed by the old man when their hands had touched and the Guide had recognised that Mickie was not a human being of Earth.

"I knew then that you were very different, but it was not till later that I realised that you were Pfafth."

"How did you realise that, X'Kaa Tz'Horzash?" Mickie felt that great things were about to be revealed.

"I told you all at that time that I was guided and helped by higher souls. It was these souls that later told me of your identity."

Mickie was sharply reminded of the conversation Markel and Kerrala had had with the Guide in the village square. "The same souls that guided X'Kaa Gaishaxan to meet with the two Pfafth and tell them the time of the Pfafth Empire was ending?"

"Indeed, Mickie, those same souls as well as others."

"From a million years ago, X'Kaa Tz'Horzash?"

The old Guide smiled. "A million years is nothing, young man. Not in the scale of Infinity."

"But how does any entity live a million years, Guide?"

"Do you remember your meetings with the Harliya tree-people?"

"Yes, Guide. They told me that they live many times, coming back to be born again after they have died in the jaws of the Long Feeders."

"Did you believe them?"

"I don't know. They certainly presented a lot of evidence, and they were always able to continue a debate with my parents that had started on a previous visit with another Harliya as if they were one and the same."

"They told you the truth. And do you recall the mention that after a certain number of such lives, they cease coming back and move elsewhere?"

"I do, Guide."

"It is from that Plane of Elsewhere that my guides live over a million years and teach me."

Mickie was trembling. He badly wanted to talk with his parents about what he was hearing, but all of them had agreed to the Guide's request that Mickie have this conversation alone, though Allie and Grant could observe it. They had promised that they would not use the telepathic powers of the Speakers or the mental radio of the Ship's communication systems to talk to each other.

"So you have always known about the Pfafth Empire and how you were once part of it?" Mickie asked.

"We have."

"This I must ask, X'Kaa Tz'Horzash. If you and your people have always known about the Pfafth, how have you hidden this knowledge from the Speakers? So many of you are in constant telepathic communication with them, surely they would have detected such information? And yet the Speakers had no knowledge of the Pfafth when they were first mentioned by the Zlan."

"We are an ancient race Mickie, as you know. We were a civilisation thousands of years before the Speakers reached their full capabilities and we have encountered telepathic races before. Only a few of us Guides know about the Pfafth, and we learned how to block off parts of our minds long ago."

"Did you know what had happened to the Pfafth after they departed X'Katcxo?"

"We knew of the terrible slaughter conducted by the Sillaron, but we did not know where the survivors went. Even my Guides could not follow them. We assumed that all had died. But then you appeared and that meant they still existed, somewhere."

"They travelled to a single galaxy and then moved themselves forward in time by one second."

The older one's eyes widened in astonishment. "Even my teachers could not see that. Time is an impenetrable curtain and we had no concept that such a thing could be done."

"It was done by twelve people. And today, there are just fifty who know how to cross that barrier. I am one."

The Guide's astonishment filled the room, Mickie felt.

"So the Pfafth live on today." The Guide spoke more to himself than to Mickie.

"They do. I was able to visit them just a few weeks ago. There are only about eighteen million of them when once they were three hundred million, and they have declined into a race with no superior powers, living on nothing but dreams of revenge."

The Guide closed his eyes for a few seconds then looked again at Mickie.

"The Pfafth were always a strange development, we felt. A race with such powers that they could rule a vast Empire, but without the spiritual maturity required to rule wisely. Really, they were just small boys given a fearsome weapon and all they did was terrorise the neighbourhood."

Mickie almost laughed at the comparison. "And yet you seemed unafraid of them, back when they ruled you. My memories of my ancestor, Markel, are that you liked us in a way that people liked puppies, and you seemed happy enough to let the Pfafth rule."

"Because we knew that such a situation could not last. The collapse of the Pfafth Empire was inevitable, given their immaturity. We chose to live in peace with our temporary masters. Within Infinity, the Pfafth had a very short time."

"And your friends on the Plane of Elsewhere told you of the coming collapse?"

"They did. Now it is time for you to learn about the Shurameen and the Kaloti."

Whoops! Here it comes, Mickie wondered if his parents were equally excited by what they were to hear.

"Why do races die out, Guide?"

"They do not die out, Mickie. They merely grow up and go Elsewhere."

Mickie rocked back on his cushion. "The same Elsewhere that your teachers live in?"

"Think back to the Harliya, Mickie. They live many lives, and while it appears to be a short, idyllic and non-productive life, they mature spiritually during that time. When their souls have learned enough, they move to a higher plane to start a new phase of existence. Eventually, all the Harliya will reach that plane and they will not live on their tree world any more. It is part of growing up, just as you grow up and move away from home to a different one."

"The Shurameen have already gone to this place, this... Elsewhere?"

"And the Kaloti are preparing for it. There will be no more Kaloti born."

Mickie's mind was reeling. "But what happens after that, Guide?"

"I have no idea, Mickie, my teachers will not tell me."

"Will it happen to you?"

"Eventually. But the role of the X'Kasxi is partly to teach others about this. We will stay for many centuries yet, even though most of us are Old Souls."

"Old Souls?"

"Just as you have grown from an infant to a child and are now a young man who will eventually become mature, then old, so does the soul grow up and age, Mickie."

"Will it happen to all of us? Kalamosians? Cassoleans? Humans?"

"Eventually, yes."

"And what of the Pfafth?" Mickie was struggling to keep his mind in balance as these astounding things were told to him.

"The Pfafth have a problem," the Guide said gently. "Even before they retreated behind a barrier of time, they were spiritually very immature. If they have been isolated from all other species for a million years, they cannot have progressed and it seems from your observations they have gone backwards. My Guides on the Plane of Elsewhere tell me they must come out of their cave or they could endanger all of Creation."

"I don't understand, Guide."

"Nor do I, young man. This is what my Guides tell me. But it seems that somehow, you must lead the Pfafth back into the normal universe so that they can return to the normal experiences of growth."

Mickie was shaking with exhaustion and overloaded mind. "I don't know how to do that," he said.

"If your ancestor was one of those who moved the Galaxy forward, the power remains within you. You have plenty of time to discover it."

"And what of the Sillaron? There are even fewer of them but they seem to have a ruler of massive power."

"There are forces of evil in the Universe, Mickie. The Sillaron must also grow again, but the force that leads them is beyond my comprehension. We will all need to work together to tackle that one."

"X'Kaa Tz'Horzash, why have you chosen this time to tell us these things? You have kept them hidden for many thousands of years."

"Because now, Mickie, several species are reaching this critical time of growth just as new dangers appear in the Universe. And the Pfafth must return to the family of all the species to play their part. And in that drama, you have a large part to play yourself."

Mickie could not take any more. "I have to go," he said.

"You have already taken more than anyone could have expected of you," the Guide said. "Go to your parents, Mickie. You still have high mountains to climb."

Mickie had only hazy recollections of the Guide standing up and leaving, then his parents entering the room, helping him up and leading him away.

Chapter 8 – Another Pfafth in The Universe

"If I was gob-smacked the last time the Guide gave us some insights into the spiritual nature of the Universe, then I'm triply-gobsmacked now." Allie sat in a comfortable lounge in the suite she and Grant shared while in the Guide's house. Grant sat alongside her and she had settled comfortable against his shoulder. Both of them cradled crystal glasses of scotch, a bottle of which had been discovered in the room with much delight. It always pleased Mickie to see them together like this. It gave him a warm sense of security that he had never experienced in the near-forgotten years on Earth.

"It will send some jolts through a lot of civilisations, when it all gets out," Grant said in agreement. "There are a lot of religions and philosophies that will be contradicted by what the Guide said."

"The religious loonies on Earth won't be happy, that's a fact," Mickie said with a grin. "But it will be many years before they hear about it, so I suppose there's nothing to worry about there."

"But what with all that spiritual stuff, and the fact that the X'Kasxi have been hiding so much from the rest of the Universe what they knew about the Pfafth, a lot of beliefs about history are going to get turned upside down," Allie continued. "You've certainly had an impact, young Mickie, since we picked you up as a frightened, miserable little kid. Just the Cassoleans alone are going through some mighty turmoil, never mind everyone else."

Mickie felt a surge of worry. "I hope nobody gets upset with me about this."

"No chance," said Grant, reassuringly. "We're all mature enough to understand that great discoveries get made, they contradict previous beliefs and that has to be accepted. Nobody's going to blame you for discovering the old Cassoleans and the telepathic skills, nor for learning about the Pfafth. It just happens."

"I hope so." Mickie wasn't entirely certain. "What scares me most though, is that the Guide seems to expect me somehow to bring the Pfafth out of their hiding place. I have no idea how to do that and I'm not sure I want to anyway."

"Mickie, regardless of the fact that you have the entire life memories of a great leader in your head, you are still a fourteen-year-old boy," Allie said with a smile. "That's the life we want you to lead from now on. If some day, the whole Pfafth thing comes up, we'll all deal with it then, and you'll get a lot of help. Just remember, you're not alone."

"Thanks." The simple word hid a great deal of emotion within Mickie. He was struggling to come to terms with what his parents had said. He *was* a fourteen-year-old boy, but the adventures of recent months had made him grow up, probably much too fast. And when he thought back to what he had been when he left Earth, only two years ago, it was like thinking about some fictional kid in a Charles Dickens novel, so detached was he from that awful life. Sometimes he wondered what would have happened if a Speaker had not heard his unconscious, telepathic cry for help. Would he have continued to be just an abused child, eventually growing up to take his revenge against his father and pay the legal consequences? Or would his Pfafth powers have begun to make themselves felt at some stage, and he performed some appalling act of violence, perhaps a mind bolt against someone hostile? Then he remembered the appearance of just one Zlan that morning in the park and the chaos and bloodshed that had been caused, even though nobody really believed the stories of the few eye-witnesses.

With that, he felt better and stood up. "Study time, I think," he said and moved to the door. "And you know what? I need to catch up both in school and with the trombone. Next planet, I think I'll pass on the visit and stay on board and do some work, if that's okay with you two?"

Grant waved his scotch glass at him. "No problem, kid! There's nothing of great interest on the next planet. Just a regular port of call to do some basic trading."

Mickie smiled cheerfully and went back to his cabin to practice the musical lesson of the day. He was enjoying the process more and more as he gradually learned to read music and play some well-known pieces from Earth. A couple of hours of that and some chemistry studies and he thought he'd give the gang a call to Hangar Ten and a game of Loopies.

*   *   *   *

"I suppose you've really become a space traveller when you're too bored to come down to a new planet and have a look!" Melkana joked. "You're sure you won't come with us?"

"It's not that I'm bored!" Mickie protested. "But I really do have a lot of school work to do, and the trombone still sounds like a wounded cow. A few days alone will be a perfect time to catch up."

"Very sensible, I reckon," Fencris said. "Just look at what's happened every time you've visited a planet recently!"

"That's right," Drellion chimed in. "Every place you go, you get people dropping in from all over the Universe, asking you to come and talk to the Great Leaders! And when you do, all sorts of horrible stuff happens."

Mickie flicked a drop of *Sle'Ach* at him and grinned as the boy's lightening reflexes let him dodge with a casual grace. "Then you should be safe this time," he said. "What's down there, anyway? Have you been before?"

All three nodded. "Nothing much, actually," Drellion said. "Technologically about on a par with Kalamos, culturally a bit more primitive, so they still have nation wars and things like that. The people are almost humanoid like us, a bit heavier build, that's about it. We pick up some minerals and sell them computer technology."

"All a bit boring, really," Melkana admitted. "It's just that we spend so much time on the Ship, it's always a good idea to get local gravity and fresh air when you can."

"Still, the best planet to miss, perhaps," Mickie said. "And as our leaping and spinning champion here said, I do seem to have had some weird stuff happening the last few planet-falls. I'll be happy to catch up with some normal stuff for a change."

"I think he's really going to practice some really wild Pfafth Loopies manoeuvres in Hangar Ten while we're away," Drellion said in a pretend aside whisper to the others.

"Heaven knows, he needs them," Fencris agreed and laughed as Mickie blew then a loud raspberry.

I wonder how I ever lived without this bunch? Mickie thought to himself.

By the end of the first day alone, Mickie was beginning to wonder if he'd made the right decision. The whole school was down on the planet, so he couldn't even take advantage of the freedom to explore the joys of checking out the interest in the Kalamosian girl, Nevinandra without worrying about how he felt about Melkana and her possible reactions, never mind his own.

He did a full hour of practice on the trombone in his cabin and explored the library of jazz from Earth that the computer held, finding some powerful and emotional Blues from the 1920s and 1930s in the USA and he tried playing some of those pieces, but gave up in despair after a few efforts.

Studies of the history of Kalamos didn't seem exciting without Melkana and Drellion to talk to about them and somehow make them more real.

Mickie realised he was bored out of his mind.

"So where are you guys now?" he asked, after establishing communications through the Ship's computer.

"We've decided to take a long walk," Drellion replied, his voice seeming to come out of empty air in Mickie's cabin, though actually being transmitted by the minute speakers in various locations around the room. "It's pretty nice country, really, and we're heading for a lake that everybody says is beautiful."

"I'm afraid my little brother is charging off into the distance," Melkana joined in. Mickie could hear the slight breathlessness in her voice. "But it looks like he's there, and so is Fencris, and .. oh my! It really is beautiful, Mickie. You should have come down here! It's gorgeous!"

"I wish I had, too," Mickie replied. "I'm bored here."

"Yeas, you should see this, Mickie," Fencris joined in. "It's the bluest water I've ever seen and it's flat calm. There are mountains on the other side and the reflection is just like a mirror. If ever a place needed a boat, this one does."

"Is it warm enough to swim?" Mickie asked.

"Let's check," Drellion said. "The beach is nice, and the water is.... let's see... yoiks! No! It's icy! There's no way anyone will get me in there!"

Mickie laughed. "Well, sounds like a great place for a picnic, anyway."

"And that's what we're about to do," Melkana said. "Let's see what we have... ooh, yummy stuff, Mickie!"

"Okay, at least I can match the yummy factor up here, but it's not the same as outdoors with you guys."

For another half hour, the four continued to talk, three of them basking on a beach on the planet, one of them a few thousand kilometres above, orbiting the planet in the vast Ship.

"I think I need to walk off that food a bit," Drellion announced after a short break. "Anyone else coming?"

"I think so," Fencris said. "Melkana?"

"No, I'm a bit sleepy," she said. "You guys go off, I'll just have a nap here."

"It should certainly be safe enough," Drellion said. "I doubt there's a soul within five kilometres."

Mickie opened one of his textbooks and tried to concentrate on the history of Kalamos, and conversation languished while the other two boys set off to walk around the lake.

"So how is it looking?" Mickie asked after twenty minutes.

"Fantastic!" Drellion replied. "This is like the lake regions near home. I can't imagine how great it would be to have a cottage...."

They were interrupted by a panic-filled scream from Melkana.

"Melkana, what's wrong?" Fencris shouted, the fear strong in his voice.

"These people!" Her voice was filled with tears and fright. "There's about ten of them, they've got knives... ah!"

"Melkana!" Mickie couldn't stop himself. He yelled in appalling terror of what was happening. Melkana's cry of pain had been horrible. "Albert!" he shouted to the computer. "Can you give me a picture of what's happening?"

"In two minutes," the Ship's computer replied calmly. "We'll be overhead the location and the cameras will see."

"Fencris!" Mickie called. "Where are you?"

"About five minutes away," Fencris gasped, obviously running at full speed.

Mickie was in agony, cursing the limitations in his Pfafth powers that prevented him from making a short-distance teleport to the scene, but until he had a clear image of where it was, he couldn't even attempt it.

There was another full-throated scream from Melkana and Mickie's blood seemed to freeze. But then he heard other noises coming from the communications device in Melkana's shoulder. In a second or two, he realised he was hearing shouts of panic and utter terror from male throats.

"Melkana!" he called again.

He could hear her sobs, deep, terrified gasps of fear such as he never wanted to hear again. But at least she was still alive.

And then the Ship reached a position in orbit where it could see the location and one wall of his cabin showed the scene.

And Mickie's world turned upside down.

Melkana was in the middle of the beach, kneeling on the sand, her head buried in her arms. Around the beach were scattered several bodies of the local people, some of them ripped into bloody parts, obviously dead. But Melkana was not alone.

She was surrounded by the Spiders of Zlan.

For a few moments, the scene stayed like that, as if frozen onto the sands of the beach. A few seconds later a shuttle arrived and Melkana's parents rushed out, stopped short for a moment as they encountered the Zlan, but the Spiders moved away and allowed them to get to their daughter and enfold her in their arms. Allie and Grant followed a few paces behind, clearly stunned by the sight, and then Fencris and Drellion ran in from the other side.

Drellion was the first to speak, showing considerable composure. "What are you Zlan guys doing here?" he demanded. "Not that we're not delighted to see you and very grateful and all that, but what brought you? Did you come to save Melkana because she's a friend of Mickie's?"

"We greet you, Drellion of Kalamos," one of the Spiders said with great formality. "But we have no requirement to save one of you because of your friendship with the Pfafth."

It was Fencris who got the implication first.

"Mickie," he said, his voice betraying his excitement and astonishment. "Now we know who the other Pfafth is."

Chapter 9 – Where to From Here?

"She was just thirteen months old when we adopted her," Mendorina said. Melkana's mother sat alongside Harrokarn on a couch in the cabin owned by Allie and Grant. Their hands were closely intertwined and Mendorina's face was still white with the shock of the events.

"We both thought that she seemed to have Mendorina's colouring, she could even have been a natural child of ours when we first saw her," Harrokarn said. "And when Drellion was born three years later, nobody could have seen that they weren't actually brother and sister. Look at them now, they look a lot like each other."

"How did you come to adopt her?" Allie asked gently.

"The usual channels," Mendorina said. "We thought we couldn't have our own child, so we applied for adoption. Melkana was found abandoned a few weeks earlier, and that's such a rare thing on Kalamos. The agency called us as soon as we filed our request. She was such a lovely little girl and we fell in love with her immediately. We never got any information about her parentage. I know that's odd, but the agency said it was a complete mystery to them how she appeared and they were never able to trace the mother."

"And neither of the kids knows about it?" Grant asked.

Harrokarn shook his head. "We wondered about telling them, but they grew up so much alike and so close, that we decided not to."

An hour had passed since the traumatic events on the beach. Melkana had been flown up to the Ship immediately and was now in the hospital suffering from severe shock and a bad knife slice across her shoulder. The latter would be healed within hours by the cellular reconstruction equipment, but her mental state was a worry. She was almost catatonic from the combined horrors of the ugly attack on her by a group of young males and then by the arrival of a dozen Zlan who had slaughtered her attackers within seconds. Her Pfafth identity was still not known to her.

"So they'll have to know the whole story soon," Allie said. "Drellion already knows she's Pfafth, so he has already worked out the obvious. How is he?"

"Remarkably cool," Mickie joined in. "I think he was absolutely shattered at first by the fact that she's not his natural sister, but he's also off the ground to learn that she's Pfafth. I think he was wondering if he was one also, but you've already told him that he's your real son. I'm not sure if he's disappointed or relieved at that."

"Nonetheless, the hospital's got him under observation as well," Mendorina said. "Just in case there's some delayed shock that could break out at any time."

"Well, now we know what it was that had the Zlan confused on Korrobodor when they came to our rescue," Mickie said. "They must have sensed another Pfafth somewhere around, but maybe thought it was my presence. But that was enough for them to have the trigger set with Melkana's mental waves and they responded to her fear when she was attacked."

Grant nodded. "Sounds about right. So now the issue is, how and when do we tell her? And how is she going to react?"

"I don't think you have anything to worry about," Mickie said.

Four faces turned to him, the question alive on each one of them.

"She just called me," Mickie said. "She heard Fencris on the beach. And she'd already come to the same conclusion. She knows."

* * * *

They looked cautiously at each other.

"Hey," he said, nervously.

"Hey," she replied. She was still in the hospital ward, lying under a blanket and her face was pale. She looked tiny and defenceless as if she had become five years younger.

Silence fell in the room.

"I had to find out sometime, I suppose," she said, breaking the spell of the few seconds.

"Hell of a way to do it," Mickie replied, a slight sense of relief growing at the possibility that she seemed to be coping.

"That's a fact," she said. "I'll never forget that horrible scene, what with those ugly men suddenly appearing with knives in their hands, then the Zlan arriving and ripping them to pieces."

"It could probably have been handled better," he agreed.

The silence resumed. Mickie stared at the foot of the bed, unable to meet her eyes.

"Hey!" she said again.

"What?" He looked up at her and her gaze was serious.

"Does this mean I get to do all those cool Pfafth things? Teleporting, mending any scratches and breaks, mind bolts and all that stuff?"

"I suppose so. It seems to come with the territory."

"How come I couldn't do it before?"

"I seem to remember that Pfafth girls developed those

talents later than the boys. You get the high empathic skills earlier and you've always had those, anyway. We just didn't know it was the Pfafth stuff."

"But didn't Kerrala develop those talents early, the same time as Markel?"

"Yes, but she *knew* she was Pfafth, so she expected to have those talents eventually. You didn't know about them. So you never even thought about trying to use them."

"I suppose."

Melkana seemed to fall into a reverie of her own. Mickie sat still, not daring to say anything that might upset her.

"You know what's funny?" she said after a few minutes of silence.

"What's funny?"

"I think I've always known. I just didn't realise it. But as soon as you arrived on the Ship, I felt... *something* familiar about you. And then when I heard Fencris say he knew who the other Pfafth was, my only thought was, well, of *course* I'm Pfafth, silly! It wasn't a surprise at all."

"That's weird."

"Isn't it, though?" She lapsed back into her own thoughts. Mickie studied her face.

"I hate to think they're not really my parents and Drellion isn't really my brother." Her voice was a sad murmur.

"But they are. They're all you've ever known and nothing's going to change. I mean, if Grant and Allie can be my parents after only knowing them two years, yours can be too, far more like real life. They're not going to love you any less."

"Mmmm." Silence fell again.

"What are we going to do about the whole Pfafth thing?" she asked softly.

"What, the blocked galaxy and all that nonsense? Nothing. I've already said I want nothing to do with that lot."

"But the X'Kasxi Guide said you had to!"

"Maybe one day. But I told my parents I just want to forget about the whole thing."

"Good. 'Cos remember, I don't have any memories of being Kerrala, like you've got of Markel, so it just isn't real to me, yet. I don't think I want to develop those skills and powers. It just isn't *me*. I want to carry on as before."

"Seems like a plan. When are you going to be fit for Loopies?"

Finally she grinned and her eyes sparkled. "Two more days. This cut is healed up, and I suppose I could try and work out how to do that Pfafth thing and heal it quicker, but I can't be bothered."

"Two days it is. We'll be ready." He stood up and made for the doorway to leave.

"Mickie?"

"Yes?" He turned back and her face was serious again.

"I don't want to have my life dictated by other peoples' ideas. I've got my own plans and being a Master of the Universe isn't one of them. And I know that we're the descendents of Markel and Kerrala, but we're not actually *them*. So if anything happens to us, it's as Melkana and Mickie, not Kerrala and Markel."

"I understand. Get fit. You're going to be whipped at Loopies in two days."

"In your dreams!"

He laughed and walked out, relived that the crisis seemed to be over and they were friends again. And his heart sang at the acknowledgement that one day, something might develop between them.

Chapter 10 – The Last Telling of the M'Sarda

"Mickie, I have X'Kaa Tz'Horzash wishing to speak with you."

The cultured tones of Speaker 356 broke into Mickie's trombone practice alone in his cabin. For a second, Mickie felt irritation. He had just reached a wonderful moment when he found he could play a piece just by ear, automatically placing the slide in the right position and blowing the note he wanted. He had carefully and slowly worked his way through several bars of *"Sweet Georgia Brown,"* having discovered the works of an English jazz band of the fifties and sixties, the Chris Barber band and heard this number played by Barber's silken smooth trombone.

But then the implications of the call hit him and he carefully placed the trombone on its stand. "Of course, Speaker," he said.

"I greet you, Mickie Dalton of Kalamos," said the soft tones of the ancient Guide from the planet of X'Katcxo, over forty million light years away.

"I greet you, X'Kaa Tz'Horzash," Mickie replied, feeling a wave of curiosity mixed with worry. *Why was the old Guide calling him now?* They had spoken only weeks before.

"I pass on a message to you from my teachers," the Guide said.

"From your teachers, X'Kaa? Those on the Plane of Elsewhere?"

"Those indeed, Mickie."

"I am deeply honoured that your teachers would wish to tell me something, X'Kaa Tz'Horzash, but I am also puzzled by this."

He could almost hear the smile in the Guide's voice, even filtered as it was through the telepathic links of the Speaker. It eased the serious concern that this conversation was causing him.

"It has never happened before, Mickie. But then, never before has a member of the most powerful species in the history of the Universe reappeared after a million year absence with such news as you brought."

"Then what is it that your teachers wish me to know, X'Kaa?" Mickie was feeling proud of the way he was conducting this discussion, remembering the courtesies due to such a venerable and powerful leader of the X'Kasxi people.

"They wish you to visit the planet M'Sardraz."

"I have never heard of that planet, X'Kaa." Mickie sent a swift mental query to the computer.

"We are quite certain of that, Mickie. It has never been visited by your people, neither Pfafth nor Kalamosian, nor by any other of the current space-going species, because the inhabitants have wished it that way."

"There is no record of any such planet, Mickie," said the computer into his mind.

"The inhabitants, X'Kaa? Then they are intelligent and civilised?"

"More than might appear when you visit them."

"But why am I asked to visit there, X'Kaa? And who asked me, your teachers or the people themselves?"

"It is the M'Sarda who asked."

Mickie's mind spun in confusion. "Then I do not understand at all. If nobody has had contact with the... the M'Sarda, how do they know about me and why have they asked me to visit?"

"They were a powerful race during the apex of Pfafth rule but the Pfafth knew nothing of them, while they knew everything about the Pfafth. They sensed your return and it was they who contacted my teachers. My teachers suggested that your understanding of what is happening in the Universe might be increased if you witness the Last Telling of the M'Sarda."

"What is the Last Telling, X'Kaa?"

"That you will find out for yourself. I have just given the planet's coordinates to your computer. You are within three day's flight time and it is important that you be there. You should also take the Melkana Pfafth-child. I believe your parents will approve."

"I shall try and do as you ask, X'Kaa."

"I thank you, Mickie Dalton of Kalamos. You will learn more about Infinity from this."

Mickie sensed the tiny break in the flow of energy that signalled the end of the contact.

"Speaker 356?"

"Yes, Mickie?"

"Do you know about the planet M'Sardraz?"

"Yes, we all know of it."

Mickie was shaken. "But you have never mentioned it!"

"There was no need to. And the M'Sarda made it clear for many thousands of years that they wish no contact with other species."

"Many thousands... Speaker, how long have they existed?"

"They were a civilisation before my species developed the Universal telepathic skills."

"So they were there at the same time as the Pfafth ruled their forty galaxies?"

"Yes."

"Can you tell me anything about them?"

"They preceded us, Mickie, as the great Universal telepaths. They studied every known intelligent species looking for the answers to the questions that all of us ask. Why does the Universe exist? How was it created? How does intelligence arise? But they kept their presence secret from almost all species. And while the Pfafth believe they created the Speakers, the race that truly developed our universal powers was not the Pfafth but the M'Sarda. They taught us how to replace them as the facilitators of communication. Without their help, we would not have become what we are."

Mickie began to wonder if he would ever come to the end of the series of shocks he was experiencing about his species.

"Speaker, does that mean you have always known about the M'Sarda?"

"It does."

"But that means you have always known about the Pfafth?"

"That is also true, Mickie."

"But you told us in the beginning that nobody knew about the Pfafth!"

"A regrettable lie. We were always under a commitment to the M'Sarda to hide our knowledge."

"But you seemed so shocked when you first told us you had found some traces of memories of the Pfafth."

"And we *were* shocked, severely so. We thought we were the only one left with any such knowledge."

"And you had no idea that the X'Kasxi also knew about the Pfafth?"

"None. The recent discovery of their ability to block that from us while using our communication powers has caused great interest among my species."

Mickie took a deep breath, deciding that this was probably not the last great shock he would receive in the story of the Universe's history.

"What is this Last Telling that they want me to see?"

"A most profound, spiritual event that ends one cycle of their existence."

"I don't understand."

"I will feed all the data into your ship's computer together with the requirements for the translator devices. Before you visit, you will learn more. But let me tell you this. No individual of any species has ever seen this moment in another species' history."

Utterly baffled and intrigued, Mickie went to talk to his parents.

* * * *

The same shuttle that had once taken Mickie alone down to the surface of Zlan to meet the Spiders' Council how descended quietly to the surface of M'Sardraz, though this time, Melkana accompanied him. She had raised no objections, nor had her parents when Mickie had told her of the discussion with X'Kaa Tz'Horzash. Nor had there been any problems with diverting the Ship's flight for a few days. Everybody with a financial interest in the trading vessel knew that they were the richest group of all the Kalamosian traders' fraternity, largely because of the find of Shurameen art treasures. And they all agreed also that the more Mickie could learn of the real history of the Universe, the better it would be.

"I know I'm Pfafth," Melkana said. "I know I'm sort of descended from Kerrala, so that gives me some responsibilities. Mickie and I will go down and see what this is all about."

Assured firmly by Speaker 356 that there was absolutely no danger, both sets of parents agreed. Albert, the computer had confirmed that he had received precise landing coordinates and also that full translation and cultural history data had been incorporated so both children would fully understand what was going on.

The door silently opening was the confirmation of touch down on the planet's surface and both children moved to the open space. The air was soft and fragrant, heavy with the scent of the ocean and the temperature was comfortably warm at what they knew was just after dawn. They had landed on a beach and as Mickie and Melkana stepped out, they realised the sand was pure white and smooth. Palm trees lined the beach and Melkana laughed as she broke the silence.

"Just like a tropical island!" she exclaimed in delight and bent down to pick up a scoop of the sand, letting it flow between her fingers as smoothly as cream. The sea was only a few metres away and the sound of the small waves was a gentle hiss as the water flowed up and down the sand.

Mickie looked around. "We're quite alone," he said.

"Of course we are, silly," Melkana replied, tracing a big "M" in the sand with her toe. "Remember what the computer told us, we'd land a little way away from the meeting site so as not to interfere. We have to walk about half a kilometre, up the beach, keeping the sea to our right."

She seemed to have recovered her normal sunny disposition, to Mickie's and everybody else's relief and she looked excited by this venture. She was no longer the pale, shocked little girl lying in a hospital bed, looking far younger than her actual years.

"You're right. Well, I for one am walking in the surf," Mickie said, removing his shoes and socks and rolling up the legs of his tunic above his knees.

"Great Pfafth thinking," Melkana agreed, doing the same, and the two of them began splashing their way along the beach, ankle deep in the warm sea. About a hundred metres along, the beach ended with a small outcrop of rock. They climbed over that to see another beach, this time extending into the far distance. They began walking in the surf again then stopped when they saw signs of life. A further short distance ahead, they saw a small crowd of people. As the children approached, they realised that the individuals were immensely tall. They seemed perfectly human in features, but none was less than two metres tall, Mickie estimated, and many were considerably taller. They reminded him of pictures he had seen of Masai tribesmen in Africa, a hugely tall, slender and graceful people.

"They're all adults," Melkana whispered. Something about the scene encouraged silence. Mickie saw that she was right. Everyone was a mature, full-grown person, not a child was to be seen. And nobody was speaking a word, nor did a single individual turn and take note of the alien visitors.

"Stay about fifty metres away," said the silent voice of the Ship's computer in Mickie's head. "They know you are here, but they will completely ignore you, so don't worry. They have invited you, but just to observe, not to partake in the events."

Mickie pointed at a spot in the shade of what looked like a magnolia tree, filled with sweet-smelling, bright red blossoms. Melkana nodded and they sat in the sand, sensing the temperature climb as the sun rose.

"Albert, there are no children," Mickie said through the silent connection to the computer.

"The Speaker's briefing was that there had not been a child born for over forty years," Albert replied. Mickie glanced at Melkana and she nodded, indicating that she was receiving the same information. He began to understand what was happening.

"They are vanishing, like the Kaloti and the Shurameen," he said, communicating to Melkana through the computer so that no words needed to be spoken aloud.

Their attention was diverted from any response as the entire group sat down in the sand, all facing away from them.

Just one individual remained standing, looking down on the assembly of perhaps a hundred people. It was a man, his face looking quite youthful compared to many of the others who seemed much older. Finally, the silence was broken.

"I am the last born to us," the man said. "And this is the Last Telling of the M'Sarda."

A small sigh ran through the seated crowd. The words and the sigh were the first sounds Mickie had heard from these mysterious people.

"I am Menshasha of the Bengoolong and this is my Telling," the man continued. "I have lived many lives and too many of those have been lives of pain for the crimes I committed against others. Once I was Hesgarosh of the Nayami and I killed thousands in my pursuit of power."

The sigh from the audience was deeper this time and Mickie saw some of them sway back and forth in grief.

"I think this is some form of confession ritual," Mickie said silently to Melkana.

"That is correct," said Albert. "My briefing from the Guide tells me that this ritual occurs only every two or three years and it does correspond to the ancient rite of confession that has occurred in many religions. The name Hesgarosh is one of a great tyrant of thirty five thousand ago who slaughtered several tribes as he tried to take power."

"Does that mean that this man once lived before and did those things?" Melkana asked, her face calm as if she already accepted the fact.

"The history and the evidence suggests that it is so," Albert replied.

The recitation of several other past lives continued for another ten minutes, and while none of the names or the episodes meant anything to Mickie, it was obvious that they were of huge import to the listeners who displayed signs of emotion throughout. He looked at the speaker again as he appeared to be coming to the end of his address.

"I am Menshasha of the Bengoolong and this has been my final Telling. I am the last to be born to you and soon we shall say our farewells."

The man sat down, tears streaming down his face and hugged a woman who was weeping the same way.

Another man, a lot older than the previous speaker rose to his feet and began a similar recitation of the crimes he had committed in numerous past lives. Occasionally, Albert interjected short commentaries about the events being mentioned. Soon, Mickie began to see the pattern. Each of the speakers was telling about long-ago incarnations when they committed appalling crimes against their own kind, but then lived their most recent lives in considerable pain or torment, forced to help others and suffer for them as some sort of repayment.

After nearly three hours, as the sun reached almost directly overhead, the ritual seemed to be coming to an end. The first speaker again rose to his feet.

"This has been the Last Telling of the M'Sarda," he said. "We here are the last of our people and I am the last to be born to us. We have paid our debts and finished this, the last cycle of the last of the M'Sarda. Now we must move on to the next chapter of Creation. Our time here is done."

A low, melodic note began from somewhere in the middle of the crowd. It was picked up by others in different harmonies and voices until it was a continuous, beautiful chord that lasted almost five minutes. Then it stopped abruptly. And in the same second, every one of the crowd seemed to drop unconscious to the sand.

But Mickie had extended his empathic senses out to them and he knew they were not unconscious.

"They're all dead!" Melkana spoke aloud. She had realised what Mickie had seen. Every single one of the people had died at precisely the same moment.

The two children got to their feet, sadness overwhelming them, and walked to the edge of the area containing so many bodies.

"This is horrible," Mickie said, trying to control his horror. "Why did they do this and why did they want us to see it happen?"

"It was merely the end of one stage of existence and the start of another," said a woman's voice.

Startled, Mickie and Melkana turned to the sound.

A young woman stood a few metres away. She was dressed simply, a white dress, bare arms, no hat in the blazing sun and bare feet around which the small surf washed gently. Her dark brown hair hung loosely down her back. There was nothing about her that could have generated such a sense of power, but she radiated strength in a way that made Mickie want to sink to his knees and hide his face. He sensed the same reaction in Melkana and without knowing when it happened, realised they were holding hands in some sort of protection.

"My name is Maragos," the woman said with a smile of great sweetness.

Mickie was overwhelmed with confusion. "But... you've been dead for forty thousand years.... you're a man.... you're a Shurameen..."

"All those things, yes," the woman said, and laughed. "Maragos is the name I have chosen and you are right, he was a man who died over forty thousand years ago when my species, the Shurameen did what you have just seen the M'Sarda do."

Both children shook their heads in utter bafflement.

"I don't understand," Melkana said. Mickie could feel how she was trembling and it reflected the same emotion in himself.

He knew he was in the presence of a power so great as to be incomprehensible.

"I was Maragos the sculptor," the woman continued. "But I was also every Shurameen who ever lived. I am the entire species that left their world forty thousand years ago."

His fear simply vanished and he knew Melkana had experienced the same.

"You had no need to fear," Maragos said. "I just made it easier for you to realise that."

"Why did we come here to see this?" Melkana asked.

"So that you could understand a little more of what you have to do," the woman answered. "But wait a moment, I think those bodies had better go."

Back where the mass of dead M'Sarda lay, something flickered. A small glow appeared then all the bodies vanished.

Maragos turned back to the two children. "In this heat..." she murmured. "Now," she said more briskly. "Young Pfafth, you know that all the M'Sarda have gone."

"To the Plane of Elsewhere?" Mickie asked, more a statement than a question.

"That's as good a name for it as anything else," Maragos said. "They had completed the cycle of physical lives and moved on."

"The Guide on X'Kasxi told me that all species do that eventually."

"He is correct. It is part of the total cycle for the Universe. But for them to move to the Plane of Elsewhere, they must have matured and grown enough to be ready."

"What happens when they move there?" Melkana asked. She seemed more able to handle these facts than Mickie was, for he was still so overwhelmed by the events of the morning that he was struggling to follow.

"That is something you need not know yet, nor should you," Maragos replied. "Each stage brings with it the wisdom to understand the next one. For now, you must only understand that complete maturity is essential for progress to the next stage. But we wanted you to see this, see that it was a very real thing that happens, this end of a complete stage of a species' existence."

Mickie finally began to understand. "X'Kaa Tz'Horzash said the Pfafth are very immature because they have been in hiding for so long."

Maragos turned her full gaze on him and Mickie trembled again as he looked into her eyes. It was like peering into the centre of a star, so powerful was the force within her.

"That is the problem," she said. "The Pfafth must return to the Universe of all beings and resume their growth. So must their galaxy. If they do not, the entire balance of Creation will be disturbed. You two must lead them out of their cave."

"I don't know how to," Mickie said. "It took eleven Pfafth to move the galaxy in time, and they had trained all their lives for that process. How can we two kids do it?"

"On your own, you can't," Maragos said. "But remember, Mickie, you two have almost all the power needed, even if not quite enough. There are other Pfafth who still retain most of the ancient abilities. Seek their help."

"The other agents." Mickie understood what she had told him.

"Indeed," she said with a smile that nearly brought him to his knees.

"Tell me again," Melkana said. "Just who are you?" She seemed far less disturbed by the events of the morning than Mickie was.

Maragos turned the force of her smile on her. "It's not easy to comprehend, I agree. And I can't tell you the entire story, because you are still too young as a species to be ready for it. But please try and believe that I am every Shurameen who ever lived throughout our history. We are now all one."

"All those millions and millions of people, they are all inside you?"

"That doesn't really explain it, but it will do."

"And you live on this... Plane of Elsewhere."

"There are other planes, child, even higher than the one you call the Plane of Elsewhere. My home is one of those."

"I don't think I understand at all." Melkana seemed cool, but not hostile, merely interested.

"It will be many thousands of years before you do, Melkana," said the extraordinary woman. "But for now, you must tackle the problem of the Pfafth. As your old Guide said, they have always been a problem race. They developed immense powers well before they gained the maturity to handle them. Now they must grow to that maturity, or they will find themselves again in the dangerous position of having power without wisdom. That is your task, young people. And now you should return to your ship and to your people."

"Will we ever see you again?" Mickie asked. Somehow, he knew that this meeting was a turning point in his life and Maragos had other parts to play in his future.

"I am always with you, with both of you," she replied. "Even if you can't see me, I will be there. But you have powers that even I do not, because the Shurameen did not have them, and it must fall to you two to bring the Pfafth back into the community of all species."

Feeling too stunned to say any more, Mickie turned to the track back to the shuttle and he and Melkana began to walk back along through the edge of the ocean. After a few moments, they both simultaneously turned back to look at Maragos.

But she had gone.

Chapter 11 – The Plane of Elsewhere

"Captain, a long time ago, you promised me I could just come and talk to you." Mickie felt nervous about calling the Captain, but his strong desire to spend some time talking to this mysterious and beautiful being had been increased by the recent events and he had finally plucked up the courage to call him.

"I remember that, Mickie and you are most welcome. Is there something specific you want to discuss?"

They sat in the Captain's cabin, the Kaloti sitting motionless in the high, elongated seat that was suitable for his tall, thin build. Most of the other seats in the cabin were more suitable for human structures, and as the other species that made up the crew were all similar to this model, any visitor could use them. Three other Kaloti-style seats were also present for the Captain's discussions with others of his kind.

The light was the soft, gentle yellow of the sun that warmed the Kaloti home world, so that the room seemed like it was experiencing late sunset to Mickie's eyes and gravity was only about half of that operating in the rest of the Ship, standard for Kaloti quarters.

"When I first asked you, I just wanted to talk to you about the Kaloti species and your history," Mickie said. "But so many strange things have happened since then that I really want to talk to you about things that you may not want to discuss."

The Captain's huge eyes widened to almost full circles, a sign of great amusement.

"I think I can anticipate the topics. You want to ask me if the Kaloti are about to move on from this cycle of existence and where we are going?"

Mickie took a deep breath. "Can I?"

"It would not normally be permitted. But I know of your recent adventures, of course, and I have learned that your mission now is to bring the Pfafth back into the community of the rest of the Universe's life forms. That is why you were shown the Last Telling of the M'Sarda and why the X'Kasxi Guide has told you of some of these mysteries. So I believe I can talk to you as you wish."

Mickie tried to gather his thoughts, aware that he might be on the edge of expanding his knowledge by even greater quantities.

"Will the Kaloti vanish soon, Captain?"

"We are the last of our species, Mickie. No Kaloti have been born for many years. The last of us will die in about forty years. I am one of that last generation."

"How long have you known that?"

"Within days of my birth. When several days passed with no more Kaloti born to us, the realisation came very fast. But we had suspected the time was coming for some years. More and more of us had reached such spiritual growth that we could remember past lives, and that only occurs when one is ready to cease returning after death to a new life."

Mickie remembered his conversation with X'Kaa Tz'Horzash. "You have all become Old Souls?"

"Indeed we have. And we have learned that such a realisation is the signal for us to move on."

"To the Plane of Elsewhere?"

"There are many names for this, Mickie. But yes, we move to another, higher plane to continue our growth. It is so similar to normal life. You know that you, as a child, went to junior school for some years until you were in the senior year. To all the other children, you seemed quite mature and old. But then you moved to a high school, where you became a beginner again, facing new experiences and growing to meet the demands. Had you remained on Earth, you might have gone to University and experienced the same cycle of growth before again moving on to start a career. This is what appears to be the cycle for all of us."

"So where does this end, Captain?"

"I do not know."

"Does it frighten you that all your people will vanish soon?"

"It leaves me sad, sometimes. We have done so much to create the Universe as it is now, by our development of the hyperspace ships. But others are learning how to pilot them. So I merely wait for what must happen and determine to play my part as well as I can."

"We will miss you, the Kaloti people, Captain."

The Kaloti's eyes opened wide again. "No need to, Mickie, for I am certain we will all meet up again, somewhere in space and time."

"I do hope so."

"No doubt about it at all. And now I must give you a message."

"A message, Captain? From whom?"

"From me. From the Kaloti. From all the species of this astounding Universe."

"But how do you have a message for me from everyone in the Universe?"

"That you will understand some day. But the message is simple, while the task is hard. You must bring the Pfafth back into the Universe."

Mickie felt the breath knocked from his body. "But.. but I don't know how to, Captain."

"There has to be a way, Mickie. They found a way to leave the Universe. There is a way back."

"But why is everyone so insistent that they must return? They don't seem to be of any value at all."

"But the Universe is incomplete without them, Mickie. And it is therefore unbalanced."

"That sounds like something the Harliya would say."

"The Harliya understand imbalance better than anyone. But enough, Mickie, I have done my duty and advised you of your task. Now, let me ask you about some of your adventures, especially with the Zlan. For I assure you, young man, those things still scare the life out of me!"

Mickie laughed, and the rest of the evening passed for two friends sharing their life histories. Only later as he tried to sleep, did Mickie think about the astounding assignment the Captain seemed to have given him. Why did the sad remnants of the Pfafth have to come back from that enormous void of one second in the future to join the rest of the Universe? And how could he possibly make that happen?

Chapter 12. A Seriously Long Distance Call

They sat around in Mickie's cabin in varying attitudes of relaxation. The Ship was in orbit round a bleak, uninhabitable plant that rotated as far from its star as Saturn did from Earth. Robot mining equipment was busy a few thousand kilometres below them, digging into the black, frozen surface to extract valuable minerals. It was not a visit for a planetary ramble.

Fencris sat cross-legged on the carpet, his usual position, while Melkana claimed the lounge and lay on her back, her hands behind her head. Mickie and Drellion occupied the two armchairs, both sitting crossways, their backs against one arm, their legs draped over the other. The atmosphere was thoughtful.

"So, have you found any of these whacky Pfafth talents, Melkana?" asked Fencris, breaking the silence.

"Nah, I decided to leave all that stuff to the Master of the Universe here," she replied.

"Quite right, too," Fencris said. "Lord knows, he's better at those than he is playing the trombone."

"Or Loopies," added Drellion. His initial shyness with Melkana after the discovery of her Pfafth origins had gone after she had burst into tears and wept on his shoulder, terrified that she had lost her closeness with her beloved little brother. It had shown him how close they were and his own fears of the broken relationship had dissipated also.

Fencris raised his head and looked over at Mickie. "You're very quiet, young Lord and Master," he quipped. "I hope you're working on the problem of bringing the Pfafth Galaxy back in time?"

"I wish I could," Mickie replied and reached down to the floor for his glass of *Sle'Ach*. "But I haven't the faintest idea of even how to start thinking about it."

"I thought you'd decided not to bother, anyway," Melkana said. "They really don't seem to be of much use to the rest of us."

"That's the problem, they don't. But the Captain told me the Universe needs them to be in balance."

"The Captain? What does he know about it?" Fencris seemed startled.

Quickly, Mickie recounted the strange conversation he'd had with the Captain a few days earlier and the others listened in bewildered silence. Fencris finally broke it.

"Everyone's ganging up on you, Mickie."

"But I don't understand," Mickie exclaimed, the stress showing in the tightness of his voice. "All these species, they all seem to have more powers, especially Maragos. Why can't they do it? What do they need me for?"

"Maybe they don't," Drellion said from the other armchair.

"Then why do they keep bugging me?" Mickie demanded, a trace of helpless tears in his throat.

"No, I didn't mean they don't need you. I mean, maybe they don't have more powers than you. Or perhaps it's a *specific* power they don't have."

A short silence hung in the room.

"Melkana, I thought I told you a long time ago to hit this kid, 'cos he was getting too clever," Fencris said seriously. "You messed up, and now look at what's happened. I think our looping whiz-kid has got it."

"Maybe somebody could explain it," Mickie said, the tension easing a little as Fencris' words made him smile.

"Well, look at the species we've met," Drellion said, sitting up. "They all have certain powers, but not all the same ones. The Speakers can't read the Zlan telepathic band wave, but the Zlan can't conduct multiple conversations like the Speakers can. The Shuramee could manipulate matter even better than the Pfafth, but they couldn't teleport. Mickie can teleport enormous distances, but not short ones like the Zlan. And he can't transmit telepathically, not all that well, anyway. Maybe Maragos, whatever she is, can't move a Galaxy in time, but the Pfafth can. In fact, nobody else but the Pfafth seem to be able to do that little party-trick. That's why they all need you."

Fencris let out a long slow whistle. "I think that's it," he said softly.

"Way to go, little bro!" said Melkana with a brilliant smile at Drellion. "It seems we Pfafth can do something nobody else can do, even if we don't know how to do it!"

Mickie was lost in thought. Then he looked round and said, "I bet there's somebody else who knows! Fencris, you met him!"

"Ah!" said a voice of great power that filled the entire cabin. "I was wondering if you remembered me!"

The shock ran through the group like a sharp gust of wind through a forest. All four of them had experienced Fencris' astounding experience of meeting the unknown entity as he searched for a way to communicate with the Zlan during their imprisonment on Korrobodor. Speaker 356 had played the memory from Fencris into their minds just as he had with Mickie, so they recognised the voice immediately. They looked at each other and by unspoken agreement, elected Fencris as their spokesman, he being the only one who had communicated directly with this unknown entity.

"Oh, hello!" he said, regaining his composure with great speed. "And we were wondering where you'd got to!"

"Explaining *that* could get complex," replied the unseen entity. "Let's just say I've been around and about."

"Where's round and about?" Mickie asked, needing to draw on some courage to address this amazing individual.

"Hello, young Pfafth!" he got in reply. "You seem to be having some adventures these days! We were fascinated to discover from you where your species was hiding out."

"You mean you didn't know?"

"We didn't, no. And in answer to your question, I think we'll need to have some longish chats about the nature of the Universe to be able to explain just where I've been travelling."

"So, just who are you, anyway?" Melkana chimed in. "You seem to have the Speakers all in a tizzy."

A chuckle resounded in the cabin. For yet another moment of confusion, Mickie wondered about the nature of telepathic communication. He heard the voice as if it was coming from a series of loudspeakers, without any specific source, but certainly somewhere in the cabin, and it spoke in English. And yet he knew that Fencris was hearing the voice speak in his own dialect of the several Cassolean tongues, while Melkana and Drellion heard the language of Kalamos. How had they heard that chuckle? he wondered. And had the others heard the *same* voice?

"The Speakers are still babies in this business of universal telepathy," came the reply. "And as they have now told you, they actually learned it from the M'Sarda, not from the Pfafth breeding technique as once believed. We go back quite a lot further than either of them, before the Pfafth, before all species, in fact."

"You were the first intelligent species?" Drellion looked startled.

"Let's say we have yet to discover anyone older than us."

"Cool!" said Drellion. "How far back does that take you?"

"Over two billion of your years."

The four looked at each other in astonishment.

"So do you have a name?" Melkana persisted.

"Not really," came the reply. "As the species that led everybody else, we never found it necessary to adopt a name. As for a *personal* name, why don't you just call me Mister Brown?"

Again Mickie wondered if that essentially English name was the same as the one given to the other three. It seemed unlikely and he decided that the others had somehow each been given a unique name by which to address this entity, much as everybody on the Ship had their own private name by which to address the computer. And it probably meant that when one of the others spoke that name, it would be translated to Mickie as Mister Brown.

"Mister Brown, you said we should have a chat," Melkana said firmly. "I think we need to talk to you about this business of bringing back the Pfafth to the rest of the Universe."

"Certainly, Melkana. And may I say you are handling the discovery of your Pfafth identity very well?"

Melkana showed her irritation. "Okay, so let's do it."

"I thought we were," said Mister Brown.

"No, not here, not like this," Melkana said. "I want to see who we're dealing with. Why don't you come here, visit the Ship?"

"Hmmmm," said Mister Brown. "I think not. My presence on board your vessel might cause all sorts of problems for the engines and computers. Why don't you come here and join me over coffee?"

"But where is 'here'?" Mickie asked. "And how would we get there?"

"I can show you the way here, just like the Cassoleans used to show the Pfafth how to get to a new location. And you can get here the way you can get around the Universe."

"But that's just me," Mickie protested. "Melkana may be Pfafth, but she hasn't yet learned how to do this. And the other two can't do it at all. We all want to come."

"Remember how Markel's father took Markel and Kerrala on their first inter-Galactic travels?" Mister Brown asked.

The other three looked hard at Mickie. He hadn't told them all the details of his dream life as Markel.

"He put his arms round them and teleported. Anything he held was transported with him."

"You mean if you touch all of us, we'll transport with you?" Drellion asked. "Are you sure? Sounds a bit risky to me."

"No, it works," Mickie replied. "I remember that it was all tested out. It's how we teleported Cassoleans to various locations for them to memorise the scenes and then teach others. Providing we were in contact, we could carry anyone or anything."

"That's correct," said Mister Brown.

Silence fell in the cabin as all four digested the implications.

"So, do you guys really want to meet this Mister Brown person?" It was Fencris who broke the small tension that was building.

"Yes!" All three of the others spoke together.

"We've got four days before the Ship breaks orbit," Fencris said. "That should be plenty of time for our chat."

"Don't worry about the time," said the great voice. "Regardless of how long our meeting lasts, you'll be back on the Ship in less than a minute."

"You can alter time?" Melkana asked.

"Not really. It will be like Mickie's hallucination of his life as Markel. Compressed."

The cabin was silent for a few seconds as they absorbed that.

"Everybody tell their parents and get their permission," Mickie said. "If it's okay with them and the Captain, we should go."

For a few moments, there was another silence as each of them established communication with their parents and explained the situation.

"He saved all our lives on Korrobodor," Grant said. "I still feel a bit anxious about this, though. You have absolutely no idea of where he is?"

"I will have soon," Mickie said. "He's going to give me the Cassolean treatment and show me the route there. But I'm pretty sure it's a long way from anywhere we've been before."

"I've no doubt." Allie's voice held some irony together with the same anxiety Grant was feeling. "But you're old enough and experienced enough now to make your own decisions. I assume the others are getting their parents to agree?"

"Yes, they are. You'll tell the Captain?"

"We will. Let us know as soon as you're back."

Mickie looked round and saw nods from the other three to indicate they were ready to go. He stood up and all four moved to the middle of the floor.

"I think... this way," Mickie said. "Melkana, stand in front of me, arms round my neck...oooh, goodie!" He ignored a laugh from the others as Melkana obeyed. "You two, one on either side of me, I'll put an arm round each waist... Okay, silence please, I need to concentrate."

Working hard to ignore the sensation of Melkana standing so close, he closed his eyes and immediately felt the sensation of images flooding into his mind.

It was the first time he had ever teleported from the Ship, rather than from the ground. The first image seemed to be from a point a few hundred metres out from the Ship and he felt a sense of awe at the vastness of the hull, stretching away into the distance. He heard a small gasp from Drellion and he looked down to see the dense blackness of the mining planet beneath their feet. He felt the trembling in all three of his friends' bodies.

"It's okay," he said softly. "It's only an image. I don't actually know where we are, but the image helps me pull us to where we're going."

"It's impossible," whispered Melkana. "But I almost feel I can remember this."

Mickie didn't reply. In the far, far distance, a minute speck glowed more strongly, and he knew this was the next signpost, somehow high-lighted by his unseen guide. He reached out with his ghostly, intangible extra arms and touched that speck of light and pulled his group towards it. He heard another gasp of astonishment from all three of his friends as they swooped unimaginable light years and seemed to pause above a startlingly beautiful spiral galaxy.

"And now that one," said the powerful voice and he saw that another distant spark had lit up for him. Already he knew they had travelled far further than he had ever teleported before, further than the Ship had ever travelled and they were in portions of the Universe never visited by any of the species they knew.

Again and again they swooped across impossible millions of light years, pausing briefly by galaxy after galaxy, shaped like spirals, like whirlpools, like footballs, some even so black that they seemed to suck the light out of the glow of other, distant galaxies.

But the journey was ending. Their guide directed him into the mass of one of the spirals, to a planet circling a yellow sun much like Earth's and to a land mass about half way between equator and north pole. They found themselves standing in daylight, under a warm sun. Mickie realised that his friends were almost at the end of their capacity to handle the experience. Their trembles had become shakes, Melkana and

Drellion both had white faces while Fencris' blue skin had an unhealthy blotchiness to it. But their experiences of the last two years had made them tough.

"Well, that was an interesting ride," Melkana said, releasing her arms from Mickie's neck and moving away, looking round the scene. Only a slight vibration in her voice revealed the stress from the teleportation.

Fencris and Drellion were breathing hard, but they were rapidly regaining their self-control.

"You Pfafth certainly know how to get around," Fencris finally said. His skin was recovering its normally healthy blue shade. "I think I'd rather do it in the Ship, though."

"I've just remembered," Mickie said, feeling a pang of regret and anger at his forgetfulness. "When my... Markel's father took us.. er.. Kerrala and Markel on that first teleport, he actually put them to sleep with a small mind bolt. And even if I'd remembered, I don't think I can control that bolt finely enough just to knock you out. I might have hurt you badly."

"All new experiences in life's rich pattern," said Drellion. "I think I'd rather go through it than miss it. Now, where are we and where's our host?"

Mickie realised they were standing on a beautifully manicured lawn. A fountain played a few metres away, and paths wound their way into the distance. To his right, trees formed a tall line, stretching as far as his eye could see, while to his left and in front of him, flower beds were filled with startling colours in patterns that held the eye, almost as hypnotically as a Maragos sculpture.

"Probably in there," said Melkana, looking back behind Mickie. He turned and saw a beautiful house. In the middle, an enormous bay window faced them, while to either side the wings stretched for at least fifty metres. The house was white, with window frames in dark brown. The roof was tiled in a coral pink. The whole effect was intensely pleasing and calming,

Mickie thought. To the right of the huge bay, a door was invitingly open.

"I'd say we're expected," Drellion said and set off for the door. Seeing no alternative the rest followed and entered a wide, sunlit corridor with stained glass windows along both sides. The passageway continued to their right, at which point a left hand turn cut off further views. To their left, they looked into a huge dining room, the wooden floor reflecting the sunlight in a subdued, golden glow. One circular table stood in the bay, surrounded by five chairs. A pure white tablecloth covered the surface.

A man sat in one of the chairs, facing them. He was leaning back, away from the table, one leg crossed, his right ankle on his left knee and he cradled what looked like a large mug of beer in one hand. As he saw the group, he put the mug on the table and stood up.

"Good morning!" he said cheerfully. "I'm so pleased you could make it!"

Mickie studied him. The man appeared to be in his middle age, but fit, lean and with a golden tan on his face. His full head of hair was dark brown and the face was strong, with a wide mouth now even wider in its welcoming smile. He was dressed in conventional grey slacks and a white shirt, open at the neck.

Cautiously, the four children moved to the table. The man moved a little closer and first advanced on Fencris and shook his hand. "I'm delighted to meet you in person after our last contact," he said. "You impressed me then with your courage, as do all of you now."

He repeated the handshake with Melkana. "All still a little overwhelming, young lady, I imagine. It's not every day somebody discovers they're a member of the most powerful species in the Universe in its day."

She looked deeply into his face, studying it intently. Mister Brown remained still as she did so, seeming to understand her need to examine him. Finally, she released his hand and stood back, letting him shake hands with Drellion and Mickie. His grip was firm, dry, very masculine, Mickie thought. Mister Brown could be anyone's favourite uncle, a successful businessman or a retired sports star.

"Please, sit down," he said. "I know this is all very disconcerting, but I don't know four people anywhere in the Universe better suited to handle it."

His gentleness and friendliness finally disarmed them all, and they took seats at the table, Mickie on the man's left, Melkana on his right, with Drellion and Fencris across from him.

"*Sle'Ach* all round, I assume?" he asked, saw their nods and waved at a point at the back of the room. A young waitress approached, already carrying a tray with four glasses of the golden yellow drink and another mug of beer. She placed the drinks on the table and walked away. She seemed young and pretty, and her short skirt set off lines that Mickie found he really appreciated as he watched her walk away.

"Is she of your species?" Drellion asked.

"Actually, she doesn't exist at all," Mister Brown replied with a smile. "I could have produced the drinks at the table by molecular changes, but I thought I'd make the scene as normal as possible. She's just an image."

"The Shurameen could do that, couldn't they," Melkana asked. "Change matter to something else. And so could the Pfafth."

Mister Brown nodded. "And so can a couple of other species in parts of the Universe you have not yet visited. But young Drellion got it right." He grinned cheerfully at Drellion who beamed back, delighted with the recognition. "All the advanced species have some extraordinary powers, and even those species not yet advanced, they will all develop some specific talent eventually. But nobody has them all. In fact, it looks like the Pfafth had a wider range than anyone so far, until they declined so sadly."

"Where are we?" Fencris enquired before taking a deep pull at his drink. "This all looks just too.... well, normal, I suppose."

"I can assure you, this is all quite real," Mister Brown said. "We're on the planet where my species originally began a couple of billion years ago."

"But is this what you look like?" Fencris continued. "The same as Pfafth, or Kalamosians or Humans?"

"Ah! Well, no! We used to look not all that different from this, a long time ago, but we sort of... developed. Anyway, it's a convenient shape to adopt for meetings like these."

"So what's your regular shape?" Melkana asked.

He smiled at her. "Believe me, young lady, you couldn't handle that! Not even four children of your maturity and experience are ready to see us as we are. But anyway, we're here to discuss far more important matters, and that's rescuing the Pfafth."

A small stir of movement ran round the table.

"I'm not sure the Pfafth want to be rescued," Mickie said. "They seemed to have withdrawn into their cosy little shell to dream their dreams of universal revenge, without actually wanting to do anything."

"And that's part of the problem," replied Mister Brown. "But they really do have to come out of that shell and rejoin the rest of us."

"But why?" Melkana said. "From what Mickie told us about his trip there, they really aren't much use to anyone. They've lost all their powers and they seem really very boring. And they are utterly terrified of the Sillaron still."

"But as you have seen, the Sillaron have also declined into complete ineffectualness," Mister Brown said. "They represent no threat any more."

"But what about their leader, the Sillaron Master?" Mickie chimed in. "I got the sense that it wasn't really a Sillaron, however much it resembled them. It seemed to have far greater powers. It *owned* the Sillaron, it said. And I only made it run. I didn't destroy it, I don't think."

Mister Brown looked pensively down at the table for a few moments. He seemed a little uncomfortable, and Mickie wondered what could possibly cause this entity any discomfort.

"That thing does certainly represent a problem," Mister Brown finally said.

"But what is it?" Fencris asked.

"I don't know."

"You don't know?" All the kids spoke in unison.

The strange being was silent again for a few moments, seeming to think about what to say next.

"Let me tell you some secrets of the Universe that nobody else knows," Mister Brown finally said. His expression was serious. "Actually, one other person has caught on, and you two kids met her." He nodded at Melkana and Mickie.

"Maragos?" they asked in unison.

"And we only learned this quite recently, in Maragos' case only about ten thousand years ago, and I saw it about a hundred thousand years ago."

"You're over a hundred thousand years old?" Fencris gasped, his eyes almost emitting red flames, so shocked was he.

"Er... quite a bit, actually. But that isn't the point. Here's an astonishing fact. There are one million intelligent species in the whole Universe. One million, *exactly*. That's been the figure since just over a million years ago when both Humans and Kalamosians reached the level of intelligence that they did, and the Speakers began to reach their true level of power. Some of the species have disappeared, like the Shurameen and like the Kaloti are about to, but as we know, they just go *elsewhere*, and the figure remains at one million, exactly. There are no other species developing to that level. We don't think it's a coincidence."

All four children were rigid with their attention held fast on Mister Brown.

Finally Mickie cleared his throat. "You're saying there have to be one million species for some purpose?"

Mister Brown nodded.

"What purpose?" asked Drellion.

"I don't know."

"And the Pfafth have a role to play?"

"Yes, but beyond being part of the universal developments, I don't know what that role is."

"And what if they don't come back into the Universe?" Fencris was totally absorbed in the story.

"Imbalance," replied the man. "And problems for the whole Universe."

"And being one second ahead of everyone else, that makes them not part of the Universe?" Melkana asked.

"That seems to be the case."

"But I don't know how to bring the whole galaxy back," Mickie protested. "Anyway, you seem to have far more power than anyone we've ever met. Can't *you* do it?"

The man turned his eyes to Mickie and stared at him. Mickie felt as if he were looking into the heart of a sun, so immense was the power he sensed and he felt his own strength wilt.

"No, Mickie, I can't do that," Mister Brown said. "Remember the truth that young Drellion revealed to you. Each of the species has certain powers, some yet to be developed. But one thing I do know, and I am the only entity that knows all the intelligent species, you Pfafth are the only species with the capacity to move objects in time."

Mickie felt his insides churn. "What you're saying is that Melkana and I are the only people who can rescue the Pfafth?"

"And the other Pfafth agents who still possess their abilities. Between you, yes, you're the only people who can do it. And Mickie, it's more than saving the Pfafth. In fact, it seems to be a matter of saving everything. The Universe. Possibly even Creation itself."

"But hang on a second!" Drellion had been quiet through the entire discussion so far, but had been following every word with close attention. "Just now, you said you knew every species in the Universe, all the one million of them. But you said you didn't know what the Sillaron Master was."

Mister Brown smiled at the youngest of them. "Your intellect remains astonishing," he said. "So what do think that implies?"

It took Drellion only a few seconds.

"The Sillaron Master is not one of the million species?"

"Correct."

The four kids gaped at him.

"Then where does it come from, if it's not part of the Universe?" Fencris finally asked.

Mister Brown smiled sadly. "That's the problem. It comes from somewhere else."

"But you don't know from where?"

"That's correct, Fencris."

"And it's still dangerous?" Melkana asked.

"More than I know how to tell you. But the first problem for you is to bring the Blocked Galaxy back in time."

Mickie's throat was tight with tension. He looked across at Melkana and saw that she too was experiencing great fear and panic. "But we don't know how to do it!" he croaked.

Mister Brown smiled. "You have one huge advantage, Mickie, you too, Melkana. For not only do we know that you *can* do it, we have a fantastic array of talents to help you find that ability deep inside your mind, just like the Speaker helped you find the teleportation ability."

He looked round the table at the four friends. Each of them seemed to be trying to absorb the conversation and its implications and none of them said a word. Mister Brown gently broke the silence.

"So now you know what you have to do," he said. "I think you should be getting home now and working out how to do it."

Chapter 13. The Group Assignment

Mickie and Melkana sat opposite each other at the table in his cabin.

"We don't really seem to have any alternative, do we?" she said. "It looks like everybody's depending on us to save those silly Pfafth." She seemed quite composed, but Mickie detected a trace of sadness in her voice. He extended his empathic sense and read confirmation of the emotion.

"I felt you do that," she said, surprised. "It was as if you touched my head very gently."

He tried to suppress his own astonishment. "But why are you so sad?"

"Because that's the end of being just Melkana," she said. "All the plans I had, they just got wiped out. You and I, we're not just kids any more. Now we're supposed to save the Universe. It wasn't really what I had in mind as a career path."

"No, I suppose not. Maybe when it's all over, we can get back to what we thought we'd do."

She shook her head. "Not a chance, and you know why. It's that stuff about *'You can't go home again'* that you told us from Markel's memory. If we do this nutty Galaxy-moving thing, we just won't be the same people any more and we won't be able to go back to the lives we'd planned."

"You're right. Everything will change. But our whole lives are all about change. They changed for you and Drellion and Fencris when I came aboard. They changed again when we found the Maragos art treasures. They changed after almost every planet we've visited. Good grief, our lives nearly *ended* during some of those visits! The only thing that stays the same with us is that things keep changing. We should be used to it."

For a second, she stared at the tabletop. Then she looked at him and her wide, cheerful grin broke the sad mood.

"You're right! This is just one more insane adventure. Okay, so how do we go about moving a whole Galaxy one second backward in time? Heavens, I can't really believe I just asked that and meant it!"

Mickie laughed in relief then had a thought. "It's time you started learning how to be a Pfafth," he said. He looked around his cabin, stood up and walked to his bookshelf. He scanned the shelves and picked out a hardback copy of Asimov's science fiction work, *"I Robot."* He walked back to the table, dropped the heavy volume with a resounding bang squarely in the centre of the surface then sat down across from her again.

She looked at the book curiously, then up at Mickie.

"So?" she said. "It's a book about robots."

"Lift it up," he replied.

She stretched out her hands, but he stopped the movement with a touch on her left wrist.

"No, not that way. No hands."

"Don't be silly."

"I'm not. You *can* do it. I can do it, I've tried it, and I remember the lesson when Kerrala and Markel did it. You're more advanced than Kerrala, even if you don't know it. Look *into* the book, every atom and then lift it."

For a few seconds she stared deep into Mickie's eyes as if looking for a clue as to how to do this thing then dropped her gaze to the book. She went silent and Mickie sensed her withdrawal of attention from everything in the room but the object before her. He held his breath.

Half a minute passed and Mickie began to release his breath slowly and as quietly as possible, trying to suppress the sense of disappointment he felt. Melkana still hadn't accepted that she had the Pfafth powers even more than Kerrala had.

The book moved. Mickie felt his insides churn. The book shifted across the table by two or three centimetres and stopped. He held his breath again.

This time the book rose smoothly off the table to a height level with Melkana's eyes and hung motionless between the two friends.

Mickie let his breath out. "I told you so," he whispered.

The book slowly lowered back to the table and when it was motionless, Melkana took her eyes off it and looked at him.

"That would seem to prove I'm Pfafth, don't you think?" Her voice trembled with the shock of what she had just done.

"Either that or a Shurameen, and you're much too small to be a Shurameen. Too pretty as well."

To his surprise, she blushed. "Aw shucks, Mister Dalton, I bet you say that to all the Pfafth young ladies you meet!"

"Every single one of them," he agreed, feeling a wave of delight at her feminine reaction.

"Well, okay, that wasn't too hard," she said, becoming all business again. "But there's a significant difference between a book and a Galaxy, and I didn't move the book in time at all. So how do we go about the main event?"

"I haven't the faintest idea," he replied. "I think it's going to take some training. Speaker 356, are you there?"

"I was wondering when you'd call," said the telepathic being from somewhere in the void. "Let's get down to work."

*   *   *   *

What followed was a lengthy period of several weeks of intensive work with the Speaker, much like the period early in Mickie's life aboard the Ship when the telepathic being had trained him how to find and use his Pfafth powers. Melkana had to go through the same training just to reach the point at which they could both start working on the major project of moving a galaxy, but Mickie had one advantage there. Somewhere, deep and lost inside his mind, he still had the memories of Markel who had actually accomplished that astounding deed together with the others of the Management Committee, and the Speaker spent many hours tracking down those memories, even though Mickie could not remember them himself.

Not at all to Mickie's surprise, Melkana learned her Pfafth powers at a far more rapid rate than he had, two years earlier.

"Watch this," she said, as they sat in his cabin again. a few weeks after the episode with the book. A glass of *Sle'Ach* sat in the middle of the table, but with a flicker, it became a small pot filled with sugar. With another flicker, it became a crystal vase.

"Wow!" said Mickie. "I've never tried that trick, and I don't think I know how to do it."

"Yes you do," she insisted. "Here, have a look."

Instantly, Mickie felt the knowledge flood into his mind. The ease with which she gave him the information and the speed at which she had learned it herself staggered him.

"Kerrala always was the brightest of all," he said in wonder. "She probably had greater powers than Markel, but she was far more careful about using them. I think you are further ahead of her than I am of Markel."

"It's almost as if I already *know* these things," she said in agreement. "I think a lot of it is because you've already gone through the learning, so we both know it's all possible and I accept it quicker."

"That's probably it," he said with a nod. "Maybe we'll actually get to the point of discovering how to do this thing."

"How's it going?"

"Slowly. I don't actually do much, it's Speaker 356 who's doing the work. He's tracing the memories of everything Markel went through, looking for that moment when they moved the galaxy, so I'm remembering a lot of everyday stuff that Markel went through that I'd quite forgotten."

"But you haven't found it yet?"

"Not yet. We just keep working at it."

As days became weeks, the fatigue built up inside them and they spent most of their time asleep when not working with the Speaker. They didn't go down on planet visits, and they found little time for socialising.

Family and friends expressed their concerns.

"We haven't played Loopies for *weeks*!" Drellion complained during a rare coffee session at the café. "We've been calling on some of the other kids in the school, but we've found nobody's anywhere *near* as good as you two. Heck, even Mickie's better than anyone else there!"

"You realise, don't you," Melkana replied. "With what Mickie and I have learned these last few weeks, we could just *obliterate* you? Remember that time when Mickie rose up above his arc to catch Drellion? Not only can we do that, we could hover in the middle, spinning all the time, or even block you from jumping."

"That's a horrible idea," Fencris said, worry showing in his face. "That would mean we could never play fair again."

Melkana touched his hand. "I didn't say we *would*! You know we'd never do that to you."

"I know you'd never do it deliberately," Fencris replied. "But can you control these powers? Would you know if you were using them, even a little bit?"

"I'm pretty sure," Mickie said. "I find I have to make a deliberate effort to use any of them, unless I'm scared out of my wits or so angry I can't stop myself."

"Like the mind bolts, or when you leaped to Speaker's Planet?" Drellion asked.

"Exactly. And I'm pretty sure I've learned how to control those abilities as well."

"Awesome!" Drellion's grin lit up the room. "Let's go and check it out in Hangar Ten!"

"Yes!" The approval was unanimous and the four ran to the Hangar for the first game in some time. Mickie was right. He and Melkana didn't use any of their Pfafth powers and they were so out of practice that the other two beat them soundly.

* * * *

And then came the time when the Speaker found the tracks in Mickie's hidden memories of his life as Markel.

"Here," said Speaker 356 and Mickie felt the surroundings of his cabin disappear like mist on a summer's morning.

He was Markel again, and he sat in the newly constructed office of the Pfafth Management Committee. Once, this group had been the supreme rulers of the most powerful species in the known Universe. Now they were fugitives from the Sillaron who had slaughtered nearly half their numbers and forced them to flee to a remote galaxy.

The twelve of them looked frightened, exhausted, much as Markel felt himself. Only a day had passed since their arrival here, barely ahead of the tidal wave of hatred and death that their one-time servants had visited on them, somehow suppressing the powers of the Pfafth that should have been able to put down the uprising with ease.

But there was no time for the rest that they so badly needed before undertaking the most stupendous task that sentient creatures had ever attempted in the Universe's history. The

Sillaron might already know where the Pfafth had gone, might already be gathering their forces to follow and complete the slaughter. The impenetrable barrier had to be created at once.

The twelve reached out to each other's minds, became one and began to stretch their control over every atom in the Galaxy. At some unknown point, they held the entire mass of every star, every planet, every free-moving comet, every grain of dust in the interstellar reaches of space and then they..... *moved* it.

And with that memory recalled, Mickie saw how it had been done. It had felt as if they had a machine of monumental power that directed its thrust at exactly the right point and moved a monstrous weight with ease and precision, as if moving a tiny lever in the control cabin of the greatest crane in the Universe and raising a whole planet. They had moved the galaxy forward in time by one second.

A million years later, Mickie had to find a way to move it back again.

Mickie returned to the here and now, staggered by what he had just seen. It simply was not conceivable that twelve people could embrace an entire galaxy and move it in a dimension that was still not understood by the greatest scientists in the known intelligent species. Not even the incomprehensible Mister Brown seemed to know how to do what Mickie had just seen a handful of people do.

Feeling some of the deathly weariness that had afflicted Markel a million years ago, Mickie ordered a drink of the energising *Sle'Ach* from the dispensing unit and drank a whole litre of it before feeling normal energy levels return.

*   *   *   *

"Oh my God!" Melkana opened her eyes and stared at Mickie. Her reaction was obvious in her choice of words. She had just received from the Speaker the same memories of Markel's movement of the Pfafth Galaxy as Mickie had been given and while she had only taken a few seconds to replay those memories, it had been a subjective period of some hours for her and the same exhaustion that Mickie had felt was now affecting her.

Mickie passed her the large mug of *Sle'Ach* that he had already poured, knowing how she would feel on returning to the present. She drank it in one go and returned it for a refill.

"Pretty astounding, huh?" Mickie said as she worked on her ·second helping. She put down the empty mug and wiped her lips.

"I still can't believe it," she said, her voice low, still affected by the shock of the memories. "I was somebody else and when we merged our minds I got all the memories of those other people, including...."

"Including Markel's life with Kerrala," Mickie finished for her. "Yes, I realised you'd get all that when the Speaker fed you Markel's memory. So now you have the memories of a hundred years of living as a man and the most powerful individual in the Universe at that time."

"I can see how it changed you," she murmured. "It's already changed me!"

"So do you think you understand how they did it? How they moved the galaxy forward a second?"

"I think I understand *what* they did and what we'll all have to do. I don't think I have the faintest idea of how it works, though."

"Nor do I, really. But when I came to, after the memories, I thought of it like moving a tiny lever in the control cabin of the largest crane in the universe and moving a whole planet. I knew how to do it, but I didn't understand the engineering behind it."

"That's not a bad way of looking at it," she said thoughtfully. "So where do we go from here?"

"We need to gather up the people who can do it with us," he replied. "Speaker 356, are you there?"

"Yes of course, Mickie," came the instant reply. For a second or two, Mickie wondered what other conversations around the Universe the Speaker was conducting at the same time, and with whom and what it must be like to do what the Speaker did.

"Speaker, will you put me in touch with my brother on Kalamos?" he asked. "And please include Melkana in the connection."

It took just a few seconds for the Speaker to locate Brandon and establish the connection.

"Hey, little bro! Great to hear from you! How's everything aboard the Ship?"

Mickie grinned, immensely lifted by the sound of his brother's voice. They'd had only a few conversations since their departure from the small solar system outside the Blocked Galaxy, but each of them had made Mickie feel cheerful at the thought of having a real life relative, one that he truly liked and admired. Brandon had been delighted to learn that Melkana had been identified as the other Pfafth.

"We're having interesting times Brandon. Melkana's here with me."

"Melkana! So nice to talk to you! When are you coming to visit?"

"Next trip home, Brandon, I promise."

"You'd better! Mickie, what's up?"

" Remember that entity I told you about, the one that helped Fencris call the Zlan to rescue us on Korrobodor?"

"I most certainly do. The way you described him scared the hell out of me! Have you found out who and what it was?"

"Not really, Brandon, but we met him."

Brandon's shock reverberated through the millions of light years between them. "You *met* him?"

"We did. All four of us, we teleported to his home planet, further away than anyone has ever been before and had a nice little chat."

"Mickie, you've always been a source of amazement to me, but I have to tell you, this beats everything! What did he tell you?"

"He said we have to bring the Pfafth back into the Universe."

Brandon was silent for several seconds, and even through the telepathic link, his voice sounded weak when he spoke.

"You have to *what?*"

"We have to reverse what Markel and his Committee did a million years ago and bring the Galaxy back into normal time."

"That's what I *thought* I heard you say, and I still can't believe it. How are you supposed to do that little trick?"

"Not just me. Melkana also. And we know how to do it. And that's where you come in. You and all the other Pfafth agents. We can show you how to do it and then we have to get together."

"I don't understand, Mickie."

"Wait a moment, and you will. Speaker, will you replay Markel's memory of that episode to Brandon?"

Ten minutes later, after recovering from the immense shock of receiving Markel's memories, Brandon agreed. He would contact all the agents and they would meet at the safe house outside the Blocked Galaxy and with Melkana and Mickie, attempt to bring it back into the same time as the rest of the Universe.

* * * *

"Only nineteen?"

"That's all I could get."

Mickie was dismayed. "I thought there were fifty agents who still had all the old Pfafth powers?"

"There were." Brandon seemed calm enough, but Mickie could detect his brother's stress, even though it had declined considerable under the extraordinary control of their bodies that the Pfafth had. "But most of them are getting on a bit after the breeding program was stopped. Eight have died over the last two years, five seem to have lost significant portions of their powers after retiring from their jobs, and the others refused to believe what we were trying to tell them. They blocked their minds to the Markel memories that the Speaker wanted to give them and we've been unable to contact them at all since."

"Is Sendagon here?"

"No, he's one of those who refused to be part of this."

"Even though he's met me and knows who I am?"

"Even after that." Brandon showed his disgust. "Some people prefer to keep living their safe lives rather than face up to reality. In the end, Sendagon was simply too frightened of what would happen if the Pfafth came back into the Universe from their hiding place."

They were sitting in the lounge of the safe house on the small planet a few light minutes from the Blocked Galaxy. So far, Mickie and Brandon were alone, Mickie and Melkana having arrived two hours earlier to find his brother had been there nearly two days already. Melkana had made this leap with her own powers, the first time she had performed the process, and she had been slammed into almost a coma by the fatigue. Brandon had carried her to one of the bedrooms and left her to sleep it off. They then spent the time catching up with each other's lives and simply enjoying the company of brothers. This time, Mickie had toured the house and found that it was more a mansion, with ten bedrooms and a large conference room that could seat thirty people round a massive, rectangular table. Robot cleaners maintained the house and rarely appeared when anyone was there.

"When they built it, they expected that we'd have regular

conferences of agents," Brandon said. "That was over five hundred years ago, and we've never yet had such a meeting. I think most of the agents who went Outside were less interested in locating you than in preparing their own escapes and places to live, just as I did. So there was little interest in meeting to discuss updates in the search for Markel. As far as I know, this the first time all the bedrooms have been used, never mind doubling up as we are."

"The nineteen who are here, do they understand what it's all about?"

Brandon smiled without humour. "Theoretically, yes. Remember, none of them has met you and they're probably not entirely convinced of who you are, though they're curious as hell to meet you! But I doubt any of them seriously believes they're going to move the galaxy back in time."

"And they're all asleep now?"

"They are. They've been dropping in during the day, the last one just three hours ago, and all immediately retired. None of them seems to have developed the immunity to teleportation fatigue the way you have. I know I haven't, and that's why I arrived as soon as we'd spoken two days ago."

Mickie grinned. "And made sure you got the best room, as well!"

"Indeed," replied Brandon. "And we'll share that one. And I'm dead certain you'll need the bed after we've done this astonishing thing. Markel's memories seemed to indicate that quite firmly."

"All of them have received those memories?"

Brandon nodded. "I made contact with each of them within an hour of talking to you, and the Speaker gave them the record. They were all as stunned as I was."

"Brandon, I honestly don't know if we can do this!"

"We'll give it our best shot, little brother. That's all we can do."

"And if we succeed, what do we do then?"

"I suggest that we pop over to see the Pfafth Management Committee and tell them what's happened. That should be an interesting meeting."

"I'll say! They'll go bonkers!"

"At the very least!" Brandon laughed out loud. "I can't wait to see that little twit, that Vemanor Markel. His whole world will come to an end!"

"We'll need to tell the whole planet very quickly," Mickie said, his own grin showing his amusement at the probable reaction of the pompous Chairman of the Pfafth Management Committee.

"I'm ahead of you! I've already asked the Speaker and he said as soon as we tell him, a whole group of Speakers will transmit the same message to every Pfafth on the planet, telling them what has happened."

"That'll mean a few million terrified Pfafth, I imagine. Even though that's what they've believed all their lives is supposed to happen, the stark reality will be scary."

"Mickie, it has to happen, you know that. Somehow we'll get everyone calmed down and then we'll work out what we do next."

"I suppose. Have you set a time for us to meet?"

"In ten hours. That's when we'll try this thing. But the agents will be waking up over the next five or six hours, so they'll all want to meet you, of course. You're the reason for every one of their careers, never mind the fact that each of them was bred with the possibility of actually being Markel themselves. Or Kerrala, in the case of the five women agents who have arrived."

"Oh! I never thought of that! Could any of them be hostile?"

"I suppose it's possible, Mickie. But that would be an immature reaction, and I think they'll get over it pretty soon."

"I hope so. We need everybody's cooperation."

"We'll get it. The future of our species depends on it."

Sixteen men and six women sat round the conference table. During the previous few hours, they had all met, some for the first time, some as old friends. The meetings with Mickie and Melkana had been varied. All the agents had been curious, a few had been courteous but distant, the rest had shown a warm welcome to the man and woman they had been expecting to find one day. Between them, the group represented the finest minds of the Pfafth species, the last group that retained the astounding powers of the one-time dominant species in the Universe.

"No point in wasting time," Mickie said. "We've all got Markel's memories and understanding of how he and his Committee did this. Let's get to it."

He closed his eyes and extended his empathic skills to each of the others round the table, sensing them do the same. Without surprise, he first gained close linkage with Brandon and began to experience his memories. He saw Brandon's early childhood, the initial excitement of his parents that their son might be the reborn Markel, then the disappointment when the shortcomings were revealed, Brandon's mixture of sadness and relief at the discovery, then his pain as the growing abuse and ugliness of his parents became revealed, the beatings, the anger... so much like Mickie's own childhood. He saw Brandon's delight as his baby brother was born, the love he held for the small mite and then his grief as it was discovered that the child really was the successful result of a million years of breeding and was removed from the family to be taken elsewhere.

His linkages expanded and he saw into the minds and memories of each of the group, sensing at the same time as they found their way through Mickie's own memories, the awe and fear as his talents became revealed, the terror of his first encounters with the Zlan and the Gelkka and the shock of discovering what he was and what his responsibilities would be. Briefly he found himself in Melkana's mind and saw her own memories of discovering she was Pfafth, and how she regarded Mickie, her odd sense of recognition when he first came onto the Ship, the increased closeness between them.... he smiled inside at that.

He saw other memories and realised that the most common among this group was the disappointment reflected by parents once their child had been shown not to be the new Markel or Kerrala. With some, the reaction had lasted for years and the child had paid for their inadequacy with a lifetime of rejection by their parents. Others had done better and their parents had been relieved not to have fathered the saviour of the race and had happily returned to a normal relationship with their children.

And all of the agents here, even Brandon he saw, held some degree of resentment against Mickie for actually being the successful result of a million years of breeding, some jealousy at his powers and yet also a willingness to surrender to his leadership.

With a soundless explosion of light, the twenty-two minds became one. No longer were any of them aware of their own identity, they were just a single entity with a mind powerful enough to move worlds. The single mind began the next stage of reaching out to the nearby Galaxy and embracing the planet on which the Pfafth still lived, wrapping it securely and spreading inward and outward simultaneously to enfold the planets further from the sun and those closer... it felt the brilliant power of the sun itself and then somehow that was swallowed into the control of the mind in that house. The speed of expansion accelerated, the entity took in more and more suns and their planets, reached further and swallowed the parts of the galaxy to the edge nearest to the Pfafth home world and began racing out to the distant edges, more and more suns, planets, comets, loose dust, all became wrapped in the power of the one mind and then with a rush, it had it all, the entire Galaxy held within its power.

And so the third stage began.

Without knowing how, the mind reached for that one point that would allow the lever to force the billions of suns and their planets to move in time. It found it, began applying the pressure, pushed harder, harder, it was not the ease with which Markel and his team had pushed the Galaxy forward, the resistance seemed much greater. Even from within the melded mind, Mickie began to sense the declining, draining power and the start of the break-up back into individuals.

Nothing happened.

They had failed.

*　　*　　*　　*

Mickie had no idea of how long he had stayed slumped in his seat at the conference table. Just as in Markel's memories, he slowly awoke as if from a general anaesthetic in hospital, every muscle feeling like wet paper, completely without strength. Even so, he saw that he was the first to move and he wondered if some of Markel's genes within him had remembered the last time this had happened and had become a little adjusted. He waited a few more minutes, realising they had forgotten to allow for this dreadful fatigue, thinking that perhaps they should have left one of their number uninvolved in the first attempt. That way, there would be somebody to bring the restorative drinks and assist in moving the exhausted agents to greater comfort.

He found he could move, felt greater strength return to his limbs and stood up, shakily. He croaked an order to the dispensing computer and a few seconds later, a sparkling jug of *Sle'Ach* appeared. He picked it up, his arm and hands trembling, feeling as if the jug weighed a ton, poured himself a glass from one of the line of glasses by the computer and drank deeply. Strength began to flow into his body.

He moved to Melkana and began massaging her neck and shoulders. As she finally stirred, several others of the group also showed signs of life. Mickie poured a glass for Melkana, put it to her lips and let her drink, seeing the miraculous effects start to work almost immediately. Ordering more jugs from the dispenser, he slowly moved round the table, pouring glasses for those starting to stir and leaving a jug within their reach for when they woke more fully.

He looked at the large clock on the wall and saw they had been outside of normal life for over fourteen hours.

Another hour passed before the last of the agents had fully recovered. All of them looked as if they had not slept for days, complexions were grey, eyes shadowed in a fatigue most people never experience. Nobody spoke, nobody even seemed to recognise anyone else in the room. Not even Brandon or Melkana looked at him with comprehension. They drank greedily from their glasses, refilled them and drank again, and that seemed to restore some normal functions. By mutual and silent agreement, they hauled themselves to their feet and shambled off like zombies to their rooms. Mickie followed Brandon to the room they had allocated to themselves and both were back in a coma-like sleep within seconds.

*　*　*　*

"So what happened?"

It was Leannina, one of the female agents who spoke. Twenty-four hours had passed since the group had left the conference room, the site of their failed attempt to restore the Pfafth Galaxy to normal time. Nobody had slept less than twelve hours, some as many as sixteen, and there had been little conversation as the twenty-two people made meals and tried to restore their bodies to normal strength and conditions. Even for

Pfafth with their full powers of recuperation, the task had been lengthy and difficult. They reminded Mickie of a scene from the memories of Markel as a child, when he had first travelled with his father and Kerrala in a Pfafth spaceship to carry proto-humans to a new planet. The people in this room looked like the utterly exhausted crewmembers who had teleported the massive vessel and its load across several hundred light years.

Now they sat in the recreation room of the mansion, sitting more comfortably in armchairs and lounges. Some still showed traces of fatigue in their faces and posture, but all looked aware and fully alert. But they also looked depressed and worried at their failure.

"I don't know," Mickie replied to the questioner. Leannina was a middle-aged woman of slim build, with short black hair and a flat, almost Asian face. Almond eyes looked unsmilingly at Mickie. "Everything went as we all remember from Markel's memories. We merged our minds, we took hold of the entire Galaxy…"

"That was one amazing experience," another agent broke in. He was a young man named Doriander, perhaps Brandon's age in his mid-twenties, and the excitement of the wonderment of what they had done reflected from bright blue eyes in a handsome young face.

Mickie smiled in response to the eagerness. "It certainly was," he agreed, remembering the exhilaration as the group mind swept through the entire Galaxy, enfolding it and understanding every molecule, every atom, every electron of the entire mass. For a second or two it hid the anxiety and fear he was also feeling as a result of the disaster of the previous day.

"But we seemed to hit a block as we tried to exert the pressure point," Brandon said, returning the conversation to the grim topic of their failure.

"It felt quite immovable," Leannina agreed. "I got the sense that we just could not move it in that direction."

"That may be the problem," another of the women, Kassiana said. "Maybe you simply cannot move an object backward in time. I can understand how it can go forward, because you create time as you move. But the past doesn't exist any more. There's nowhere for the Galaxy to go."

"But the rest of the Universe is still in the past, as far as the Pfafth Galaxy is concerned!" protested another man, an older one, perhaps in his sixties, Mickie estimated, then recalled the man's memories from the merger of their minds and saw that he was actually over eighty. "So the past is still there for it to move to," the man continued.

"Mister Brown told me it was possible," Mickie said. "And with that guy, I have to believe him."

Nobody needed to ask who Mister Brown was. Like Mickie's recognition of the older man's age, everyone now had everybody else's memories and they had experienced the meeting of the four children with the strange entity.

"Then maybe we just don't have the strength," Sellmar, another of the agents said. "After all, Markel and his Committee had been training for years for that task, and they were all intensively practiced in using all their powers. I know that we still have them, but in reality, the only ones I've used are teleportation, some empathic readings and an occasional low-level mind bolt."

A low murmur ran round the room. It contained agreement and sadness, mixed with considerable worry that Mickie read with his own empathic talent.

"It's a horrible possibility," Brandon agreed. "Even with the million years of breeding in Mickie and Melkana, it's still possible that we don't have the total strength for this."

"Maybe we were pushing at the wrong spot," Melkana said. All eyes turned to her. "Maybe we pushed at the spot where Markel and the Committee had pushed before to move the Galaxy *forward*. Shouldn't we be pushing at the opposite point?"

The room was silent for a few seconds.

"I think Melkana has got it," Brandon said finally. "In which case, how do go about finding the correct pressure point? Markel's Committee was only interested in moving the Galaxy forward and we have the memories of how that was done. All we have now is the principle, but we have no idea of where the reverse point is."

"But can it be too hard to find?" Mickie asked, trying desperately to raise the flagging spirits of the agents. He felt a wave of fear that they might decide to give up and just leave things as they were. Some of them, he knew, would prefer that already, having considerable doubts about exposing the Pfafth to the terrors of the outside Universe.

"We certainly have to give it a try," Brandon said, recognising both the deepening depression in the room and Mickie's worries. "Here's what I suggest. We give ourselves another day to restore our strength fully. Then we go into the first stage again, we create the single mind. With that ability, we must surely be able to examine how we identified the pressure point that moved the Galaxy forward and then work out the opposite point."

Most of the agents seemed to agree, if not that enthusiastically, but Mickie sensed the remaining doubts.

"Would you please recall what Mister Brown told me at our meeting?" he said urgently. "We don't have any choice. It's not just the Pfafth we're trying to save here. It's Everything! The whole Universe. Possibly even Creation itself, even if we have no idea how or why. We *have* to do this."

It worked. As the agents recalled Mickie's memories of that encounter on a far distant planet, they regained their commitment to this task. The meeting broke up as the members went their own ways to prepare for their second attempt to move a Galaxy backward in time.

Chapter 14. Old Alliances Again

Perhaps they hadn't been properly prepared the first time, Mickie thought. The group was back together, this time in the recreation room, once more seated in lounges and armchairs so as to be more comfortable and secure when they returned to their own self-awareness. And this time, one of their number had been left out, so that somebody could help immediately with the restorative drinks or any other emergency when the time came.

The faces were different too. The first time, Mickie had still sensed doubts and fears about what they were about to attempt. Now there were no reservations. Having gone into Mickie's memories and seen how deadly serious Mister Brown had been about saving the Pfafth, they all know how critical this was. There would be no holding back this time.

"Everybody ready?" asked Mickie and received a silent assent from each of them.

And in some unknown passage of time, the white, silent explosion happened again and they were a single mind that held an entire Galaxy within its control.

This time, the Mind did not aim at the pressure point that it had recognised from Markel's million-year-old memories. It knew there was no value in that. This time, the Mind began to examine the galactic mass of stars and planets from a different perspective. If *that* point pushed the Galaxy *forward* in time, where was the point to push it *backward?* With no sense of time, it might have been a few moments or it might have been for many hours, the Mind pondered on the question. It examined the gravitational flow of the solar systems, of the comets, of the entire Galaxy and it began to see a pattern, a series of interlinked movements of the stars, how the Galaxy was really a single engine that played its part in the grand, stately dance of the entire Universe of similar galactic engines. With that comprehension, it understood something that Markel and his Management Committee had not. Without this one engine playing its part in the coordinated machine of the millions of other galaxies, the entire balance would eventually start to decay. It was not just the Pfafth who had to return to play their part in the Dance of the Universe, it was the Galaxy that held them, also. Just as a high-powered engine would eventually explode as one minuscule flaw would expand and cause stresses that threw the total system into collapse, so would this Galaxy's absence eventually cause imbalance in the Universal mechanism.

The Mind looked beyond the Galaxy and examined the sparkling gold plain of Universal Time and the jet black, bottomless ravine that represented the one-second gap between the Galaxy and normal time. Each of the individual minds within the group mind had learned to cross that ravine, but they had never understood its nature. Now the Mind began to work on that problem and slowly developed an understanding. If *those* were the forces, then the point at which to push so as to close that gap would be..... *there.*

It almost seemed easy, now that the Mind had learned the nature of Time and its relationship with Gravity and the movements of solar systems and galaxies. It placed itself to look at the point at which pressure had to be brought and concentrated, and began to push.

It sensed movement, but still not with the relative ease that Markel's group had experienced. There was still massive resistance, still a sense of trying to push a huge boulder out of its dent in the ground. The Mind summoned every particle of its power and pushed again, feeling its energy draining as if there was a short circuit.

The Galaxy shivered, moved a fraction and fell back to its place in Future Time.

And nothing happened.

The Mind trembled with fatigue and let the individuals within it go as they wished.

They had failed again.

"Twenty-seven hours," Leannina said. She was the agent who had stayed out of the merger of minds and it was as well she had done so, because not one of them had the strength to lift their heads when they returned to their own selves. It was four hours since they had woken and Leannina had been busy assisting each of them with drinking the *Sle'Ach* and this time administering a helping of energy pills. None of them was yet able to stand up and go to their beds.

"Twenty-seven hours, not one of you moved, you looked like corpses," Leannina said with a slight shiver.

"But is everyone back okay?" Mickie asked. Even getting the words out was a major effort and he could feel the drain on his system that it caused, even after several litres of the restorative drinks and pills.

She shook her head. "Allarkel is dead," she murmured. Mickie recognised the name as the elderly agent and a wave of sadness washed over him.

"What did you do with him?"

"I carried him out, converted his body to dust and let him blow over the planet," she replied.

Mickie tried to move his arms and realised he was regaining some degree of strength. Around him, the others were starting to stir, some even getting to their feet and within another twenty minutes the room was empty but for Mickie, Brandon and Melkana.

"Not encouraging," Brandon whispered, the maximum strength of his voice.

"We've got to keep on trying," Melkana said, her voice a little stronger than Brandon's. "Now we've seen what's at stake, we can't back away."

"But if we couldn't do it then, why would we be able to do it another time?" Mickie said, feeling despair wash over him. "Obviously we don't have enough power."

And a familiar, cold, merciless voice resounded in Mickie's mind.

"*No,*" said the Zlan. "*You don't. But we can provide it.*"

Mickie grinned at the other two, relishing their surprise at the sudden change in his attitude.

"Our friends have come to help," he said.

*   *   *   *

The general atmosphere around the room was of revulsion and fear.

"I know from our history texts that the Zlan were once our allies and protectors," Kassiana said. "But very few of us have seen one of those beasts, apart from Brandon and you two," she continued, nodding at Mickie and Melkana. "I know I haven't and the idea of being in the same area as one, never mind sharing our minds with them, honestly, it frightens me beyond belief."

A murmur of agreement ran round the room, several of the agents shifting with obvious discomfort at the concept. Having already experienced how closely their minds had merged to form a single entity, doing it again with a species so alien as to be terrifying was an act that made them shiver.

"I know," Mickie said. "I've learned to trust them and be friends with them, as well you all know from my memories. But I think I have almost as much difficulty as all of you with sharing our minds with giant spiders."

"What I don't understand is how they know they can help," Brandon spoke up. "I thought Mister Brown said we were the only species that could move objects in time?"

"He did," Mickie agreed. "And I agree, that's a puzzle."

"Why don't we ask them?" Kassiana said.

"We must," Brandon said. "But the Zlan can only communicate with one mind at a time. We'll need coordination. Mickie will you ask the Zlan if they'll work with the Speaker here?"

Mickie nodded and sent out a mental query, hoping one of the Zlan was listening.

"Of course, young Pfafth," came the instant reply. *"We have been monitoring this discussion."*

"Somehow I thought you would be," Mickie said.

"The issue is far too important to worry about privacy ethics," said the cold Zlan voice.

Mickie nodded at Brandon.

"Speaker 356, please link the Zlan to everyone in this room," Brandon said.

"You are linked," said the calm, measured voice of Speaker 356.

"We know how to help you because we monitored the two attempts to move the Galaxy and we have received Mickie's memories of Markel," said the icy voice, and Mickie saw everyone in the room flinch. He realised that he and Melkana were the only ones who had heard the Zlan communicate before and he remembered how frightened he had been in the

beginning. He saw faces go white and people drew back sharply in their chairs as if to distance themselves from the deadly voice.

"Listen, everybody," Mickie said urgently. "Go back into my memories and review every contact I have had with the Zlan. Look at how they helped me escape from the Speaker's Planet. Look at how they saved us from the Gelkka, on Merrison and especially on Korrobodor. The entire reason for existence for the Zlan has been to serve the Pfafth for over a million years. They are the very best friends we have in the whole Universe."

He watched as the agents fell silent, reviewing in their minds the memories they had got from Mickie's life during the mind merging process. Slowly, the tense bodies relaxed, arms fell away from the tight fold so many of them had adopted as unconscious protection, white faces returned to normal colouring.

"Okay," Brandon said, exhaling slowly. "So I have a question for the Zlan. You worked out how to do this just from the Markel memories and the two attempts we have made?"

"No, not those incidents alone," said the silent voice of the great Spider. *"Ever since Mickie first experienced the life of Markel, we have been working on this problem. Our best minds have looked around the Universe, examined every scrap of scientific data that we could find and worked together to determine how it was done. But it does not mean that we could do it ourselves. The ability remains uniquely Pfafth. But we know how to direct additional power to your talents and that is what we will do."*

"But why?" demanded Leannina.

"Because of the prime imperative that the Pfafth themselves bred into us a million years ago, to save the Pfafth from danger. It is obvious that remaining in hiding now presents great danger to both the Pfafth and all other species. We have been looking for an answer ever since we realised the problem."

"And the Zlan have the greatest intelligence of any species in the Universe," murmured Mickie. "We may have some powers they don't have, though not many, but we don't have that gigantic intellect. They've worked out what Markel's group did."

"We have also worked out just how much power you were short of in that last attempt," said the cold Zlan voice. Mickie could have sworn he detected a trace of pride in the telepathic communication and he smiled. The horrific Zlan became more human almost every time he met them, he decided.

"How do you recommend we proceed, then?" he asked.

"Take two more days of rest," the Zlan replied. *"We will send ninety of our people to that planet when you are ready. That is the additional force we have calculated you need."*

"There is no room for you in this house!" Leannina protested.

"And we are well aware that such a presence would terrify you," the Zlan replied. Mickie heard the same ironic tone that he had heard on the planet of the Sillaron when offered a ride on the back of the biggest Spider he had ever seen. *"We will simply remain close to the house. That will be sufficient."*

Mickie sensed the departure of the Spider from the communication link. He looked around the room and saw expressions ranging from hope, excitement, anxiety, to some fear still.

"Let's get some rest," he said. "We have a very difficult time ahead of us."

They all knew that this was the last time they could try. Already, several of them were feeling effects to their bodies that would take all of their considerable powers to heal and might take weeks, possibly years to complete. Even Mickie was sensing some damage within himself, but hadn't yet tried identifying it, worried about what he might find. Brandon reported much the same. Only Melkana seemed completely unaffected by the stresses of the last few days and she had become Mickie's greatest moral support.

"This time," she said confidently. "This time, we'll do it. I know the Zlan will give us the extra strength we need, and we've found the right spot, we all know that."

She and Mickie had been the only ones who had ventured outside the house when the Zlan contingent arrived. The others had confessed their fear, even with the knowledge of how much the Zlan were committed to serving the Pfafth and were completely incapable of harming any of the agents. Mickie was highly impressed by Melkana's attitude. After all, her only encounters with these monstrous Spiders had been briefly on Merrison, then during the appalling slaughter of the Korrobi and finally when her Pfafth origins had been discovered and the Zlan destroyed her attackers. Despite the ugliness of those events, she had come outside with Mickie and seemed at ease as the Spiders greeted them, ninety of the giants towering over the two children.

"They're friends!" she said when Mickie commented on her reaction after they had come inside again. "Just look at how often they've saved us! And they seemed happy to see us. Somehow, any fears about spiders I used to have as a kid have gone completely."

An hour later, the group met again in the recreation room. One of the agents had volunteered to remain outside the exercise, whether from fear of melding his mind with the Spiders, or worries that his physical deterioration from the two previous attempts might have permanent effects this time, nobody asked. They all knew they would need considerable assistance when they returned to their own identities.

Mickie initiated the mental links and sensed the start of the merger of all the minds in the room. But he managed to control the process before the soundless explosion happened and reached out to the waiting Zlan outside the house. He sensed the first contact and deliberately probed deeper, suppressing his fear.

With astonishment, the process became exhilarating. He read in the Zlan's mind the joy of the huge intellect that permitted a solution to the crisis overwhelming the group of Pfafth and the deep satisfaction gained from serving again. He realised how serious had been the deprivation among the Zlan, conditioned so deeply to serving the Pfafth and having none of them to help fulfil that conditioning. He saw the intense joy that erupted throughout the Zlan world as Mickie appeared and was recognised, and the astonishment as the Spiders rediscovered the nature of their conditioning and a chance to serve again. He relived their anguished rage as Mickie vanished when the Korrobi seized them and the suppressor was used to block his call for help. Then he was one of the Zlan that roared into the midst of the Korrobi blood-drinkers, the fury overwhelming him as he killed, killed and killed again then settled down to the exhilaration of the hunt as his people sought out the misshapen beings and took them home to feed their young. He saw the excitement as a web was shaken by captured prey, the wondrous delight of racing to the trapped creature, biting it and knowing there was food in plenty again.....

The white explosion took away individual memories and now a new, greater Mind existed. Already, the Mind sensed that it had much greater power than before and it swept through the controlling process of embracing the Galaxy within its grasp. Now it encompassed not just the Galaxy, but also the golden plain of Universal Time and the black ravine that separated them. It focused on the point it had discovered before and put all its strength to it. The impossible weight resisted, it seemed determined to stay where it was.... then the Galaxy trembled, it rocked gently.... extra power surged from somewhere and drove hard against that inconceivable mass..... and like a huge locomotive on rusty rails, grudgingly, unwillingly it began to move. Slowly, then more smoothly as if oil had reached the ancient rails, the titanic mass of stars, planets, moons, comets and interstellar dust shifted, the black gash in the golden plain narrowed and the two edges closed together in a perfect seal like the matching of flawlessly engineered pieces in a huge machine.

The Blocked Galaxy of the Pfafth had rejoined Universal Time.

Chapter 15 – The Return of the Pfafth

Melkana, Mickie and Brandon sat in the public rows of the large hall in the Management Committee building in Markel City on Pfafth home world. They occupied the same seats Mickie and Brandon had occupied the last time they attended the meeting of the Committee. This time, the rows were all full with over a thousand people apparently disturbed, excited and frightened. The murmur of voices filled the hall and occasional louder or high-pitched exclamations punctuated the low rumble of sound.

"Rather more than last time," Brandon murmured softly to the other two.

"And they seem frightened," Melkana added. "Could they have noticed the time shift?"

"Hard to know," Mickie said. "But maybe our first two failed attempts shook things around a bit. It will be interesting to see if the Committee has an answer, but it sure looks like people are stirred up about something."

The trio had teleported themselves to the safe house in the fields a few kilometres outside Markel City. A week had passed since their successful return of the Galaxy to normal time and they had all needed that time to restore their strength. The Zlan were apparently unaffected by the effort for they had leaped off the planet without a word as soon as the shift was complete, and there was no sign of them once the Pfafth group recovered enough energy to go outside.

As expected, the house was empty when they arrived and a gravity car was sitting in the garage. The three rode in, left the vehicle to park itself and walked into the Management Committee Building without rousing interest. Only one comment had been made during the ride. Melkana had looked around as they entered the city, sniffed mildly and uttered a single word. "Boring," she said, and subsided, ignoring the grins of the two men. They had walked in, taken their seats and sat quietly while the throngs entered. Nobody gave them a second glance.

The rumble of conversation ceased as a door slammed open at one end of the giant room and the same procession of men and women walked up to the table as they had in Mickie's last attendance.

"I see that little twit Vemanor is still the Chairman," Brandon said. "This should be interesting."

"I declare this meeting of the Management Committee open," the Chairman said in his thin, unimpressive voice.

"Hello! They've abandoned all those prayers and stuff," Mickie said quietly.

"I imagine that happened after our dog and pony show here last time," Brandon said with a grin. "Now they know you're back, there's no point in praying for your return."

Vemanor looked very uncomfortable. "We now all know that tremors shook our world last week, though no damage was done. But something happened two days after that, when many thousands of people reported a spasm of dizziness that in fact seems to have affected every single person on the planet, according to our research. Those people in the night side of the planet also reported that there was a short period of instability in the sky, with stars going out of focus for a few seconds."

"So, what caused it?" shouted a man's voice from the middle of the auditorium.

"We don't know," the Chairman replied, discomfort showing in his posture and expression. "Our scientists are working on it."

The room became turmoil, people standing up, shouting at the Committee members, at each other, arguments breaking out in different locations.

In unspoken agreement, the three newcomers stood and waited patiently for silence to return. Slowly the thousand or so people noticed the immobile trio and sensed that they were critical to the proceedings, the room becoming quiet as the attention spread through the hall.

Mickie broke the silence.

"Chairman Vemanor Markel, we have met before. My name is Mickie Dalton, but I was born on this planet and named Markel before this Committee sent me to Earth to grow up."

The only sound to break the silence as he paused was the gentle hiss of some indrawn breaths around the chamber.

"This is my brother, Brandon, and you already know him as one of your agents," Mickie continued. "And this young lady is named Melkana. But like me, she was born here. At that time, she was given the name of Kerrala when your scientists realised that she too was the intended result of the breeding program they had been conducting for a million years. She was then sent to Kalamos to grow up. We three, with another nineteen of your agents and much help from the Zlan, we are the cause of your disturbance."

He looked around the room. Almost every face was turned to him. Many people held their hands to their cheeks as the shock of what he was saying reached them. Some had closed their eyes and seemed to be muttering to themselves, perhaps praying.

At the Committee Table, the same blank shock was displayed. Vemanor seemed incapable of speech.

"What we did," continued Mickie, "was to fulfil one of the

prophecies made a million years ago. This planet and this Galaxy have returned to the same time as the rest of the Universe. The barrier has gone. That was the cause of the disturbances, for it took three attempts before we succeeded with the help of our greatest allies, the Zlan. But there is no more *"Outside."* You are part of the Universe again."

He waited for this to sink in then resumed.

"However, that's the only prophecy Melkana and I intend to fulfil. We are not here to teach you all your old powers. If you want to regain them, by all means work at it but you're on your own. We are not here to lead you to a war against the Sillaron for the Sillaron have declined just as you have and they offer no threat. And if you want to try and regain control of the forty galaxies you used to own, you're free to try. But I don't fancy your chances because other species have arisen who will not permit it."

"Good going, Mickie," Melkana said softly. "Let 'em have the ugly truth."

"I intend to," he whispered back and turned to the Committee Table again. "We have one more task," he continued. "And that is to destroy those guardian robots parked around the Galaxy that prevent other ships reaching you. Once we've done that, I hope you'll return to the community of species out there and become part of us all without being the Lords of the Universe as once you were. I hope you'll come out of hiding and start to grow up."

He looked down at Brandon. "We've done the courtesy bit with the Committee. We've let them know first. Time to have the Speakers broadcast the news to the world."

Brandon nodded and went into a quiet reverie as he communicated with Speaker 356. The trio then watched as the crowd in the hall started to receive the telepathic messages from the Speakers. While all of them knew about the Speakers from their history texts and occasional news items from agents who travelled Outside, this was the first time any of them had been contacted telepathically and the shock was obvious. The room was deadly silent and then a slow murmur traversed the chamber as the people began to absorb what they had heard.

Mickie looked at Melkana. "Do you want to say anything?" he asked.

She shook her head. "No point," she whispered.

Mickie looked back at the Committee table. All the Committee members looked shaken, though Chairman Vemanor seemed almost catatonic. He clearly was unable to take any further part in the proceedings. But one of the other men stood up, walked round to the head of the table and took the Chairman's gavel, pounding on the table until silence had been restored.

"My name is Allandor," he said loudly. "I am the Manager for this continent and I think I have to take over for a few moments while our Chairman composes himself." He stood up straight and looked hard at Mickie.

"How do I address you?" he asked. "Are you now Chairman Markel?"

"My name is Mickie Dalton. Maybe I was once called Markel, but I have no memories of that time. And I am most certainly not the Chairman. Why not call me Mickie? All my friends do!"

The words seemed to ease the tensions in the room.

Allandor smiled. "Then this time, Mickie, may I extend our welcome to you? We were less than gracious last time."

"Thank you, Allandor. I think we caused some stress for the Committee on that occasion, so it was not surprising."

"Mickie, now that some of the million year old legends have been completed, mainly that we are back with the rest of the Universe, what do we do now?"

Mickie shrugged. "I can't really tell you. But once we've destroyed those guardian robots around the Galaxy, trading ships from other species will start to visit. I hope you will travel around like you used to. It would perhaps be a good idea to see if you can learn to teleport again. Get out and colonise this galaxy. Catch up on history and learn about the species that developed while you've been here, especially the ones you had a hand in developing, like the Kaloti, the Zlan and the Speakers. But I don't suggest you try that Empire thing again."

"We are all still worried about the Sillaron," broke in Allandor. "But you indicated that might not be a problem."

"The Sillaron declined. But danger still exists with a being that was the Sillaron Master. It's been absent for a while, but I think it's hiding somewhere. We can help you with some defences against it."

Allandor was silent for a few seconds. "So it's up to us?" he finally asked. "You're not staying to help?"

"There's nothing I can do," Mickie replied. "You just have to come out of your hiding place and be part of the Universe again. The Speakers will help a lot. The Ships that will soon start visiting you will also help. They can answer almost all your questions about what's been happening."

Mickie realised the entire chamber was deathly silent, listening to the exchange.

"Welcome back," he said. "The Universe needs you just as you need it. But we have to be on our way. I'm sure we'll drop in now and again, it *is* our home world, after all. But we have friends and family we want to see, so until we meet again, goodbye and good luck!"

A few moments later, Brandon was back on Kalamos, and Mickie and Melkana were on the Ship again.

* * * *

"It's hard to believe that there's something you can't do!" Melkana appeared to be quite at ease as she talked to the mysterious Mister Brown.

"We are an advanced race, but we're not Gods," Mister Brown replied. His voice came from everywhere in the cabin, but just where his physical presence, if there was such a thing, was located was unknown. "Just as we discussed before, every species has its particular abilities, sometimes these are possessed by several species, but nobody, not even my race has them all."

"So you're saying that only a Pfafth can dismantle those guardian robots?" Drellion said.

All four children were sitting in Mickie's cabin. Two days had passed since Mickie and Melkana had arrived back on the Ship from their meeting with the Pfafth Management Committee and their recounting of the adventure and the returning of the Blocked Galaxy to normal time had occupied many hours. Their parents had been equally enthralled and news of the events had raced through the Ship. Only when the Captain had suggested a commercial call to explore the newly-opened galaxy did Mickie remember the urgency of the issue of the guardian robots that would have to be disarmed first. Memories of the events when they had first taken the Ship to the area were still painfully fresh in everybody's minds.

That was when they had contacted Mister Brown to ask his advice and been dismayed when the astonishing entity had confessed his inability to do anything with the robots.

"We've looked at them," Mister Brown said. "We can get close to them, but that's the limit. We can't see how they've been sealed."

"Can't you change the metal into something else?" Melkana asked. "That's one of the abilities we both have."

"Ah, there's the cleverness," Mister Brown replied. "It's obvious the old Pfafth had some real geniuses. Somehow, they incorporated into the atomic structure of the materials a key that only responds to Pfafth brain waves."

Mickie remembered something. "When the doorway

opened to the vaults on Shurameen, could that have been because I touched the door? Was there something similar in the metal?"

"It looks like it," Mister Brown replied. "Which means one of the Pfafth agents must have helped the Shurameen secure those vaults so that nobody would ever get in there, except for one of their own."

"Maybe some sneaky Pfafth was planning to take the treasures himself some time, and get stinking rich?" Drellion grinned at the idea as he made the comment.

General amusement greeted his words.

"So if Melkana had touched the metal, it would probably have opened for her, as well?" Fencris said. "That could have caused some confusion!"

Melkana looked startled at the thought.

"But anyway," Mickie said, bringing the conversation back on track. "It means a Pfafth has to do it. At least a Pfafth has to get access to the inner workings."

"That's what it means," Mister Brown agreed.

"But how many of those things are there?" Drellion asked. "If they're surrounding a whole galaxy, there surely have to be *millions* of the things?"

'That's what Brandon, said, that's a fact," Mickie said thoughtfully. "How about it, Mister Brown, do you know?"

"Eighty three million, one hundred and three thousand," replied Mister Brown. "But it's logical that all of them will respond to just one being dismantled. I'm sure the original Pfafth would not have wanted to dismantle millions of them when the time came. So I'm quite certain that when a Pfafth turns any one of them off, the entire network will close down."

"Why wouldn't they have made one as the central controller?" Drellion asked, looking intrigued.

"Too big a risk," Fencris replied, thoughtfully. "The Pfafth that set this up had already planned that it would be a million years for their program to come to the end. The chances that they'd keep the record accurately of which was the control robot wouldn't have been too good, and then they'd have had to disarm all of them, one by one. And anyway, it might have failed, just as others might fail. But if just one was disarmed by a Pfafth getting inside by using the powers only the Pfafth have, then I think that would be the signal for all of them to turn off."

"Young man, you have an impressive sense of logic," Mister Brown said.

"It still won't be easy," Fencris continued, failing to hide his pleasure at Mister Brown's comment. "We'll have to work in zero gravity, in deep space, wearing spacesuits and with no idea of how to open up the thing, or what to do when we have."

"What's this 'we' thing?" Mickie asked.

"Hey, you don't think I'm going to let you go out there and tackle the problem on your own, do you?"

Mickie hadn't thought about it, but he realised immediately that Fencris had a point. Doing it alone, hanging in deep space a long way from the ship was an idea that terrified him. Playing in low gravity in the hangar was one thing, working in a spacesuit, something he had never tried before, in absolute zero gravity was quite another. He cheered up a little at his friend's words.

"But why you?" he asked. "Shouldn't I go with an engineer who may understand how the robots work? Or another Pfafth, one of the agents maybe?"

Fencris snorted. "You saw how fast the other Pfafth vanished as soon as you'd done that galaxy-moving trick! Brandon's the only one you could trust, but he's no scientist. And there's not a techie on this Ship who knows anything about how those robots might work, so you might as well just use this natural genius and man of overwhelming modesty!"

After the laughter had faded, Mickie realised Fencris was probably correct. Whatever those robots were, none of the engineers aboard would have any knowledge of the technology that drove them. And Fencris was a genius. Mickie had slowly learned over the past year or so that the Cassolean's natural talent and grasp of technology was already legendary back on his home world where every major university was competing for him to enrol when he finished his galactic travelling.

"We'd better learn about wearing a spacesuit and practicing zero-gravity work," Mickie said.

"I thought you'd never ask," Fencris said.

*   *   *   *

Putting on a spacesuit was remarkably easy, Mickie found. Stepping into the main garment was like putting on a snowsuit to ride a snowmobile, though quite how the front opening from neck to waist sealed itself he couldn't see.

"It's quite secure," Grant assured him. "The two parts form a molecular bond so that they actually become a single unit when you press them together. When the helmet is removed again and you pull on this little tag here, the molecules remember that they were once separate and return to their original state."

They were in Hangar Ten again, standing by the Loopies square where they had spent so many enjoyable and hectic hours. Gravity was at Ship-standard as Mickie and Fencris put on their spacesuits, supervised by Grant and Fencris' father Devenar who seemed unconcerned by what his son was about to undertake. But Grant was also very calm and controlled, though Mickie could sense the worry his father was feeling, so he assumed Devenar was not quite as cool as he appeared.

"Same with the gloves," Grant continued. Mickie slid on the remarkably light gloves and pressed the wristbands onto the sleeve of his spacesuit. Just as with the front seal, he could no longer see a line of separation between the two pieces of fabric.

"They seem very light for space-walking in absolute zero temperature," Mickie said doubtfully.

"Very advanced material," Grant reassured him. "Your hands will be quite warm enough and you have sufficient flexibility to manipulate tools. Let's do the helmet."

Carefully, Grant lowered the helmet over Mickie's head and down to the shoulders where it clicked into place. Grant took Mickie's right hand and placed it on a small switch above his right ear.

"Press that," he commanded, and the faceplate moved aside, sliding into the helmet. "It can't happen accidentally when you're in vacuum, because the switch is deactivated," he said. "But when you get back in here, you'll be amazed how badly you want to breathe fresh air again and you won't want to wait till the helmet is removed."

He moved Mickie's hand to another switch above the faceplate. "And that's the light," he said, as a powerful beam radiated from the top of the helmet. He switched it off again.

Mickie turned and looked at Fencris, also with his helmet in place. Apart from the lightness of the suit, it could have been the model used for any number of science-fiction films he had seen back on Earth.

"The backpack carries two hours of air," Grant said. "But you'll be pulling along an additional two hours each in the extra tank. When you get the warning buzzer that you're down to fifteen minutes, just take this nozzle by the waistband and plug it into the point on the tank. It takes only about a minute to refill your suit tanks. But the suit is programmed to warn you next time that you're down to thirty minutes supply. If you hear that, get back to the shuttle."

"Let's get gravity down and have these kids practice," Devenar said. "Leave your faceplates open at first until you get the hang of it. I've attached the safety lines."

Mickie checked, and saw that both he and Fencris had thin

cords attached to their belts. The safety lines were some twenty metres long and attached at the other ends to a point on the floor.

The two adults stepped back a few metres from the white line of the Loopies square while Mickie and Fencris grinned at each other and moved inside the area.

"This should be a giggle," Fencris said. "Now you'll see how Loopies trains you for the real thing."

Mickie felt like the floor was dropping away as if in a high-speed elevator, but the experience was familiar enough not to unnerve him. But instead of the normal ten percent gravity they used for Loopies, the setting was reduced all the way to zero.

"Just remember," Fencris said. "There's nothing to stop you now until you hit a wall or a ceiling unless the line stops you. Move very gently, because if you have to grab hold of anything, you still have mass and you can jerk a muscle or break something quite easily."

Mickie nodded and looked to the middle of the playing area. A large metal cylinder about three metres long and a metre in diameter had been left there, hanging on a line about ten metres up in the air. It still floated at the end of the line because nothing had moved it yet.

With a nod to each other, the two boys gently pushed off the floor toward the cylinder with no more than a flick of their toes. Fencris judged it perfectly and reached the middle of the cylinder, grabbing hold with both arms. Mickie was less accurate and was on a course that would take him to the far end of the object. But as he reached it, Fencris' collision pushed it further away and he missed completely, continuing until the safety line brought him to a halt and he began to drift back along the way he had come.

Meanwhile, still clinging to the cylinder, Fencris was drifting further away, but the cord on which the cylinder had been hanging pulled him like a pendulum further up to the ceiling until his own safety line stopped his progress. Both boys were now drifting helplessly with no firm surface to use to regain control.

"Albert, set gravity at ten percent," Mickie ordered, and they drifted down to the floor again while the cylinder resumed its position at the end of the cord, swinging gently.

Once on his feet, Mickie ordered a return to standard gravity and the two adults walked up to them.

"Not easy, is it?" Grant commented. "The trouble is, we have no idea if these robots are made of any magnetic materials that you could connect to, or if there are any sorts of handholds or points to tie yourselves to when you reach it."

"We should have thought of that before we started all this," Mickie said, annoyed at himself. "Speaker 356, will you connect me with Brandon? Make the conversation open to everyone here."

"Hey, little bro," Brandon's tone sounded a few moments later. "What's up?"

"We're trying to plan how to tackle the guardian robots. It's a zero-gravity job and it's proving difficult. Do you know anything about the manufacture of those things?"

"Not a thing, Mickie. Nobody has actually seen one in living memory and the plans for them must have been lost thousands of years ago."

"So it's likely there's not a living soul knows what they look like or how they work. And we can't get near enough with the Ship to see one. Have you any idea of what their range is? How far would the Ship have been before the effect cuts in?"

"That one I do know," Brandon said. "There was something about that in the ancient histories of the Great Flight. And the distance wasn't all that great, about two light minutes."

"That's not that huge," Grant joined in.

"Still a heck of along way without any sort of ship or shuttle," Brandon said.

"Okay, Brandon, many thanks, I'll call you later and tell you how we're doing here."

"You do that, baby brother! Say hello to Melkana for me."

"Fencris, let's give this another try. What if we try and pass the cylinder, one on each side, and we hold onto a stretch of the safety cord so that we at least snag the thing?"

"Good idea. I'll go low." Fencris took hold of Mickie's safety cord about three metres from his belt and the two boys jumped off again. This time they were more accurate and Mickie passed over the top of the cylinder while Fencris passed below it. Their momentum carried the cylinder forward and upward on its own cord, but both boys were now hanging on to it as it began a slow, lazy climb up to the ceiling from where its cord was suspended. A few second later the group collided with the hangar ceiling with a painful force and began descending again. Once more, Mickie resumed gravity forces and they returned to the floor.

"This is tougher than I'd anticipated," Fencris said, his irritation showing in his tight body attitude as he stood up from an untidy landing.

"Grant, how do the people who actually build spaceships manage it?" Mickie asked. "They work in orbit, in zero gravity, and they must do the same when they service the Ships."

"They wear gravity belts," Grant replied. "But the belts work by interacting with the nearest large mass, like the massive object the crews are working on, so it's not difficult. The problem for you is that you'll have to leave the Ship and travel a long way before you reach the robot, and we still don't know how you're going to do that. And the robot is probably too small to have an effect on the gravity belts."

But Mickie had retreated into his own mind. Suddenly he recalled the day when he had arrogantly insisted on a lower gravity setting for a game of Loopies, then turned ten complete somersaults and driven his body upwards from the apex of his jump. He turned his mind inward to the memory of that incident, remembering the anger, the need to try out a new ability...

"Fencris, one more go," he said with a small smile. "And this time, link your right arm in my left. Albert, zero gravity."

Fencris realised something new was happening, because he didn't argue, merely linked his arm as instructed and they jumped lightly toward the cylinder. As they got within a couple of metres, Mickie applied his recalled ability, gathered all the atoms of his and Fencris' body in his mind, saw the gravitational forces and..... brought them to a halt, motionless by the cylinder.

Fencris seemed unsurprised. "Well, okay, that seems to have sorted out that little problem," he said. "Now let's try working on this thing."

Their exercise was to remove a plate from the side of the cylinder. Various tools had been brought with them, attached to their suits in a series of pockets. Even with the light, thin gloves, it was a clumsy and frustrating process of taking tools out of the pockets and undoing the plate. They'd been given some screws to undo, some nuts to unwind and it was a long, irritating process before they had the plate freed and removed. The biggest problem was in trying to apply pressure on a screwdriver or wrench, because without holding on firmly to something, they found themselves turning round the tool, rather than the tool turning. It was finally solved when Fencris wrapped several metres of cord round the cylinder, clung to that while simultaneously clinging to Mickie's legs as he tried to turn the nuts and screws.

"Albert, ten percent gravity, normal after we reach the floor," Mickie ordered when they were finished. A few moments later, they were gathered in discussion with Grant and Devenar. Their helmets and gloves removed, Mickie and Fencris climbed out of their spacesuits and realised they were sweating heavily.

"And that was with the faceplates open," Grant said. "In the actual exercise, you'll be fully enclosed, in the dark and in open space. We have to hope this is going to work. And we haven't found a way of getting you there, yet."

An hour later, showered and in fresh clothes, Mickie got together in his cabin with Fencris and the other two friends to discuss the issue of where the robots were and how to get to one.

But as Mickie recited the difficulties of releasing the plate, Melkana squeaked in dismay.

"Michael Dalton, Master of the Universe Designate and Idiot First Class, have you no Pfafth brains at all?"

Astonished, he stared at her.

"I ask you," she said, appealing to the others. "What is the point of providing the man with God-like powers but not the brains to use them?"

"Oh lord," Mickie muttered in embarrassment. "I'd forgotten. I wasn't very good at that trick."

"What trick is that?" Fencris asked, eyes glowing bright red with amusement at Melkana's words and her laughter behind them.

"This one," Melkana said. She picked up a tray from the coffee table around which they were sitting. In the flicker of an eye it had become a glass jar, immediately followed by a pile of sand on the carpet. "Molecular change," she said. "Even Our Glorious Leader can do that one, though not as well as I can!"

"You mean instead of sweating ourselves silly for an hour hovering by the cylinder, you could have just changed the plate to dust?" Fencris was not angry, just amused.

"It's not something I've found a need for," Mickie mumbled. "It never occurred to me!"

"And you probably won't need it when we're out there," Fencris added. "Remember what Mister Brown told us, it will almost certainly open to a Pfafth anyway!"

"So that just leaves us with the problem of getting there and what to do when we get into the thing," Mickie said, glad to change the subject. "I just wish I knew what they looked like."

"What's wrong with us?" Drellion said sharply, sitting up from his armchair with a bound. "We must be getting old and stupid! Why don't we ask Mister Brown?"

Melkana slapped her forehead in irritation, just as the familiar, powerful voice resounded in the cabin.

"I was wondering when you'd remember me," Mister Brown said, the amusement evident in his tone. "What can I do for you?"

"The guardian robots we were talking about before," Fencris said. "Have you seen one?"

"Oh yes, of course. Here's one."

Just as when Albert projected images in three dimensions in the centre of the room, a new image appeared. It was also a sphere, but not a smooth, round one. Instead, it consisted of a series of flat plates. But what grabbed Mickie's attention and also Fencris' judging by his pointing finger was the series of metallic handholds at numerous spots around the sphere.

"Hah!" said Fencris. "Well that solves one problem! We can strap ourselves to the thing as we examine it or if we need to apply pressure on anything."

"Most unlikely that you'll need to," Mister Brown replied. "As Fencris just said, molecular change won't be needed. After all, I can do that party trick myself, but I couldn't get inside a robot. I'm certain it will open to the Pfafth touch."

Mickie was studying the image. "How big is that thing?"

"Ah!" said Mister Brown and the image of a man appeared next to the robot. The object was about three metres in diameter.

"So how do you think we might get to it?" Mickie asked. "And can you pinpoint one for us to aim for?"

"Certainly I can show you one to aim for. And I think you can work out the rest yourselves. It's always best if you do."

There was a small silence in the cabin. Mickie sensed disappointment in the other three, much as he was feeling himself. Did this incredibly powerful entity not know how to solve that problem? It seemed unlikely.

"Let's lay it out," he said. "We know the Ship can't get to within two or three light minutes of the robot. The engines will fail, computers will go nuts, the food supplies will turn out sewage."

"So the same will happen to a shuttle, won't it?" Melkana asked.

"Yes, but in a shuttle, you won't need food or the computers, because you could always use the Ship's computers!" Drellion was excited as he began to see some solutions. "There might be a two or three minute transmission each way, depending how far away you are, but you could still get answers from the Ship if you needed any."

"But still no engines," Mickie said. "We still can't get to the thing."

Fencris laughed. "Yes we can!"

"How?" Mickie was baffled.

"Slingshot," said Fencris. "But it depends on whether that ability of yours to move mass objects is strong enough to stop us."

Mickie began to see what Fencris was suggesting. "You mean if we take the shuttle away from the ship while we're at a safe distance..."

"Line it up and accelerate toward the robot..."

"We get up to ten percent of light speed....."

"And when the engine fails, you just keep going!" Drellion jumped to his feet with excitement. "It won't matter what the robot does to the engine or the computer, you don't need either!"

"But when we get there...." Fencris was serious again.

"I have to be able to stop us." Mickie was suddenly swamped with doubt. He had no idea if he had enough power to stop a two-tonne shuttle travelling at a tenth the speed of light and bring it to a stop with pinpoint accuracy.

"Exactly." Fencris could see the doubt in Mickie.

"And there's another problem," Melkana said. All eyes turned to her. "If you can't disable the robot, you won't have the engine in the shuttle available. How would you get back?"

"Couldn't Mickie teleport us?" Fencris asked. "Can you, Mickie? From a point in deep space to the Ship, also in deep space, can you do that?"

"No, I can't."

"Er... yes, you can." Mister Brown returned to the conversation.

"I can?" Mickie was more amused than astonished by the flat statement. "I thought we Pfafth could only leap between planetary bodies?"

"That's because it's all you've ever tried. Every time you've needed to go to a new location, you've needed help in visualising the location until you knew it. And the Pfafth so rarely travelled by Spaceship that the idea of teleporting from one never occurred to them."

"You mean you'd provide the visualisation?" Fencris asked, intrigued by the possibility.

"Precisely!"

Each of the kids absorbed the information they'd received in their own way and silence lasted for several minutes.

"So just two problems for us, Mickie," Fencris said eventually. "First is getting there, or rather not overshooting the mark and flying helplessly till we die of starvation, and second is whether or not we can disable the thing when we get to it."

"That's about it," Mickie agreed.

"And we could test the first one before we get there," Melkana pointed out

"I think we'd better," Fencris said with a wide grin.

*   *   *   *

"We've come for the ride," Drellion announced as Mickie walked up to the small shuttle. Melkana simply smiled cheerfully.

"I shouldn't really allow this," Grant said. "But it's only a test, so you might as well come along and see how we do."

The four children followed Grant into the small, circular lounge and took their seats.

"I'll do the piloting," Grant explained. "I'm sure you'll see why. The Ship's computers can handle the controls to set us off and cut the engines, but by the time Mickie has slowed us down, if he succeeds, we'll be a few light minutes away. It will be quicker if I bring us back, rather than wait the extra time for the Ship to handle it."

The observation screens came alive with the image of the Ship hovering just a few hundred meters away. As he had been speaking, the shuttle had left the Hangar and moved away.

"Okay, ten seconds to get to one tenth of light speed, Mickie...... and cut the engines."

The Ship vanished as the shuttle flung away under the awesome power of the gravity engine.

Mickie concentrated, trying to peer deeply into the walls of the shuttle, seeing every molecule, every atom, working to get hold of each part of the shuttle as before, he and his team had taken hold of a galaxy. Suddenly he had it and he started exerting his strength to stop the incredible forward speed. The struggle built up and he felt the strain on every cell he had, it was like applying the brakes to a locomotive, nothing seemed to be happening... he fought harder and harder and harder, felt his energy start to dissipate... he was losing the battle. Then like a flood of cold water over the head of a thirsty man, new energy appeared, he sensed the shuttle slow and then stop. Weariness enveloped him as it had when they had moved the galaxy, but he raised his head to see Melkana drooped in her seat showing the same fatigue as had hit him.

"That was you helping?" he whispered faintly.

She nodded weakly. "I think I'd better come along on the real trip," she croaked.

Chapter 16 – The Last Barrier

The voice that rang through the Ship was horribly familiar.

"You will come no closer. You have received one warning that you ignored. This is the last one. Your engines will not function unless you direct yourself away from here. Your computers will remain inoperable. The Galaxy you see before you is banned. Do not attempt to get to it. You may leave or you may die of starvation. The choice is yours."

This time, however, there was no fear ringing through the vessel. The Ship reversed direction and moved back along the path it had taken to get to the galactic guardian. When it was a light minute along its track, it stopped. The crew completed a pre-planned series of diagnostics and the kids did their own informal test by pouring some *Sle'Ach* from the food dispersal unit and chatting briefly to the computer by whichever name they used for personal identification.

Everything was normal. They were out of the range of the guardian robot.

"Okay crew, showtime!" Mickie announced, feeling far less confident than he was trying to show. He, Melkana and Fencris were already in their spacesuits, helmets on and faceplates open, and with his words, they climbed aboard the shuttle.

"Let's go," he announced and the shuttle lifted, floated towards the hangar door that was dilating like a camera shuttle and flickered through the temporary gap in the force field that kept the air inside the Ship. The screens came alive with the view of the enormous vessel, which diminished sharply as the shuttle moved back another hundred thousand kilometres.

"The idea is that we'll accelerate toward the Ship and the computer will cut our engine just as we draw level," Mickie announced. "Mister Brown provided the precise location of the nearest robot, which is now three light minutes away, and the computer is aligning us to meet it. So at our speed, it will take us thirty minutes to reach it."

"And how do we know when to start decelerating?" Melkana was not looking her normal serene self. There were too many unknown possibilities to meet in the next few hours.

"The shuttle computer timed how long it took us to stop in the trial," Mickie replied. "It was eight minutes and twenty seconds. We should start slowing ourselves with nine minutes to go and work it from there."

"Okay, let's go," Fencris said with some impatience, and as if the shuttle had heard and obeyed, it began its furious rush back toward the Ship. A second later, Mickie saw the brief flash as they passed the Ship.

"Engine is..." began the computer speaker, and then the warning message started.

"You will come no closer. You have received...." then that too cut off as the shuttle hurtled further inward.

"Everything has shut down," Mickie murmured.

"But not light and gravity," Fencris said. "The same happened the first time. We still had life support, just no power, computers or food."

"Hey, I just had a thought," Mickie said. "When the Ship's computers shut down, we still had translation facilities. We were still able to talk to each other, just like we can now."

"Curious, that," Fencris said, nodding his head. "Maybe the Pfafth had developed something along the same lines for talking with alien species. They left us with life support for some hours, enough for us to retreat, so maybe they thought future ships would have mixed species crews and we still needed to communicate in order to get away."

"I just hope that thing doesn't have anything else to throw at us," Melkana said, her nervousness showing."

"No real point," Fencris replied. "Without food or power, the crew would die. At least we got the option of retreating that time. Once past the point, the Ship would just float helplessly at sub-light speeds and take centuries to reach the Galaxy with no chance of being near a habitable planet. And anyway, the Galaxy would always be a second ahead of it, so the Ship could never reach it at all. No point in having any other weapon to hit us with."

"I hope so," she replied, a little comforted by the logic. Mickie hoped Fencris was right also, but said nothing. Carefully he examined his old wristwatch he had brought with him from Earth. As a simple mechanical object he had assumed it would be immune to whatever the robot was broadcasting and he had been right. It was ticking away cheerfully.

For twenty minutes they sat silently then Mickie nodded at Melkana.

"Brake," he said.

It seemed easier this time. Though still weary, he realised after some uncounted time that they had stopped, though he was not sure how he knew that. *How can I tell?* he asked himself.

Fencris poured a large glass of *Sle'Ach* from the flask they had brought with them, knowing they could not rely on the computer to provide it, gave it to Melkana and repeated the process for Mickie. Feeling much better within a few minutes,

Mickie decided not to bother about the question of understanding his position in limitless deep space.

"Can anyone see the thing?" he asked. "Are the observation screens working?"

"Damn, we never thought of that!" Fencris said angrily. "No, they're dead."

"So how are we going to find the robot?" Melkana asked, a trace of panic in her voice.

"Well, you could ask me!" Mister Brown responded. All three let out a gasp of relief.

"You know, for three of the finest intellects in the Universe, we've missed several points," Fencris said, still clearly annoyed.

"So how far from the robot are we?" Mickie asked, smiling at Fencris.

"Why don't you come outside and take a look?" Mister Brown replied.

They looked at each other and in unspoken coordination, closed their faceplates. Mickie advanced to the door, expecting it to open into space automatically as the air was drained from the shuttle's interior. But nothing happened and he nearly banged his helmet against the hard metal.

Ignoring the muted laughter from the other two, he turned back. "Another thing we forgot," he said. "No computer power to open the door."

"But not a problem, either," said Melkana, her grin evident behind the transparent faceplate. "Everybody grab a lifeline, tie it their belts, okay?"

Aware of what she was about to do, the others did as she did and attached short safety lines to their suits.

"Ready?" she asked, saw three nods and turned to face the door.

The hard metal melted away. The deep black of space was revealed and a sharp blast of air took hold of all three, sweeping them toward the open door until they hit the limit of the safety lines.

"You're really good at that," Fencris said in admiration. "I wish I could do it! Okay, let's get outside."

Re-attaching themselves carefully to full-length safety lines that connected to reels with several hundred more metres available, they slowly pulled themselves out of the empty doorway. One line was attached to the tank of air that they would carry with them, should the task take longer than their suit capacities. His heart in his mouth, Mickie found himself in an empty void in zero gravity. Off to his right, the Pfafth Galaxy was a sheer, vertical wall of stars. But it wasn't like on the Ship where they were still safely inside the Hangar. Now the sensation of endlessly falling was awfully real. He swallowed and took charge.

"Okay, remember when we teleported to see Mister Brown? We seemed to be hovering over the galaxy then. This is just the same. We're quite safe."

He heard the heavy, raspy breathing of the other two in his helmet. The three clung to each other as they had that time, and slowly Mickie sensed the easing of their terror.

"Right," he said. "Where's that robot?"

All three turned their heads as much as possible, but could see no sign of the guardian robot.

"Try moving yourselves to the top of the shuttle," said the voice of Mister Brown in his earphones.

Carefully exercising his power to move objects, Mickie pushed the group as directed. Concentrating hard on the motion and looking carefully at the nearest part of the shuttle so as to judge the movement he inched their way along but his concentration was broken by Fencris' startled exclamation.

"Well, scramble my nadgers!" he said, a phrase Mickie had never heard before. He looked up. No more than fifty metres away, on the other side of the shuttle was the strange, multi-faceted sphere of the guardian robot hanging silently.

"Unbelievable!" Mickie breathed. "We nailed it, absolutely nailed it."

"Let's not hang around here more than we have to," Fencris said. "Can you two pull us all over there?"

Without further words, Mickie felt Melkana initiate the drive and the three of them approached the big sphere, grabbing hold of the handles conveniently placed at several locations. With a firm tie to the object, Mickie felt more relaxed and lost some of the sense of falling. But he forgot the air tank trailing behind them and a second later it crashed into the robot, causing a cry of panic from all of them.

"We're really not very good at this stuff," Fencris said sharply as he tethered the tank to one of the handholds. "I can see why people normally get some weeks of training before they try it."

Mickie regained control of his breathing. "Right now we need to see if there's an opening anywhere," he said. "Probably easiest if Melkana and I just scan this monster and see if we can detect anything at all."

Still holding on with both hands, Mickie sent his gaze deep into the metal of the flat surface in front of him. He began to see the molecules, even the atoms and he tried to exert effort to changing the metal into dust, but nothing happened. Perhaps the metal was impervious even to a Pfafth, he thought, feeling a trace of worry. Carefully, he released one hand, stretched for another handle and pulled himself to another panel. The same effort resulted in similarly zero results.

"There's a panel here with a symbol on it," said Fencris. "Somebody come and have a look. Melkana, you're nearest."

"Coming," she said, and Mickie saw her move over to Fencris as he switched his attention to another panel.

"I've tried pushing it," Fencris said. "But nothing happened, so why... *Bramingzed!!!!*"

The translator gave up on that one, but it wasn't needed to hear Fencris' shout of astonishment. Barely audible was Melkana's own squeak of surprise.

"What happened?" Mickie shouted, a twinge of fear running through him.

"It opened when I touched it," Melkana said, her voice ragged from the shock.

"What, like the dome on Shuramee did?" Mickie hauled himself over to the other two as he spoke and stared into the opening.

"Just like that," Fencris said. "Hey, I was right, if Melkana had touched it, the dome would have opened for her, too!"

Conversation faded as the three helmets banged together over the gap in the surface. Remembering the switch for the lamp, Mickie touched it and a glowing white beam lit up the interior. The other two did the same and every crevice was illuminated.

The view was disappointing. Mickie's first thought was that it looked like nothing but the innards of the computer system at school back on Earth, just racks of electrical parts.

"Not all that sexy, is it?" Fencris commented, echoing Mickie's thought.

"I keep thinking that the Pfafth were a hugely advanced race technologically," Mickie said. "But the fact is, they got most of their powers from the natural abilities they had. They didn't really have to develop the sort of technology that the Kaloti or the Cassoleans have. And this is million-year old equipment, anyway."

"What are you thinking, young Pfafth?" Fencris' tone indicated he might already be ahead of Mickie.

"He's thinking what we're all thinking," Melkana said. "The main protection for this thing was the fact that only a Pfafth could open it. After that, the materials are obviously designed to last a long time, but the technology is relatively simple."

"So you think...." Fencris' grin was visible inside his helmet by the light reflected from the beams.

Melkana was silent, concentrating. Suddenly part of one rack melted away as she converted the molecules to some other form. Mickie did the same with another rack and within a few minutes, the interior was nothing but dust.

"Of course," said Fencris. "It might have been booby-trapped to blow up when somebody did just that."

"No chance," said Mickie. "I'm certain that the Pfafth creators of these things reckoned that if a Pfafth had opened it, it could only be to dismantle it. And no other species could open it, as it was tuned to a Pfafth mind."

"Ah... I'm sure you'll be pleased to know," said the powerful voice of Mister Brown. "All the other robots around the galaxy have just gone dead."

"In that case," said Mickie. "Can we get back to the Shuttle? I really do *not* like this space-walking stuff. I'll get the air tank."

A few minutes later, they drifted in through the empty space where the shuttle door had been.

"The observation screens are on," said Melkana. "The computer must be alive and the engines will work."

Fencris walked to a point next to an observation screen and flipped open a panel Mickie had never seen before. "They do," Fencris concurred. "The manual controls are functioning."

"Then can you get us back to the Ship at full speed?" Mickie asked. "I need to get to a washroom and I can't do it in a vacuum."

* * * *

"There's something very odd about the way the robots all died at the same time," Drellion said.

209

They were back in Mickie's cabin, lounging in the styles that suited each of them after a hard hour of Loopies. Mickie was on the floor, leaning up against an armchair. Melkana was lying flat out on the settee and the other two sat in armchairs, Drellion crosswise, his knees over one arm, his back against the other. Two days had passed since they had destroyed the one guardian robot and so switched off the rest. The Ship had taken advantage of being the first trader in the region and was busily engaged in seeking planets with valuable properties.

"What's odd, little brother?" Melkana asked lazily.

"That galaxy is over a hundred thousand light years long and nearly eighty thousand in diameter at the middle," Drellion continued. "The Pfafth didn't have any form of telepathic communication systems, so each robot could only have signalled others at light speed. It should have taken years, *thousands* of years for all of them to get the signal and switch off."

"An interesting thought," agreed Fencris. "Once the Speakers had developed their telepathic talents, nobody bothered with any other communication technologies, because there wasn't any need. And the Pfafth didn't have the Speakers, but they didn't bother because they could teleport anywhere long distance, so they only needed simple radios and telephones for ordinary use on a planet."

"So where did that instantaneous signal come from?" Drellion asked. "Mickie, do you remember any such developments from your Markel history?"

"Not a thing," Mickie said thoughtfully. "And anyway, there are no telepathic machines, so that can't be the way the robots did their thing."

"Isn't it funny how having all those amazing powers was actually a real disadvantage?" Melkana said. "It meant the Pfafth never had to develop real science, so other species did it instead, and when they got marooned in their galaxy, they went backward very fast."

"Yes, I don't remember any culture of scientific research in Markel's day," Mickie replied.

"I think I know how they did it, though," Fencris chimed in. "They would have *had* to develop such a technology for the robots. If they hadn't, our young Loopies whiz-kid here is right, it could have been many thousands of years before the Galaxy was safe to approach after the first robot got killed. I'd say that their engineers who designed the robots would have learned quantum mechanics."

"Hey, even scientists on Earth were working on that," Mickie said. "It's fascinating stuff, I wish I'd read more about it. But how would it help?"

"I've been playing with it," Fencris admitted.

Mickie laughed. He suspected that Fencris' "playing" was decades ahead of the best scientific research back on Earth. "So how does quantum mechanics come into it?" he asked.

"There's a particularly fascinating experiment we do," Fencris began. "You put two particles together, charge one positive, the other negative, then separate them. Now, if you switch the charge of one of them, the other one switches also. No idea what's happening, we can't detect any signal, but it happens, *instantaneously*. But here's the fun part. It doesn't matter how far apart those two particles go, even light years, and it still happens instantaneously. So if you have a whole collection of particles and they get charged up in binary code, just like bits and bytes in a simple computer, you could send a message across the universe in no time, if there's a receiving collection of matching charged particles somewhere. I reckon that's what they did, put a transmitter receiver made up of charged particles in each robot and as soon as one died, it send out a "switch off" message to all the rest and they got it immediately. Simple, really."

Mickie wasn't sure which impressed him most; the idea of non-telepathic communication across the universe, that his

Pfafth ancestors had developed a method to use it, or that Fencris had been playing with the idea and had identified what had happened.

"It sounds like the answer," he said, trying to sound cool.

"So how about dinner?" Fencris said and roused himself from his armchair. "Last one to the restaurant is a dead robot."

"Even if that's not the answer, it happened," Drellion said cheerfully, also getting up. "We seem to have run out of adventures, Mickie."

Drellion was, of course, quite wrong.

Chapter 17 – Peril on Earth

"Mickie I have a call from Earth for you."

"From Earth? I don't think I know anyone on Earth who could be calling. Unless it's my uncle Pallotar, but I heard he'd returned to Kalamos."

"It's your friend Paul."

"Paul! Wow! Yes, connect us, please!"

"Mickie?" Paul's voice sounded hesitant. "Are you there?"
"Paul, this is just fantastic! I feel rotten that I haven't called you myself, but things have been a bit frantic."

"This feels strange, Mickie. I'm sitting in my room, and it sounds like your voice is coming from about a metre away! I hope my parents don't hear me yakking to myself! They'd have me certified!"

"It's okay, Paul. I bet you'd hear them coming up the stairs. So what's happening? What brought on this nice surprise?"

"Mickie, do you get any news from Earth?"

"Not really. I've seen the odd news program about my disappearance, but that's all ancient history now."

"There's something very weird going on here, and it's so weird I wondered if it had anything to do with aliens and stuff like that. Jeez, I feel stupid even saying that! But I decided to try and contact you, anyway. That Speaker is amazing! He responded as soon as I tried calling him."

"So what's causing the problem?"

"Have you ever heard of a place called Shahristan?"

"Shahristan? Somewhere on Earth?"

"It's a little kingdom just north of Bhutan."

"Hang on a sec, Paul, I'll just check my Atlas. Albert, display Shahristan and surrounding countries on Earth."

A large globe of Earth appeared, hanging in the middle of Mickie's cabin. A small section was lit up, and the names of the surrounding countries were displayed. Mickie saw Bhutan, to the north of Bangla Desh and east of Nepal with the tiny state of Sikkim in between. On the northern border of Bhutan was Shahristan. It was minute, just about the size of a small county in England. Apart from the small border with Bhutan, the rest of the country was surrounded by China.

"Okay, Paul, I've got it."

"Mickie, who were you talking to?"

"Oh! That's Albert! He's the Ship's computer and it can do just about *anything!*"

"The computer is called *Albert?* You're kidding me!"

"Well, not everybody calls it that. It's just the name I use so I can have personal communications with it and use it for stuff like this. Everybody has their own name for it."

"It sounds wild!"

"It's fantastic! But anyway, what's the problem with Shahristan?"

"It seems to have almost vanished. It was on the news the other day. Nobody has been able to get in or out. There have been no communications with anyone there for some weeks, no phone, fax or Internet connections, nothing. The last people who got out about a month ago said something weird has been happening. It's gone silent, nobody allowed to sing, play music or anything, and they get hurt if they try."

Mickie's heart lurched. Something unpleasantly familiar echoed in Paul's words. "Hurt? Did they say how?"

"That's one of the weird things. Almost as if they got a

really horrible migraine that lasted a few minutes. But then it went away."

Mickie began to feel a creepy sensation running up his back. "So what happens when somebody tries to get in?" he asked.

"I don't really know," Paul replied. "I think they've started suppressing the news now. But the first comments were that nothing worked. Motor engines stopped for no obvious reason, a couple of military jets crashed when they flew over and now they've stopped talking about it. But that's why I've called you, because that doesn't sound like anything natural at all."

"No Paul, you're right. It's not natural."

"You mean it really is something from outer space?"

"Yes Paul, it is. Earth has finally had its invasion by aliens. And things could really get nasty."

"You mean you know what's happened?"

"I think so. I'm pretty sure of it."

"Can your people help? You sound like you have a lot of power there."

"Paul, you have no idea! I'll be there very soon."

"You mean you're quite close?"

"Er... well, no, but I'll still be there very soon."

"Can you fix it?"

"I don't really know, Paul. But I'll tell you all about it if I do. But hey, what's happening back in Manchester?"

"Oh, same old, same old. Your silly old parents get nastier and smellier, and I saw your sister the other day!"

"Ye gods, what's she up to? Did you talk to her?"

"I did. She wasn't friendly, but she seemed as cranky about her parents as you were. Anyway, she's going to university next year, somewhere away from Manchester!"

For ten minutes longer, two friends chatted about the usual sort of stuff any normal kids would talk about, no matter that they were twenty million light years apart.

* * * *

The silence was what hit Mickie first. Not an abnormal silence, but the mystical, beautiful silence of remoteness. He stood in the middle of a plain, but in front of him was the fantastic sight of the foothills of the Himalayas. They glowed with a pearly whiteness, as if the light came from within, rather than reflected off the snows of eternal winter. The sky was a brilliant blue, sharper, almost incandescent in its beauty, while the air was pristine, as if never touched by any industrial pollution. Standing still, Mickie felt warm, but the odd light breeze had a chill to it.

"Oh my!" he said aloud. "I always wanted to see those mountains."

He turned around, and saw the city of Brindalore, the capital of the tiny kingdom of Shahristan, just three kilometres away. He knew that only twenty kilometres away was the border with China, while Bhutan lay to the south, another five kilometres away. He had never dreamed as a child that one day he would see these places.

Brindalore looked like a place of spires. Breathing deeply of the magnificent clean air, Mickie began to walk to the capital city. Forty minutes later, he stood before the city entrance guarded by two marble statues of Buddha, three metres high. Both had their palms held up to him in salutation. He returned the greeting in the same manner.

"You don't deserve to have your place mucked up this way," he said aloud and continued in to the city.

It seemed deserted. He walked along the sandy road for a few hundred metres before it became a sealed roadway, but he saw no vehicles. The buildings were all low, nothing more than two storeys, but as he reached the centre, the spires of several structures soared above the rest. Finally, he saw a person.

"Good morning!" he said cheerfully in English. His studies with Albert had told him that, like Sikkim, Shahristan had once been a British territory, but had retained its sovereignty under a hereditary monarch after the British had left India and English remained as one of the official languages.

The man gaped at him, open-mouthed in astonishment, then turned and ran into a nearby building.

"Well, okay, I suppose you didn't expect to find some Western kid dressed in jeans and a sweater, walking in from the Bhutan border," Mickie said aloud. "But I thought we might have had a chat about what's going on."

Walking on a little further, he came to an open square and at last he saw more life. People were strolling around, some shops seemed to be doing business and he even saw what he had been hoping for, an open-air café. It had a dozen tables, each sheltered by a large umbrella. He walked up and took a seat. Two or three other tables were occupied by groups of middle-aged men. The three men in the group nearest to him were dressed in Western-style business suits but wore white turbans.

A waiter approached him. He seemed nervous.

"Is English okay?" Mickie asked gently.

"Er... yes," the waiter replied, and the exchange caught the attention of the nearest group. The three men stared hard at Mickie.

"Tea, then," Mickie ordered. He had the cash to pay for his order. He had been surprised to find that the Ship had a stock of various Earth currencies and he had a wallet filled with Indian Rupees which he had learned would be accepted in Shahristan. An hour with Albert before leaving had taught him a lot about this little Kingdom.

As he waited for his tea, he looked around. The silence was overwhelming. No motorcars, no industrial noise, nothing but the sound of people walking and just the murmur of soft conversations. There was no music in the café. With the background of the Himalayan foothills, the scene was immensely powerful. Despite the worry about the danger here,

Mickie drew in the sense of mystery and vastness the way a man inhales the flavour of a fine wine.

"What brings a Westerner to our little nation?"

The voice came from the next table where sat the three men in turbans.

Mickie turned to face them. "Just tourism," he said.

"There are no tourists in Shahristan these days," said one. His face was impassive, revealing nothing.

"There is this one," Mickie said, trying to reduce the tension with a smile.

"And when did you arrive?"

"Just an hour ago."

"Then you are no tourist," said another of the men.

"Why is that?"

"You carry no bags and no hotel here could have checked you in. And nobody has left or come to this country for four weeks. How did you get in?"

"I flew in."

"You didn't fly in." The tension in the faces of the three was becoming obvious. The waiter placed Mickie's tray with a tall glass of tea in a silver holder and a plate of small biscuits on his table and withdrew rapidly, as if afraid.

Taking his time, Mickie put sugar in his tea and stirred it with a long spoon. He took one of the biscuits and chewed slowly on it.

"Why would that be?" he asked.

"Because no engines, no motors, no communications have functioned for many weeks," said one.

"And no music has been allowed," said Mickie. "Yes?"

His comment had an effect. The three men looked at each other, fear showing in their expressions.

"Who are you?" demanded one of them.

"My name is Mickie Dalton."

"And who is Mickie Dalton?"

"Somebody who wants to meet the forces that have taken over this country."

"You are just a boy. You think you can demand such things?"

"Can you let these forces know I'm here?"

This caused a laugh, though not one of great humour.

"And you think that if we tell these smoke things that Mickie Dalton is here, they'll invite you to supper with the royal silver?"

"Smoke things?" Mickie felt the hair on his neck stand up. His suspicions had at last been proven correct. The Sillaron were here.

"I think you know something about what is happening here. I ask you again, who is Mickie Dalton?"

"Somebody who can help. Who are you?"

The three men stared at him as if examining him to test his honesty. One of them finally spoke.

"I am Major Ramesh Murali."

"Major? The army?"

"Shahristan has no army. We only have a ceremonial band for the King's royal occasions."

"And your band has been silenced?"

"How do you know such things?"

"I've met these things before."

The silence at the other table was palpable.

"So you do know what they are?" The major finally spoke.

"I think so. You said smoke *things*. There's more than one? Tell me about them. You've seen them?"

"We've seen five," the major replied.

"Five?" Mickie was shaken. Could there be five Sillaron Masters here? He could not begin to think why so many of the monsters would have taken over this small country, or how so many of them could have got here. "Can you describe them?"

"Like pillars of black smoke," one of the other men said.

"The smoke seems to revolve, but sometimes we see a white face inside the smoke."

"What are they?" the major interjected, his distress evident. "From what pit of hell do they come?"

"Major, it would be wrong of me to tell you that. I'd be breaking some very strict laws."

"Then can they be killed? This country cannot live like this."

"How do these things enforce their will?"

"They hurt us," the major said. "They appeared when my band was practicing. Several of my men collapsed with pains in their heads like they've never experienced before. The things said there'd be no more music."

"They told you that? How did it sound?"

"It was very strange," the other man replied. "It was as if the voice was inside my head." He rubbed his face, sad weariness showing in his eyes.

Mickie was still puzzled by the number of the Sillaron here. "How big are these things?" he asked.

"Perhaps a little over a metre high," the major said. "About as wide as I am."

A metre high? That shook Mickie. The Sillaron Masters he had met were at least three metres high. Something was not right here. He took a sip of his tea to cover his confusion. "And where do these things live?"

"The royal palace, where else?" The major looked angry.

"And where has the King gone?"

"He stays. He says he will not be driven out by monsters."

"Where is the royal palace?"

The major merely pointed to Mickie's left. He looked in the direction to see that the entire side of the square was one single building, built like all the edifices he had seen so far of a lovely, warm, yellow stone.

He stood up. "Get your bandsmen ready, Major Murali. We will need them soon."

The major did not move. Anger showed in his face. "A boy gives me orders? You are what, fourteen, fifteen? And you tell us what to do?"

Mickie looked down at him. "Not an order, Major, more of a suggestion. But consider this. I arrived just an hour ago when no troopers have made it here, no aircraft have been able to fly overhead, no vehicles will run. Maybe you should consider that my suggestion could be worth following?"

For several seconds, the two stared at each other. Then one of the other men at the table stood up. "I think this boy is a man, Ramesh. We should get the band ready."

Mickie smiled at him. "Pick a good tune," he said. "Wear ceremonial gear and watch for my signal." He turned to walk across the square.

In the middle, he stopped. He looked around and saw not a single soul in the area. But shadows at windows told him that he was being observed.

"Like a scene from '*High Noon*,'" he muttered to himself. "But I think Garry Cooper was taller than I am."

He touched a button on his belt. Just as at the huge Abbey on the planet of the Sillaron, music began to sound from the tiny speakers round his waist. But it was not the massive, impressive tones of the Bach Toccata he had used then, but a gentle melody sung by a soprano voice. Mickie waited.

His wait was short. He didn't see from where they came, but suddenly there were five Sillaron standing outside the Royal Palace. He sensed the mind bolt coming at him, but it was so weak it took almost no effort to raise his guard. The bolt merely touched him, like a child's slap. But he stopped the music and looked at the five smoky shapes. They barely reached the height of his chest. These were not Sillaron Masters.

"You were told that such sounds would not be allowed!" The voice was heard in his head as with any telepathic communication. He sent out his empathic senses toward the Sillaron and saw the worry and astonishment in them. But the minds he detected were... he could not be sure what he was sensing. Quickly he tested his other abilities and as he had expected, the suppressor was in effect.

"I chose to disobey," he said.

"You *chose*? You disobey us? We will kill you for that!"

"Don't you want to know who I am before you try to kill me?"

"Why is that important?" Mickie sensed the anger and the growing disturbance in the five Sillaron.

"I am Mickie Dalton. I am Pfafth."

This time, the disturbance became wild panic and as the five small shapes writhed and white faces peeped out at him, Mickie finally realised the nature of the Sillaron. They were children!

One of them seemed to find some courage.

"Then we will do as our people have done before, Pfafth. We will eat your soul."

Behind him, Mickie saw the military band lining up. They were wearing uniforms like the Royal Guards outside Buckingham Palace, he saw with amusement. Red tunics, bearskin headwear, they could have been in a London postcard, except for the Asian faces. Shahristan's British Colonial ancestry was revealing itself.

"I think not. Do anything silly and we will hurt you badly." He turned to Major Murali and nodded. Immediately, the band broke into a noisy march. Mickie waited just a few seconds and waved to stop the music. He turned back to the Sillaron. They were bent double with pain, smoke drifting away from their main mass.

"You see," Mickie said. "And that's just the minor pain we'll cause you. Your mind bolts are useless now." He turned and walked over to the bandsmen.

"Major," he said. "You are going to need all your military discipline in a few moments. Brief your men, Tell them that regardless of what they see appear in the square, they must stand firm. There will be no danger."

The major swallowed. "Something will appear? What?"

"Humanity's worst nightmare, Major. But I promise you, there is no danger."

The major stared at him for a second but nodded briefly then turned to his men as Mickie walked back to his position.

Mickie touched the crystal round his neck and felt the force of the suppression field dissipate. He sent his call.

Two seconds later, two giant spiders appeared behind him and the panic in the young Sillaron became uncontrolled fear. The smoke writhed and a high-pitched humming sound came from them. Behind him, Mickie sensed the waves in the lines of the bandsmen as fear radiated from them, also.

"And now we get serious," Mickie said. "You will not eat my soul. Unless you behave, my Zlan will instead take you as food sources for their young and you will take weeks to die while the spiders feed on you."

The humming increased another to a new pitch, a sound Mickie decided was a signal of acute distress.

"Go!" Mickie said to the Zlan. "Your presence is causing havoc here. But return immediately I call you."

Soundlessly, the two monsters vanished and Mickie sensed some easing in the tension in both the Sillaron and the bandsmen.

"They said that the Pfafth could do nothing when the suppressor was on," came a tentative voice into his mind. Now the youth was obvious. Mickie realised he was dealing with a frightened child.

"They were wrong," Mickie replied. "I found the answer to that thing a long time ago. What are you doing here?"

"We stowed away on a Kaloti Ship," came the reply. "We just wanted to do something different. Then we saw a shuttle being prepared to land somewhere, so we got in that. We didn't know where this planet was."

It must have the shuttle that came to collect his uncle, Pallotar some weeks ago, Mickie realised, and Pallotar had been doing some research in this area.

"How did you get a suppressor?"

"The Master dropped it in the Abbey when you killed it."

So these kids had been there when Mickie had destroyed the Sillaron Master on their home planet? No wonder they were terrified when he had announced his name.

"So you should have known I could counter it."

"We didn't think," replied a Sillaron. Mickie struggled to stop laughing. It sounded like any human child caught out in silliness.

"Do your parents know where you are?" he demanded.

"No."

"So what am I going to do with you? You've committed serious crimes against this world."

"Please don't kill us," begged one of the shapes before him.

"I won't, but your punishment must be severe," he said. The two Zlan appeared again behind him. Mickie saw a waver in the lines of the royal band but the men stayed where they were. He turned back to the Sillaron. The hum of acute distress was loud in his ears, like a wasps' nest when a stone has been thrown in to it. Mickie decided that any possible resistance had collapsed in the face of the Zlan's presence.

"I will send you home," Mickie said. "Your own people can deal with you."

The humming subsided.

"But you will have to wait here until a Ship arrives to carry you," he continued. "So you'll surrender that suppressor to me and you'll stay in the city's prison. If you try to escape or throw a mind bolt at anyone, not only will the band start playing very loudly, they will send for me again and my Zlan will not hesitate to claim you as hosts for their young."

"Young Pfafth," said one of the Zlan. "We have a suggestion."

"What is that, my friend?"

"We will carry them home immediately."

Of course! Mickie felt annoyed with himself for not thinking of that.

"We suspect that might be punishment in itself," continued the great spider.

Mickie laughed out loud. The Zlan continued to astonish him as they revealed this sign of a sense of humour.

"On second thoughts," he said to the Sillaron. "You can be home in a few seconds. But for that, you have to ride the Zlan."

The humming reached an ear-paining pitch for some minutes as the young Sillaron faced up to the terrifying idea, but logic eventually took over. Showing every signs of blind terror, the smoky shapes somehow crawled to the backs of the giant spider, and with a small pop they were gone. Mickie walked the few steps to where they had been and picked up the blue crystal of the suppressor device.

Behind him the band struck up a melody unfamiliar to Mickie, but it had that dirge-like quality possessed by almost every national anthem in the world. From the front door of the palace, a young man appeared. He was dressed in an ordinary business suit and was accompanied by another, even younger man wearing a uniform similar to that of the military band. The younger of the two spoke.

"His Majesty, King Siranom the Third!" he announced loudly.

Mickie stood still while the two approached him. The band went silent.

"We owe your our lives and our country, Mickie Dalton," said the King and reached out his hand.

Mickie was British enough to have some idea of how to respond to royalty. He bowed his head as he shook hands. "I'm glad I could help, Your Majesty," he said.

"We are puzzled," the young King said. His accent was flawless British public school. "What were those things and how did you deal with them?"

"Your Majesty, it would be best if you don't know," Mickie replied. "But they will never appear again, I can assure you."

"Then another question. I heard you tell those things your name. But what is *'Pfafth'*?"

"That also is something I can't tell you, your Majesty."

The King looked hard at Mickie. "You can't? Or won't?"

"The laws on these matters are very strict, Your Majesty. Please believe me, it is better if the full story remains unknown."

The King seemed to think for a few seconds then accepted what he had heard. "Nobody will ever believe what we have seen," he said. "From where in God's name did those hideous spiders come? And yet they seemed to obey you, though we heard no communication between you."

"That too would be best hidden," Mickie said. "It is too early for Earth to learn what is out there."

"So those things, you, all of you, you are not of Earth? I think we are relieved to know that. But you sound like an Englishman, from.... hmmmm... Manchester, I think?"

"Manchester is where I spent most of my life, your Majesty. But I was born elsewhere."

"And now you should be getting back to this ... elsewhere?"

"I should, yes. My parents and friends are waiting for me."

"But I hope you can stay to dinner and at least tell my wife and me about some of these mysterious things."

"I have never dined with a king before," said Mickie.

The other man grinned like a schoolboy and suddenly became very normal. "Then you'd better stay. My chef does the best apple crumble and custard in the world."

Struggling not to laugh too hard, Mickie accompanied the King inside. Behind them, the band struck up a melody. To Mickie's delight, it was Gilbert and Sullivan's Overture to *The Pirates of Penzance*." Here he was, two thousand metres above sea level, on the border with China and near the foothills of the Himalayas and he felt almost as if he was back in England.

Two days later, Mickie received another contact from his friend Paul.

"Mickie, what did you do?"

"Let's say I applied some pest repellent," Mickie replied. "I really can't tell you any more. What happened on Earth?"

"It's all very odd," Paul said. "There are no official announcements at all. The news channels just talked about repairs to all the communications links and some vague references to terrorist threats, but nothing specific has been said. But some of the rumours are really wild! One of them said something about giant spiders appearing! You wouldn't know about that, would you?"

"Giant spiders? Jeez, that sounds horrible! No, can't say I know anything about giant spiders, Paul."

"Are your really sure, Mickie? I remember when you disappeared, there was some rumour about those hooligans muttering about Giant Spiders. Are you hiding something?"

Mickie remembered the arrival of the Zlan in the park in Manchester. But he knew he must not let Paul know about such things being real. "I'm really sorry, Paul, there's nothing I can tell you about that."

"Oh!" Paul sounded disappointed. "Oh well, it sounded pretty good. When will you get back here?"

"No idea. But how about you come on a trip with us when I do?"

"You're on! I've no idea what I'll tell my parents, but I'll do it!"

"We'll work something out. See you then, old buddy!"

Chapter 18 – Some Rest & Recreation

"The Planet of Dreaming Crystals," Allie said with a smile. "Without a doubt, the most astonishing place in the Universe."

"After all the places we've seen, that sounds impossible!" Mickie replied.

"It's the one place we all look forward to visiting," Grant joined in.

The three of them were sitting at lunch, something Mickie always relished. He had still never got over the pleasure of sitting with his new parents and talking, instead of the old nightmare memories he still occasionally suffered, of a smoke filled room, noisy slurping from his father, the hacking coughs from his mother and the ever-present fear that his father would find some reason to beat him.

"But in three years, we haven't visited before?"

"It's out of our normal trade routes," Grant explained. "But sometimes, we make the effort to visit when we think the crew is getting fatigued and stale."

"So what's it like?"

"Almost impossible to describe," Allie said. "There are two sides to the place. One is the sunsets when the weather is right. Then you'll see the Dreaming Caves when you get there and I'm not going to try and explain those."

"The Dreaming Caves?"

She nodded. "Be prepared for the most astonishing experience of your life."

Mickie returned to his dessert. He'd been able to get the Ship's computer to produce custard the way he liked it and he still loved to treat himself to apple crumble and custard. After being astonished by the quality of that dessert served by the King's chef in Shahristan, he'd had to apply some effort to persuade the computer to review the ingredients and recipe, but finally he believed he could show the Royal Chef a thing or two.

Despite Allie's words, he still doubted the Universe had anything left more astonishing than what he had seen in the last three years.

"Looks like the perfect conditions," Allie said as they left the shuttle.

"What are perfect conditions?" Drellion asked. None of the kids had been here before, and all were intrigued by what they had heard.

"Big, lumpy clouds like those," Grant said, pointing at the fluffy cumulus clouds. "And clear skies where the sun is setting."

"I'd say about an hour to sunset," Fencris said, shielding his eyes and checking the sun's altitude.

Mickie looked around him. The shuttle had landed on a large, featureless plain that looked like dull, frosted glass. More than fifty people had descended from the Ship with him and most were now walking around, the children running and playing games of chase. Gravity was quite high, probably even higher than Earth's, so Mickie began to walk briskly round the plain to work out his leg muscles and soon the other friends joined him.

"What is this stuff?" Drellion asked.

"Crystal," Melkana replied. "Dad said that any area like this was once a cave and the crystals grew there. But they grow so fast, eventually they fill up the cave and break it up, and the whole hill or mountain breaks up also. But now it's outside, and the crystals break up and get rubbed down by weather."

Mickie looked harder. Now he could see that the surface was just a little bit transparent and he could see down perhaps a centimetre. Long lines extended in parallel to his left and right, looking like splits in the surface.

"So what's this about sunsets?" he asked generally.

"I think that the sun shines through the crystals when it gets really low," Fencris said. "So I imagine we might get nice colours on those clouds."

Mickie shrugged. "Well, okay, I imagine that's pretty neat. Don't know what everybody's been raving about, though."

"Nor me," Fencris agreed, and the other two nodded their similar views.

Around them, many adults were laying out seats that they had brought with them, others were spreading blankets and preparing picnic baskets. Mickie saw Allie and Grant already sitting on a blanket and she waved at the group to join her and Grant. They sat down as the first edge of the sun hit the distant mountains.

And Mickie discovered that it wasn't just the colours.

The first note sounded like the gentlest note from an organ, so high it could barely be heard. It grew in volume and the note became a chord and swelled rapidly until it filled the heavens. Mickie felt a wave of utter delight and happiness and he threw his head back, only to see that the colours were playing in the clouds like a fireworks display such as the world had never seen. Every imaginable shade of every colour and some he had no name for exploded among the massive halls of the clouds, ran through the valleys and up the sides, down the others and flung themselves into the spaces between. And the music grew even more powerful and complex, the chords multiplying and varying as they grew until the sound became the most glorious symphony and choral work he could ever have dreamed of. Tears of absolute joy and happiness filled very fibre of his body and he sensed that the others around him were experiencing the same abandoned, total happiness.

The beautiful music began to fade as the sun dipped further and the ecstatic colour display diminished until there was just a simple red glow at the base of the clouds.

For ten more minutes the crowd from the Ship sat there in complete silence, then finally a few of them stirred and rose to their feet, began packing up their chairs and blankets. The air had become significantly colder.

"Back to the shuttle," Allie said softly. "We'll sleep back aboard the Ship. Too cold to camp out here."

Almost in a daze, the four children followed the adults back to the shuttle and took seats for the short ride back up to the orbiting Ship.

"The crystals begin harmonic vibrations as the heat radiates away in the evening," Grant explained. "There are whole ranges of mountains made entirely of the material, so that scene occurs in many places round the planet."

"Can we come back again tomorrow?" Mickie begged.

Grant smiled in understanding. "We'll do that each evening for the next three days. But tomorrow, we'll come back to a different spot about midday and you'll find out about the Dreaming Caves. If this evening blew you away, the Caves will shatter you!"

Mickie closed his eyes and tried to relive the ecstasy of the Crystal Sunset. Whatever the Dreaming Caves would bring, he knew he couldn't wait to experience that rush of utter joy and happiness that the evening had brought.

*   *   *   *

At noon, the Shuttle descended again, but this time they landed in a small valley.

"There are about seven or eight caves here," Allie said. "Bring your seats with you, and a blanket, because it gets cool in there."

"So what happens?" Melkana asked

"Somebody has to be outside the cave to come and get you later," Allie said. "Today, it's my turn, first. It's a bit like looking at a Maragos statue, you lose track of time. But when you find a spot, just sit down and relax. These crystals are somehow telepathic and they'll let you dream your innermost dreams and play them back into your mind. They'll be so real, it will be like living the actions."

"That's cool!" Melkana said with a grin. "Can I pick any dream?"

"Sometimes. But usually the crystals find something you didn't really know existed and the dreams are extraordinary."

"If the crystals are telepathic, does that mean they're alive?" Mickie asked.

"We're not sure. Nobody, including the Speakers can communicate with them, so we think not. They're probably more like the empathic leaves from Harliya, they trigger moods and old memories. But to be safe, there's a universal ban on trying to cut away a crystal and take it off the planet. Okay, in you go, we'll come and get you in about an hour."

Intrigued, Mickie carried his cushion and blanket into the cave Allie pointed out. About ten more people came in with him, and they all selected a spot with reasonable privacy, but the four friends stayed within a few feet of each other. The cave seemed very light, not at all gloomy, and massive stalactites grew from the ceiling, while equally huge stalagmites rose several feet from the floor. Every step and every sound made by the people settling down became an echoing chord from the crystals, a little like the music of the previous evening, but slowly silence fell.

Mickie began to feel as if a curtain had surrounded him and

separated him from the rest of the cave's occupants. Blackness grew, not a frightening darkness, but a warm, friendly cover and protection from the world.

The gentle, smooth sounds of a trombone began to be heard, close, but not loud, and....

He was on a stage, the silver slide trombone in his hands. Behind him, the trumpet player and clarinet player held their instruments but didn't play. Only the double bass and drums provided a firm beat. And he was playing... he was playing beautifully, the silken smoothness of Chris Barber, he was playing with absolutely consummate ease and perfection the introduction to his favourite piece. And beside him, the tiny frame of Otillie Patterson let go with her powerful, commanding Blues voice, singing *"Kay-Cee Rider."* This was ecstasy again, playing so beautifully, backing up the amazing power of her voice as the crowd in the darkness in front of them moved in rhythm, gripped by the beat, by the emotion, by the melody. Otillie approached the end of her first phase and he built up the power of his trombone to take his solo and then blasted into the opening bars as the audience roared their approval and stood up to sway in time. No matter how many times he played, the exhilaration of what he was doing sent a thrill of delight through his body. Otillie came back in for her second phase and in the shadows, he could see the joy in people's faces, their complete enthrallment with the music, he and the band had become one with the crowd, it was power, it was beauty, it was perfection. As applause bellowed into the lights of the stage, he.....

.... was walking onto the dance floor, hand in hand with Melkana. He was in a tuxedo, gold cufflinks flashed at his wrists. Melkana was in a blue ball gown that hugged her body, her hair was swept up above her head and a diamond tiara flashed amid the coils. She came into his arms and they danced, the music showing them both exactly how to move, their bodies coordinated and perfectly in time. Her eyes flashed as she looked up at him and a delicate perfume of flowers rose into his nostrils. Other couples swayed and turned around them, but he knew that nobody looked as elegant, as handsome and as magnificent as he and his beautiful partner.....

The bright yellow ball dropped from the ceiling dome and he leaped from his position hanging on the strap at the side. He got there just a split second before the opponent did, neatly gathered the ball, flicked it down and to the side to Grant, who caught it perfectly. Mickie carried on to the side wall, turned neatly so that his feet met the wall first, superbly timed so that he pushed off again to join the team manoeuvre, flicking the ball round the circle, from the man just below the ceiling as he slowly dropped, to the man at the side, to the man at the base who flung the ball to bounce off the top of the far wall, against the ceiling and back into Mickie's net to repeat the circle. And at the end of the planned move, Mickie flung it perfectly into Grant's racquet as he twisted, turned and rifled the ball into the black disk against the far wall. The buzzer sounded, the number flickered up to "3" and Grant yelled with exhilaration, turning to Mickie and calling "Great pass, son!" Mickie grinned back, revelling in how well he had played in the same team as his father and....

"Mickie! Mickie! Time to wake up!"

He opened his eyes to see Allie bent over him, smiling broadly.

"Quite an experience, eh?" she said. "Come on, it's getting cold, there's hot coffee outside. And now Grant and I get to dream in here."

Realising he was chilled, he gathered his blanket round his shoulders and walked out into the sunshine, gratefully accepting a mug of coffee and sipping it.

"So what was your deepest desire?" he heard Fencris behind him. He turned to see his friend doing much the same as he was, sipping hot coffee while huddled into his blanket.

"Not what I expected," Mickie admitted. "I dreamed I was playing in a jazz band back on Earth, that group I told you about."

"Chris Barber? Hey, you really must want to play that trombone! Just the one dream?"

"Er.. no, I had one of playing Gravity-Ball in Grant's team and sending him the pass for the winning goal."

"Nice one!" Fencris said with a cheerful laugh. "Just those?"

Mickie felt unwilling to tell him about Melkana and the Ball.

"That was it. How about you?"

"A Broxy hunt back on Cassolea. I was the one who went in for the kill, man it was wild, the thing nearly had me, but I got the knife right into the spine!"

"Just one?"

"Well, no. I dreamed I was getting the Global Prize for Physics at the University for my work in Quantum Mechanics."

"You'll have both those come true!" Mickie said. "Hey, Drellion, Melkana!"

Mickie stopped, a little embarrassed to see Melkana. Oddly, she seemed slightly flushed.

Drellion recited with delight his dreams of playing in the world's Gravity-Ball league and of flying an aeroplane in an aerobatics championship.

"Melkana?" Fencris finally asked her. "What about you?"

"Oh... well... I played the flute in the city's symphony orchestra," she said. "It was lovely. Then I played the solo for a flute concerto."

"It was utterly amazing," Drellion spoke for them all.

The other two boys wandered away to meet some others from the school and compare notes, leaving Mickie alone with Melkana.

"Actually, I did have another dream," she said, not meeting his eye as she drank her coffee."

"Oh yes?"

"You and me. We were at a ball. You looked pretty cool in a tuxedo."

He caught his breath. "And you looked fabulous in a blue gown with your hair up. I had the same dream."

This time she looked at him, her face flushed again. "I suppose with our empathic talents, that was going to happen."

"I suppose so."

"I'll tell you this, though. For a Pfafth, you don't dance too badly!"

He laughed, and they both felt at ease again.

Four hours later, after another mind-bending concert of the crystals and colour display in the clouds, they returned to the Ship, with everybody agreeing that the Planet of Dreaming Crystals was indeed the most amazing and beautiful place in the Universe. Mickie found that the Crystals had been right about the wish to play the trombone well, and he renewed his efforts and frequency of practices. The dream about Melkana hadn't really surprised him and as for wishing to play Gravity-Ball on his father's team, that was no surprise at all.

* * * *

"Hey, wow, this almost *never* happens!" Fencris looked excited, but so did everybody else in the observation lounge.

The astounding mass of another Ship hovered just a few kilometres away as they orbited Harliya. The harvesting schedules of both had coincided and the two Ships had arrived within four hours of each other.

"But won't that cause an excess of cutting down trees?" Mickie asked when the news of the meeting had broken.

"No, not at all," Grant replied. "We've both been allocated areas and amounts to cut, but they're in different hemispheres, so there's no risk of over-cutting. The Harliyans are very, very careful about such things, as you know."

"So how many Ships like this are there, anyway?" It occurred to Mickie that he had never thought to ask before.

"Only eleven," said Grant. "That's why it's worth travelling like this, because we can never keep up with the demand for the stuff we obtain."

"So what would happen if all eleven turned up here at the same time?"

"Can't happen. The schedules are coordinated back on Kalamos, so we almost never meet another Ship. This is the first time in my experience."

"So do you know anybody on the other one over there?"

"Oh yes!" Both Allie and Grant laughed. "Several of that crew were in the same training program we were on. There's going to be a gathering of lots of friends over the next few days."

"Ah, but there's something even more critically important happening!" Grant was hiding a smile, but Mickie could sense the enjoyment in his father's mind.

"What's that?" he asked.

"They've challenged us to a Gravity-Ball match, Ship against Ship, prize to be determined."

"Wow! Are you on the team?"

"Don't know yet. We're having trials all day today and tomorrow to pick a team and then develop some team tactics. The problem is that we've never put a single team together, only individual departmental ones. So there are no agreed tactics and not everybody will have played together before."

"When's the match?"

"Three days from now. I've assigned my deputy to work on the planet and I'm going to be trying out for the team. Wish me luck!"

Mickie found the next three days enormous fun. While he still had a school schedule to meet and his increased trombone practice took more than his usual free time, the kids still found time to go and watch the Gravity-Ball trials in Hangar Ten.

The oblong playing area had been erected, as had the seating stands, twice the number that had been there for regular games as both crews would attend.

"You mean their entire crew will be over here?" Mickie asked during the afternoon practice session.

"Every last one of them," Fencris said. "You don't need to leave anyone aboard, because all the operations crew have the control units in their bodies. So they can monitor everything that's happening and adjust things, even while they're over here."

"Okay, I see." Mickie turned his attention to the players working away inside the playing arena. There were several Cassoleans in the trials, but Mickie noticed that he had yet to see an X'Kasxi player in any team so far.

"They can't," Drellion replied to Mickie's question. "They're reptilian in origin and cold-blooded, so they just don't have the speed for long periods that warm-blooded species have. They can move very fast, but can't keep it up for more than a few seconds. Gravity-Ball would kill them."

Even after more than two years aboard the Ship, Mickie found he was still learning about the facts of multiple-species life.

Evenings were times of considerable boisterous revelry. Mickie found that the two crews contained large numbers of mutual friends originating from university days or from the training programs required for joining such a Ship. The dining room was consistently packed, as were the several coffee lounges and bars in the social areas. The noise level was higher than he had ever known it and everywhere he saw cheerful gatherings, mostly reliving old episodes of earlier times and other places.

The kids from both Ships got together also. Some joint lessons were held and Mickie found himself the object of considerable attention, as some of the tales of his exploits had spread over the planets of the species present. Melkana found she was also busy with inquiries. The trick of changing matter was particularly in demand.

"Change it into a cat!" one girl demanded, putting a book on the table.

"I can't make something alive," Melkana protested, to the girls' obvious disappointment. The book became a vase of plastic flowers instead, and that was enough to draw small sighs of astonishment from the dozen or so kids gathered round. The girl laughed and immediately ran off with the souvenir of her encounter with a Pfafth.

"And you can lift things up, just by thinking it?" another boy enquired. "Show us!"

Obligingly, Melkana raised a small cushion a metre into the air, then moved it and dropped it over the boy's head, to everybody's amusement. He blushed, obviously smitten by her.

But the Spiders were the chief objects of fascination.

"You mean you actually *rode* on one?" The girl's face was a mixture of awe and horror. "How could you do that?"

"Easily," Mickie said, enjoying the reaction. "I just climbed up its leg and sat on it."

The wave of mixed revulsion and fascination that ran through the group almost made Mickie laugh, but he restrained his reaction.

"Honest," he said. "Once you get used to them and actually talk to them, those spiders are really quite good fun."

By the time they'd covered the adventures on various planets and how Melkana also discovered that she was Pfafth, many hours were taken up, though the teachers seemed not to mind, realising that one day, these tales would be in the history books anyway.

And Fencris too, came in for his share of huge interest, especially among the Cassoleans. As the one who had rediscovered the lost Cassolean talent of telepathy, he had probably generated more change and excitement on his home world than anyone else in Cassolean history and many hours were spent telling awe-struck groups of his encounter with Mister Brown and how the Zlan appeared on Korrobodor to save the crew.

Naturally, with the upcoming Gravity-Ball match, the kids also played some Loopies matches. Melkana quickly fashioned a silver cup out of various pieces of scrap, and a knock-out tournament between pairs was drawn up. Mickie and Melkana sat out, knowing that if they won even a single match, they'd be suspected of using special Pfafth powers. But to their delight, the team of Fencris and Drellion emerged victors after a whole day of matches. But Drellion found even greater rewards. Many of the girls from both Ships realised that not only was the Loopies Champion a remarkable athlete, he was a charming and good-looking boy also, and he was suddenly the object of much feminine attention. It was some days before the smug grin wore off his face.

But finally, the evening of the great match arrived.

"I'm on the team!" Grant announced with delight, just an hour before play was to start. Allie and Mickie both laughed with pleasure.

"Fantastic, Dad!" Mickie almost glowed at the idea that his father would be in the arena that evening.

"Only a reserve, mind you," Grant added. "But the captain said we'd all get a game. This is such a historic event, we've all got to be part of it."

"And have they decided what the prize is going to be?" Allie asked.

"Just a trophy," Grant said. "We all agreed that we couldn't put up anything of value, because the whole crew could lose. One suggestion was to put the entire haul of wood and leaves from this trip, but then we came to our senses!"

"I should hope so!" Allie replied. "Just imagine how resentful people could get if they lost large amounts of their income!"

"That's what we decided," Grant agreed. "Staying friends was more important."

And with that, he went off to change for the match.

Hangar Ten was like a fairground. Masses of people milled around in the area by the arena, most carrying drinks or chewing on various items. Mickie could see that picnic hampers were all over the place as the two crews had obviously decided to make a real party of this event. Feeling the cheerfulness and excitement of the occasion, the four friends searched out a place in the stands and eventually found two pairs of seats, one behind the other and claimed them, Fencris and Drellion in front, Mickie and Melkana behind. Mickie looked around but couldn't see Allie at all, but decided she was probably in the mass of people around the crystal lattice walls of the playing area.

The lights within the arena flickered a few times, a signal to the crowd to take their seats and soon the two banks of seats on either side of the arena were full. Mickie was interested to see that the crews had not divided themselves on either side, but had mingled in both tiers of seats.

The lights in the main area of the hangar went down and those in the arena rose in brightness. From the entrance doorway, a line of ten players walked in, dressed in their colours of deep, royal blue. Cheers rose from all parts of the seats as the visiting team approached the walls and all of them entered the playing area. They walked normally round the floor, so it looked like gravity was still set at Ship standard. Mickie noticed that the visitor's team was made up evenly of Cassoleans and Kalamosians. But he also saw that in addition to the racquets, they were carrying spears, heavy weapons two metres long with a wicked looking head at the end

Cheers rose up to a crescendo again as the home team entered the hangar, this time in colours of red with white vertical stripes on the shirts. Grinning cheerfully, Mickie saw Grant in the middle of the line. But instead of entering the arena, they paused outside, and the hangar went silent.

Inside, the visitors' team had placed their racquets against one wall and the ten men lined up in two rows of five near one end of the arena. With their spears held in their right hands, they stood straight, but began a tapping in unison on the ground.

"Oh my, we're getting a *Dregarl!*" Fencris exclaimed with obvious delight. He turned to the others. "It's a traditional Cassolean war dance from hundreds of years ago. It's done before a Broxie hunt back home. Just watch, this is wild!"

Mickie had once watched an international rugby match on television when the New Zealand All-Blacks had played against England. The Maori war dance - the Haka - that the New Zealanders had performed before the game had thrilled him to the core and the Cassolean Dregarl that he now saw had the same effect.

The tapping grew louder and became a driving beat. But while the rear line continued with that beat, the front five developed variations, a complex rhythm almost like a flamenco beat. But with a loud, wordless shout of a single syllable and a crash of spears on the floor, they men fell silent and motionless. That lasted just a few seconds. The beat started again, but this time the left foot of each man also banged on the floor on the opposite beat of the spears. The man at the end of the front row began a chant in a rhythm that matched the drumbeats. He shouted one phrase and the remaining nine came in at the end of it and shouted another phrase, twice as long and all the while the complex, hard beat of the wood and the feet kept perfect timing.

Then it changed. A huge crash of the spears on the floor and there was a moment of silence. Another combined shout of a single syllable, and both lines of men twirled their spears, stopped in perfect unison, crashed the spear's base on the floor again then fell into a crouch, the spears now pointing directly at the men of the other team. The chanting was taken up again, a complex rhythm supported by a stamp of the left foot, occasionally broken by a hard slap of the left hand against the dancer's thigh and at other times by a lift of the right foot and a hard stamp on the floor, always with the spear pointed at the opposing team.

Mickie found his heart beating faster, matching the increasing tempo of the driving rhythm. But the rhythm seemed to change without any obvious switching. It moved from 4/4 time to 3/4 time back to 2/2 and then almost randomly through the series, always in perfect unison, always backing up the men's chant. It was wildly primitive, exciting and almost frightening. Mickie tried to imagine being opposite those spears pointing at him, and decided it would freeze his heart. With no obvious signal, there was one final, thunderous crash of feet and spears together and stillness resumed.

Without knowing when, Mickie found himself on his feet with all the other six hundred or more in the hangar, applauding wildly. The applause from the home team was equally enthusiastic and Mickie saw wide grins of appreciation on their faces.

"That was astounding!" he shouted over the noise to Fencris. "Can you do that?"

Fencris grinned and nodded. "Before every Broxie hunt," he called back.

"But what does it mean?"

"It's a chant of honour for the bravery of the animal we hunt. It promises that we will kill cleanly and that the animal's spirit will enter us and strengthen our souls."

"Wow!" Mickie was impressed.

"I can hardly believe that the Kalamosians on that Ship have learned a Dregarl!" Fencris shouted. "They were *fantastic!*"

After a few minutes, the audience settled. Five of the home side entered the arena, the other five, took seats outside the transparent wall. Mickie was delighted to see his father in the opening team. Somebody must have issued the instruction to the computer, because the men began moving in the slow, gliding manner of very low gravity. A few moments more and they had taken their positions on the straps at points on all four walls. The referees took up stations outside, a whistle blew and the bright yellow ball dropped lazily from the ceiling. The game was on.

The visitors' player reached the ball first. He had leaped early, not from a side wall but from the back and he timed it perfectly, netting the ball while flying toward the home side goal. But instead of letting loose his shot at goal, he flung the ball against the end wall near the side. The ball banged hard against the wall and flew back to the visitors' own goal wall. But before it reached that wall, another player shot up from the floor, caught the ball in his racquet and rifled it against the side wall so it bounced right across the arena where another player caught it deftly and moved to shoot at goal. He didn't make it. Even as the applause sounded for the surprising move that seemed to have caught the home team off balance, he was tackled hard by Grant, rammed into the wall and lost his racquet, the ball floating lazily in mid air before it began drifting down. Grant had been followed closely by another player who took control of the ball, flicked it sharply across the arena to a colleague hanging by a strap. That player had his feet against the wall and as he caught the ball, he shoved himself hard toward the opponents' goal wall. He made a move Mickie had not seen before. As he flew in the arc, he flung the ball down to the floor, judging his own speed well, and catching the ball again as it bounced back to him. But as he tried to do it again, he too was tackled hard, the ball hit the ground but was taken on the rebound by a visitor.

A hard shot at the goal was well intercepted by a home team player who launched himself off a side wall and caught the ball in his left hand, bounced it off the other side, caught it in his racquet and hurled it down to the other end. But that too was intercepted and the game fell into a riot of flying men, weaving in intricate patterns in three dimensions with nobody able to make a serious shot at either goal.

The stalemate broke when a weak shot at the home goal was taken by Grant who pushed himself off the rear wall to the side wall and then at an angle toward the visitor's end. He turned three perfect loops in his trajectory, bringing a whoop of delight from the crowd and causing three consecutive tackles to miss. As he passed within five metres of the rear wall, he slammed the ball against the surface. It rebounded straight back, but the botanist, Mendor was flying fast straight at the goal from a hard push-off from his own goal wall. He caught the ball and rammed it from just a metre away against the black goal circle. The light flickered to display a glowing "1" and the buzzer sounded but the noise was completely hidden by the yell of delight from the crowd. But the goal had come at a price. Mickie saw the pain in Grant's face as he gestured at the knee he had injured some months earlier. He floated down to the exit and then limped out. Mickie could see that his father was drenched in sweat. He caught his eye and the two exchanged grins before Grant took a water bottle and drained it.

"Drat!" said Allie. "Back to the hospital ward as soon as this is over."

One of the visitors must have signalled for a time out, as the lights flickered and play stopped. The break was clearly welcome to all the ten men in the arena, as they all fell into positions of exhaustion, breathing hard. Two players from each side walked out of the playing area to be replaced by reserves from their benches.

Play resumed, and the battle was long and hard, with little advantage to either side. Mickie could see that there were very few rehearsed moves of great complexity, obviously because the teams had not had any time to work on their tactics. But at the half-way mark, the score remained as it was, just a single goal to the home side.

More player exchanges and battle resumed for the second half. During one brief, hard period of just two minutes, each side scored one more goal and that was where the count stayed as the final minute approached. But then there was a rapid flicker of blue shirts, the ball almost vanished in a blur of fast, short passes before appearing in a lightning-fast smack against the home team's goal. Mixed yells of jubilation drowned out the groans of dismay. Mendor signalled furiously at the umpire nearest to him and a time out was called with just forty seconds remaining. Mickie saw a rapid discussion between the players, signals were flashed and players were exchanged.

"It's the entire Botanist team!" Fencris exclaimed. "They've brought on that whole side!"

"That makes sense," Drellion said, nodding furiously. "They're the best side on the Ship and they've got their own moves."

Mickie saw the reasoning, though his disappointment at seeing Grant walk back to the reserves' bench was still strong.

Play started, and Drellion was proved right. The Botanists fell into a practiced configuration, moved rapidly in a well-practiced series of moves and then into their trademark manoeuvre that Mickie had seen the first time he had watched a match. The ball was flicked at astonishing speed round the ever-changing formation, the visitors looked completely baffled and then from nowhere, Mendor slammed the ball into the goal and the buzzer sounded as the lights flashed for the end of the game.

For just a few seconds, jubilation and disappointment fought each other in the crowd, but to Mickie's delight, the mood rapidly became one of mass celebration at a superb match. Drinks appeared from hamper baskets and an impromptu party began.

Two hours later, the entire Ship's crew again stood in the hangar to wave farewell as the visitors left in four of their own shuttles to return to their Ship just a few kilometres away in the same orbit

Chapter 19 – The Pfafth Rebellion

At last, Mickie's routine became what he had wanted from the start. Weeks followed months in the normal life and pattern of the trading ship. They tracked their regular paths between the planets that bought and sold products, the Ship flicked out of hyperspace just minutes away from the target planet, Grant and his trading team conducted their business and several days later, the Ship began its ferocious acceleration run to reach light speed and make its brain-twisting, sideways jump into hyperspace again. The holds were filled with pharmaceutical plants from Zlan, coffee from Mayoowani, diamonds and gold from Kamotar, leaves and timber from Harliya and assorted minerals from planets in many galaxies.

The visit to Mayoowani was tense, as both the Ship's crew and the Gelkka ignored the dishonouring of the Warrior Code that had occurred on Gelokk. Grant agreed to supply the medical supplies that the Gelokk home world so badly needed, but when the Ship reached there, the kids stayed aboard, declining the chance to visit the surface. But a chance piece of information from the Speaker indicated that massive factional fighting was starting on Gelokk and civil war was near. Mickie wondered how that could happen with a Sillaron Master running things and if the developments could mean that the Sillaron had left. And if Gelokk's government collapsed, perhaps the military rule on Mayoowani would not last much longer.

School classes occurred on a set timetable, and Mickie became more and more educated on the structure of the Universe, navigation principles between galaxies and the histories of the various races and their planets. Slowly, he also acquired fluency in the language of Kalamos, his adopted home world, knowing that it was the only additional language of another species, other than Pfafth that he would be able to master. A little more rapidly, he acquired some skill in his trombone, finally being able to read music and play by ear as well, and the regular but impromptu musical sessions he had with Fencris and Melkana became one of his greatest joys. On his own, he frequently played the Chris Barber track that had been in his dream and tried to copy the melody.

And by an unspoken agreement, he and Melkana ignored their entire Pfafth history. They never mentioned the recent events and employed none of their Pfafth powers, except on one occasion when Melkana sprained her wrist during a Loopies session. She repaired it in the same way Mickie had once repaired his broken ankle, by exploring the break with her powers of molecular change and resetting the bone.

Grant's knee healed under the ministrations of the Ship's medical staff and he returned to playing Gravity Ball as the new schedule of games began between the twelve teams in the Ship's league. The kids watched every game and Mickie became more and more impressed by the skills required to play. And when Drellion received a special approval to join the junior league, two years before he reached the normal age because of his exceptional athletic talents, there was much celebration.

This was the happiest time Mickie had ever known. At last he was in a real family and the times he spent with Grant and Allie were deeply satisfying as they talked over his experiences and he learned more about theirs and what they did in their jobs. The friendship with the other three became closer as they grew up, and while they ignored their Pfafth ancestry, Mickie and Melkana still knew they had a special bond. He never thought at all about his old life on Earth.

It couldn't last.

"Mickie, I have your brother wishing to make contact." The cool voice of Speaker 356 broke through into Mickie's trombone practice session. The Ship was in orbit round a dull planet that had much iron ore but no atmosphere and no inhabitants. Only the mining crews were on the surface.

"Brandon! How great! How's my big brother?" Mickie was delighted with the call. The two had made arrangements to spend a week together the next time the Ship returned to Kalamos, but that was still some weeks ahead.

"We have problems on home world, Mickie." Brandon's voice echoed tension and worry. Mickie's cheery mood faded immediately.

"Brandon, what's wrong?"

"I was there last week," Brandon said. "I thought I'd drop over to see how they were coping with being back in the normal universe again and to talk with the Management Committee about starting contacts with other species."

"And what did you find?" A sense of deep anxiety began to grow in Mickie.

"Something's gone wrong. There's a new Committee in place, all the old members retired under pressure, it seems. The new ones had no interest in discussing establishing links with the rest of the Universe. They didn't want to travel on the Kaloti ships, they refused to talk with anyone via the Speakers and they were appalled at the idea of people starting to work at regaining their old Pfafth powers."

"Brandon, this is incredible! What's causing that?"

"That's not the worst part, Mickie."

Mickie felt a shiver of cold run down his back. Somehow he knew this was going to be unpleasant.

"I think we'd better visit together. You need to see exactly how bad things have become. Join me at the safe house in twelve hours and we'll go in together. But Mickie, dye your hair and eyebrows, change your appearance. I doubt anyone will recognise you from our last visit, but play safe."

"For Heaven's sake, Brandon, what's the problem?"

"I think the entire Pfafth race has gone insane. They've declared war on you."

*   *   *   *

They chose a different coffee shop on the main square of Markel City, just in case the waitress might recognise them and link them to the events in the Management Committee Hall. Mickie had dyed his hair black and cut it very short. Some assistance from the Ship's medical officers had temporarily altered the lines of his cheeks and made them plumper. A casual eye would not recognise him. Brandon too, had made some cosmetic changes in his appearance, shaved his head and altered the lines of his face.

"Something nasty happens every day, it seems," Brandon said. "Ah! Yes, here's today's parade."

Mickie turned his head to the far side of the square. A huge parade was entering, carrying signs that he at first struggled to read in the distance, but he was shocked and frightened when they got closer. One said '*Markel Has Betrayed Us.*' Another said '*Markel Has Stolen Our Birthright.*' And there was one just saying '*Markel the Traitor.*'

"They seem to hate you for not fulfilling what they believed were the ancient promises," Brandon said, hiding his lips behind his coffee cup.

"Good grief!" It was worse than anything Mickie had anticipated.

"I remember when I first brought you here, you said they were crazy. Well now you're even more right, Mickie. I think the entire Pfafth species has gone insane and the inmates are in charge of the lunatic asylum."

"And you think this is because I didn't help them start a war?"

"I don't know if that's really it. After all, there were huge numbers of people who never wanted a return to that nonsense. You saw yourself how the battles broke out when the two groups met. But now there's no sign of any sanity at all."

"Do you think we should go to see the Management Committee?"

"No, Mickie, that could be fatal. Right now, if the mobs knew you were here, they'd run riot and for all your powers, I think they'd tear you to pieces."

"So what should I do?"

"For now, just hang tough, kid. I've been talking to some of the agents and they've agreed to join me in scouting out the scene. With the old Committee gone, there's nobody there who will know us except our parents, so we should be safe enough. But we need to know what happened, why the old Committee vanished and who's influencing these events."

"Brandon, take care!"

"Not to worry, little brother! I'll keep you informed."

Outside, the crowd was becoming louder. Mickie extended his empathic senses and was appalled by what he saw. There seemed to be no intelligent thoughts at all. Every mind he touched was a turmoil of rage, of hatred and... something else. He sensed an absence of control in those minds, as if another force had taken over and was driving that mind in unknown directions. Many people were armed with clubs and these began shattering the windows of shops and offices. From somewhere, a torch was lit and thrown into one of the buildings.

Flames swept upwards as if the building were constructed of dry wood.

As if being directed, the mob seemed to focus on one side of the square. Mickie saw a young man, perhaps in his late teens standing and watching the crowd. A loud scream rang out from some unidentified source.

"Kill Markel!"

The crowd's fury racked up several more notches and they began a headlong rush straight at the youth. Mickie saw faces twisted in rage and hatred. The young man turned in panic and ran, but the mob easily caught him and surrounded him. Mickie could not see what happened, but the screams of fury as more and more rioters tried to get to the man told him the horror of what had happened.

"My God," he whispered. "They killed him."

"As they will do to us if they find us," Brandon whispered, the shock of the murder showing in his face.

And even that paled into nothing compared to what Mickie saw next.

The black pillar of smoke rotated rapidly in the far corner of the square as if watching the action. It reached as high as the three-storey building behind it. A white face flashed briefly from the darkness.

The Sillaron Master was here.

The mob's attention turned on the coffee shop in which Brandon and Mickie were watching the events. With terrifying speed, the crowd began to advance on the building. Brandon leaped to his feet.

"Jump, Mickie! *Now!*"

And as the glass shattered under the impact of a large brick, the two men leaped back to the safe house on the planet outside the Pfafth galaxy.

"It's just not possible!" Mickie shouted as both men arrived in the spacious lounge of the safe house. "The Sillaron are the absolute worst enemies of the Pfafth. How could they have allied together to attack me? It's *madness!*"

Brandon's face was pale and he was breathing hard. "I don't think even a couple of our best mind bolts would have stopped that mob," he said hoarsely.

Mickie was pacing furiously up and down the room. "And where were the Zlan? They've never failed me before."

"*We are ashamed,*" came the cold tones of a Zlan. "*We became alerted to your danger, but the mass of Pfafth minds totally wiped out your own mental signature. We had never before thought it possible that we would have to save a Pfafth from other Pfafth. It paralysed us.*"

Mickie's heart slowed its frantic beating and he was able to take control of himself. "I understand, my friends," he said. "That conflict was totally outside your conditioning."

"What the hell *was* that thing, anyway?" Brandon asked, also showing signs of a return to self-control. "It looked like a Sillaron, but I'd never heard of one that size."

"It's not a real Sillaron," Mickie replied. "It looks like one alright, but Mister Brown said he didn't know what it was, or where it came from."

Quickly, Mickie filled out those details of the terrifying Sillaron Master that Brandon had not heard from him before.

"There has to be a number of them," Brandon said when Mickie had finished. "You obviously killed the one on the Ship when Grant used the laser hammers on it. And when you used very loud music to destroy the one on the Sillaron home planet, it wasn't prepared for it like the one on the Ship was. Which means they're probably not telepathic and they haven't communicated with each other."

"I think you're right," Mickie agreed, impressed by his brother's logical reasoning. "We'd already found out that the Sillaron were using Cassolean telepaths. But it's weird. Those things are so like the Sillaron and they were utterly in command. But they're different, somehow."

"And how! I tell you, little brother, I have absolutely no idea what to do next. I'm beginning to wish we'd left those idiots marooned in their galaxy one second ahead of Time."

"I know what you mean! But remember what we saw when we pushed the galaxy back. If we hadn't, the entire Universe would eventually fall off balance. And the Pfafth had to be back with all the other species in the same way."

"I suppose." Brandon seemed uncertain.

"We need to find out more about the Sillaron Masters," Mickie said. "Speaker 356, are you there?"

"Yes, Mickie. That was a very dangerous episode."

"Indeed it was. Have you been able to identify any way of reading those Sillaron?"

"I regret not. As before, we have been able only to identify the trace signature of their minds so that we can detect their presence. But as to reading those minds and communicating with them, I'm sorry to admit failure."

"What about those Sillaron Masters? Any luck there?"

"No. I can only tell you that the mental waves are very similar, but not identical. However, there is far greater power in what you term the Sillaron Masters, almost as if they are a more advanced form of the ordinary Sillaron."

"A more advanced form?" Brandon was white-faced, seemingly in deep shock. "Just as you and Melkana and all the agents are more advanced forms of the rest of the Pfafth? My god, Mickie, do you think the Sillaron have bred some form of Super-Sillaron? Perhaps to hunt down the Pfafth after they vanished?"

They stared at each other for a few seconds.

"I think you've hit it," Mickie said, his throat dry. "But if that's the case, the experiment got away from them. That's why Mister Brown couldn't identify them as a separate species."

"Somehow we need to be sure of that. But it still doesn't explain why the Super-Sillaron allied themselves with the Pfafth. It doesn't make sense."

"Almost as if getting me was more important than all the other Pfafth."

"You and Melkana, perhaps," Brandon suggested. "The very peak of Pfafth development."

Mickie shivered at that thought. Then he had a brainwave. "Speaker 356, can you locate Velkazim on Cassolea?"

"Stand by," replied the Speaker.

"Brandon raised his eyebrows. "Velkazim?"

"He was the leader of the Cassolean group we found on the Sillaron planet."

"Ah!" Brandon obviously understood what Mickie was getting at.

"I have Velkazim," the Speaker announced.

"Velkazim, what a pleasure to talk to you again," Mickie said.

"It is my pleasure," replied the Cassolean Mickie had first met as the leader of the isolated group of Cassoleans living on the Sillaron world. "How can I help you?"

"Velkazim, in all the thousands of years you were living among the Sillaron, did you know of any experiments to breed a superior, advanced race of Sillaron?"

"How could you have learned of that?" The shock in the Cassolean's voice rang through the Speaker's connection.

"You mean there *were* such experiments?"

"They had been going on well before the Pfafth vanished," Velkazim replied. "The Sillaron had hated the Pfafth from the beginning, because they didn't have the powers the Pfafth possessed and so could not rule the Universe. They let themselves be used as Regents to rule for the Pfafth, because that was the next best thing, but always they resented their second-class role. But they never lost the dream of taking over from the Pfafth. I never learned what happened with those experiments."

"They succeeded," Mickie said. "But perhaps too well, because the created became the rulers."

"Velkazim, this is Brandon. I am Mickie's brother."

"My honour, Brandon."

"Velkazim, just to be sure. Could the Sillaron teleport?"

"No, they could not."

"And they had no telepathic powers?"

"Only minor. They used us Cassoleans for that."

"Could those abilities be bred into their own species?"

"Telepathy could be enhanced, Brandon, and only with a planetary range, but not teleportation. One thing we have learned is that a species may develop its powers if they have even the minimum at the start, but they cannot develop a power that is not present in the species at all."

"We owe you a great deal," Mickie said. "You are adjusting to life back on Cassolea, I take it?"

"It is wonderful," Velkazim said with enthusiasm. "To be back with our own kind and free of that tyranny is magical. Our people are in great demand as teachers of the newly-rediscovered telepathic powers."

"That is good," Mickie said. "Our best wishes to all of you."

With a few more pleasantries, the conversation ended.

"So what next, Brandon? What can we do?"

"I have no idea. At the moment, all I can think of is that those monsters are exactly where they've been aiming to be for a million years, right in the middle of our people who are completely defenceless. They could do what they've threatened all along, kill the entire race of Pfafth."

"But if they do that, the Pfafth can never grow up and mature. Both Maragos and Mister Brown have said that would lead to a catastrophe of some sort." Mickie felt as if his guts were filled with sewage.

"I know." Brandon looked grim.

"How did they get there?" Mickie asked, trying to think of anything but the horrible possibilities. "They can't teleport."

"I imagine several ships have already visited this galaxy," Brandon said thoughtfully. "They must have hidden themselves aboard. They seem to have that ability to reduce themselves to almost nothing when they want."

"So when we brought the Galaxy back into normal time, we signed the Pfafth's death warrant?"

"It looks like it. Now we have to find a way of saving them again."

* * * *

The conference call between the agents was not fruitful. They all remained at their homes or on the planets they were visiting, while Speaker 356 facilitated the group discussion.

"We think there are a number of these things on the planet, but we've no idea how many," Brandon said, after relating the events of his and Mickie's last visit to home world.

"And there's no way of killing them?" asked Doriander.

"There is, but I can't see how to apply it," Mickie replied. He related how the laser hammers had been used on board the Ship. "We can't carry those hammers and go hunting them."

"Can't we make a more portable version?" Leannina suggested.

"Probably," Mickie agreed. "But the problem is in finding the Sillaron Masters. As Brandon said, we don't know how many there are and they seem to be able to hide in the tiniest of places. There just aren't enough of us to cover the whole planet."

"But you said loud music caused them a major problem, almost killing them," broke in another agent. "Can't we just blanket the planet with musical notes?"

"Not any more," Mickie said. "It worked once, on Sillaron world, but the one on the Ship had obviously developed some sort of protection, so they've probably all got that now. I think if we tried it, they'd take it out on our people on home world."

"We should have left the galaxy where it was," grumbled Kassiana.

"That was my first reaction," Brandon said. "But you know what we learned as we moved it. If we hadn't brought it back, the entire Universe would eventually have fallen apart."

"I suppose." Kassiana seemed unconvinced, but subsided.

"You said that the Sillaron seemed able to detect you and directed the mob against you?" Doriander said.

"It seemed that way," Brandon agreed.

"Do you think they'd recognise the other agents the same way?"

"Almost certainly," Mickie said. "I reckon they detected the extra power we generate as Markel or Kerrala descendents."

"Which means we'd be detected soon after arriving, if any of us go there." It was another agent, named Jastonar who spoke, the first time he had done so.

"That's a big problem," Mickie agreed.

"And those suppressors cancel out our powers. Could we carry the counter devices?"

"We've only got six in total," Mickie said. "But if they turn the mob on us the way they did before, you'd have very little time to get out. It's horribly dangerous. I really don't think any of you should go."

"So how can we even find out how many there are?" Kassiana asked, emoting distress.

"It's impossible," Mickie said. "The Speakers can identify the mental signature of a Master, but not identify one from another. And when they go into some form of hiding, there's no trace that the Speakers can detect. So they just can't tell us how many there are in total."

"So the only way we can be sure of killing those things is by destroying the whole planet," Kassiana said, tears in her eyes.

"And all our people at the same time," Jastonar added.

"And we still wouldn't know if all the Sillaron Masters were there, anyway," Mickie said, feeling his own fears rising as the full extent of the problem became clear.

The meeting broke up as the agents addressed their worries each in their own way.

* * * *

"Mickie, I have a request for a contact," said the cool, unemotional tones of Speaker 356.

Mickie was puzzled. The Speaker normally announced who the caller was.

"No identity, Speaker 356?"

"None specific. But I have never received a call on this band before. I have identified it, however, as one of the Sillaron."

Mickie's blood seemed to chill through his body. "A Sillaron? One of the Super-types or an ordinary one?"

"A normal one, judging by the power of the communication."

"But you said you've not been able to communicate with the Sillaron?"

"It's using a Cassolean as an intermediary. This is clumsy, but it's working."

Mickie took a deep breath. "Put it through."

The voice that came through his shoulder unit was hesitant, not the freezing hate-filled hiss that he had heard before from the Sillaron Master.

"Mickie Dalton," it said. "I was one of the Sillaron present when you arrived with the Spiders on our planet."

"Do you have a name?"

"My name is not important and you would not comprehend it if I gave it to you."

"Why are you calling me?"

"To see if I can help you."

"A Sillaron offering to help a Pfafth? Why should you choose to do that? And how can you possibly help me?"

"I have learned of how you treated some of our children on Earth. You could have destroyed them but you chose not to."

"Perhaps I just saw a demonstration that kids will be kids in almost any species."

"Perhaps. But one of those children was mine and I'm grateful for his safe return. When you visited our planet, you saw that we had declined. We are few and no longer the powerful race that once ruled the Universe on the Pfafth's behalf."

"Yes, I saw that. That was also part of the reason I did nothing to your children on Earth."

"And we know that the Pfafth have declined in the same manner and are nothing now but a footnote to history."

"Yes, that's so." Mickie could hardly believe this conversation was taking place.

"This war has no point, then. What possible reason could there be for killing each other?"

"And that is why you've contacted me? To agree that the conflict is pointless?"

"I believe you have already seen that. You could have had the Zlan slaughter us that day, but you chose not to."

"There seemed no point." Mickie didn't bother telling the Sillaron that the Zlan had found no food value in the Sillaron, so no slaughter would have occurred, regardless of what he had wanted.

"There was always revenge for the millions of your people we killed."

"It was a million years ago and would have achieved nothing but more hatred."

"But that's the problem. We may be about to do the same to your people again."

"You mean with the Sillaron Masters that you bred?"

"How could you know that?" The shock in the Sillaron's voice could be heard even through the several levels of transmission.

"It was obvious."

"The Sillaron set out to create a form that finally could overcome the Pfafth," the mysterious caller continued. "And we also were able to develop the suppressor devices that cancelled out the Pfafth powers. With those, we overcame our masters, your people."

"But then your creations took over the Sillaron?"

"Yes they did. They were bred to have nothing but hatred for your kind, nothing but an endless bloodlust. But we got it wrong. They hate every other species just as much and they will not stop until they own the Universe and every life form within it."

The words brought forth memories in Mickie's mind of the old tales of Frankenstein and his monster. Had similar events and stories existed in other species also, he wondered? "So have these things continued to breed and increase?" he asked.

"They cannot," the Sillaron replied. "We created only ten, thinking we would destroy you all with that force and then they would die out. So we ensured that they can't breed, they can't increase in numbers."

"Just *ten*? And the ones we've met are the very same your people created a million years ago?"

"They are. That was another mistake we made, not realising they were effectively immortal."

"But musical sounds seem to harm them?"

"Our brains cannot tolerate sharp variations in pitch and volume. At an intense level, such sounds kill us. Our other creations, the Drudya suffered the same problems because we created them from our own cells, just as we created the Sillaron Masters."

"One that we encountered had developed a protection against such an attack. We had to use extreme measures to kill it."

"So you have killed two? Then there are just eight, but those eight can still hide from you while killing Pfafth at their leisure."

"And that's what they now intend? To kill all remaining Pfafth?"

"Probably. As a start."

"When you created them, was it your intention to copy all the Pfafth powers?"

"Not really. The scientists who did this certainly wanted telepathy, which the Pfafth did not have at the time, and they achieved that, but only short range. They also wanted teleportation skills, but we failed to develop those. We already had the mind bolts, though not to the power your people had. But the suppressors gave them the real edge, so their main intent was to create a species that would never rest until they had destroyed your people. But we were successful with another ability we gave them, to be able to influence the minds of mass populations, suppress their thinking capacity and be capable of little but obedience to the Sillaron orders. That is how they have ruled the Gelkka, the Drudya, those on Merrison and others."

It occurred to Mickie how close he and Brandon had come to disaster back on Pfafth home world. The Sillaron Master had not applied the suppressor to try and prevent the two brothers leaping away. Maybe it didn't have one, but Mickie had not been carrying one of the countering devices either. They could easily have been trapped and killed by the mob.

"So now we've spoken, and I thank you for the information," Mickie continued. "You're correct, a war is senseless and would achieve nothing. But the Masters, what can we do about them?

"You must destroy them. That you have already killed two shows that you can kill the rest. If you don't, all life throughout the Universe is at risk."

"We'll work on that. Because even if they only destroy the Pfafth, the Universe faces dreadful consequences."

"I don't understand."

"And I can't explain it. Sillaron, I hope we can meet again under happier circumstances."

"Let us hope so."

The first friendly conversation between Pfafth and Sillaron ended.

"Speaker 356, will you pass on that conversation to all the Pfafth agents?"

"It's done, Mickie."

"Thank you, Speaker 356."

Chapter 20 – The Final Encounter

"Mickie, I have your brother."

"Brandon, hey, how are you...."

"Mickie, listen carefully. I only have one chance to tell you this."

Brandon's tone chilled Mickie. Something dreadful had happened.

"Mickie, I'm on home world. I'm standing in the main square, surrounded by several thousand Pfafth who will kill me at a moment's notice. There is a Sillaron Master standing just a short distance away. Somebody here has developed a drug that blocks the Pfafth powers except for the telepathic link to the Speaker. I was injected with it before I knew what was happening and now I'm a captive. I can't leap, I can't change matter and I can't throw a mind bolt. The Sillaron have only short-range telepathy, so I am being made to pass on their words to you through the Speaker."

"Brandon, how did this....?"

"Shut up and listen, Mickie. The Sillaron Master has instructed me to tell you this. They've realised that the Pfafth present no threat to the Sillaron Masters. They will take over all life in the Universe as they choose. But there remains just one threat to them, one hurdle. And that's you. You and Melkana are the only Pfafth with the powers still to hurt them."

Mickie heard a short gasp of pain from his brother. "Brandon! What happened?"

"Shut up, Mickie. Here's what has happened. The Sillaron Masters have been able to exert their power over the Pfafth here on home world. We found out that all eight of them are here. They were able to turn the Pfafth against you, but that's no longer necessary. They want you and Melkana to surrender to them. If you don't, they will start killing Pfafth, several hundred a day until you do surrender. You have twenty four hours to decide."

Mickie had to apply every ounce of self-control to permit him to speak in a firm voice. "I can't speak for Melkana. But I'll surrender at once if that will save the remaining Pfafth."

"Not good enough, Mickie. They want both of you. Anything less and the killing starts."

Mickie renewed his efforts to stay in control. "Tell them I'll give them a reply in a few hours."

"Do whatever you believe to be the best thing, Mickie. I love you, little brother."

Mickie cut the connection before he lost control of his tears.

* * * *

"So that's the situation." Mickie looked round the group in the Captain's cabin. His parents sat together, Melkana's parents sat next to them. The four children sat in one group while the Captain occupied his massive chair. The adults all looked horrified. The Captain wore no expression that could be identified, though his eyes seemed smaller than usual. Mickie wondered if that signified sadness, the opposite of the wide-eyed expression that was laughter to that beautiful species. Only his three friends seemed unaffected, as if this was just another in the series of adventures they had shared over the last three years. Melkana particularly looked serene, almost happy.

"We have to go," Melkana said. She might have been discussing attendance at a school function for all the horrors implied in her words.

"No way in hell!" Grant was more furious than Mickie had ever seen him. "Captain, why don't we just blanket the planet in laser hammer shocks? That will kill those Sillaron."

The Captain's musical hum hit a high pitch before the translator cut in.

"That would also destroy the planet!" he said. "It will kill all the Pfafth also."

"Better than living under the rule of those horrors," Grant snapped.

"It is not the time of the Pfafth to die," said the Captain. "That solution is not viable."

"We have to go," Melkana said again.

"You can't!" Mendorina, her mother wailed in anguish, tears rolling down her cheeks. She buried her face in Harokarn's shoulder, her pain all too obvious. Melkana got up and went to sit with them, holding her mother as she was the one to give comfort, not the one facing death.

"What alternative is there?" Mickie asked. He too felt quite calm. The decision had been made. "There are nearly twenty million Pfafth, and you all know what we've been told. They must mature, they must reach the stage that the Shurameen, the M'Sarda and the Kaloti have reached, or the entire Universe faces a problem. Melkana and I don't count in that scheme of things."

Allie and Grant looked frozen. Mickie smiled at them.

"You do understand, don't you?"

"It isn't why we rescued you from Earth," Allie said, struggling with her own tears.

"Nobody knew anything at all about the reality when you did that," Mickie replied. "We didn't know about the Pfafth, we didn't know about the Sillaron, we knew nothing about the imbalance of a Galaxy out of Time or a species separated from the Universe. If all those imbalances can be corrected by Melkana and me giving ourselves to the Sillaron, it seems a small price to pay."

"We had such dreams for you. And for Melkana," Allie said, gulping hard.

"Hey, I'd take the last three years over a lifetime of what I had on Earth," Mickie said with a smile. "It's been a good deal."

Drellion had hidden his face in his lap and for the first time, Mickie saw tears in the glowing red eyes of the Cassolean Fencris.

"There are some things to get organised before we leave," Mickie said.

*   *   *   *

"Brandon, tell the Sillaron that Melkana and I agree to surrender, but there are conditions."

"They are furious Mickie. They say you have no power to impose conditions."

"But I do. If all the Pfafth are to die, then I can take the Sillaron with us. If they do not agree, the Ship will blanket the entire home world with laser hammer vibrations that will break up the surface and destroy the atmosphere. The Pfafth may die, but it will be more merciful than a slow death to the Sillaron. And all the Sillaron will also die."

Ten seconds later, Brandon replied. "They will hear your conditions, Mickie."

"Then tell them this, Brandon. First, they will release the Pfafth immediately. That includes you."

"They agree."

"Good. Second, they will accept our surrender on the planet where we have our safe house. Melkana and I will meet them there."

"They demand to know why."

"Because I don't trust them. If the mob was able to capture you, they could take us two the same way and then they would still have the Pfafth."

"They refuse, Mickie. They say they'll kill two hundred people a day until you show up."

"Brandon, tell them this. I don't care. They can kill a thousand a day if they want. We've already seen that the Pfafth are nothing. They're a disgrace, a failed species and I want nothing to do with them. So if they don't want to come and get us the way I said, they can do what they want. But of course, they won't get us that way. And then we'll be coming for them. Because if they start killing all the Pfafth, that's when we start the laser hammers over the whole planet, and they can't get away."

"I'll tell them." Mickie could hear the shock in Brandon's reply. Two minutes passed before the conversation resumed. Brandon's voice sounded strained.

"They agree. But they can't teleport! How will they get to that planet?"

"Tell them they must ride the Zlan."

"They must *what?*"

"Hitch a ride on a giant spider. If they want us, they can come and get us."

"Mickie, they're having fits! All eight of them are here, and they're racing all over the square like frightened kids. It's almost worth it to see this."

Mickie waited for some minutes before Brandon came back to him.

"They agree, but they demand that you instruct the Zlan to leave once they have brought them to the planet. They want no attack from them. But they must also be assured the Zlan will return them to home world once you're...."

"Once Melkana and I are dead, yes. I agree."

"Mickie...."

"Brandon, stop. We've decided what has to be done. You know that the Pfafth species must go on or we will have a problem for the whole Universe, though the Sillaron don't know that. Melkana and I are not worth having that crisis for."

"I've told them Mickie and they agree. When?"

"In two hours."

"It's agreed."

"Good. Now, has that drug worn off?"

"Yes, almost."

"Then as soon as you can, get yourself out of there and join us here on the Ship."

Mickie and Melkana stood outside the house on the small planet. In that house, they and the other agents, together with the Zlan had shifted the nearby galaxy back in time one second and returned it and the Pfafth to the Universe.

The day was mild and dry as evening began to fall. The air smelled of springtime. For the first time, the two young people held hands.

"Who would have thought it would come to this?" Melkana said softly. She seemed unafraid and Mickie once more wondered at her perfect complexion and serene air.

"We seem to have done a lot in our three years," Mickie said. "Still, I'm glad we've got to this point and I can hold your hand."

"It was always coming," she said with a smile.

The peace was broken as the Zlan appeared. Eight of them silently exploded into existence on the pleasant lawn. A light breeze from the displaced air touched Mickie's face and blew a strand of Melkana's hair backward for a second. On each of the Zlan, a mass of black smoke seemed to hover over the middle of the mountainous backs. For a minute, nothing happened, as the smoke gathered itself, took shape as a pillar again and drifted down to the grass surface. Mickie decided the Sillaron had been shattered by the ride and their fear of the Zlan and they needed a while to recover their composure. He felt no regrets at their terror.

"This is a shameful business, Mickie Dalton," said one Zlan. *"This conflicts with all our conditioning."*

"It's nothing," Mickie replied. "Our deaths will preserve the Pfafth, and that's the key. But Melkana and I wish to express our gratitude. The Zlan have saved our lives on many occasions."

"We understand. But it does not reduce our distress. In these years, we have learned to honour you for your courage. Being a Pfafth is no longer the only reason we would protect you."

"Then we both thank you. You have been our good friends. But your commitment to us is now over. The Pfafth have returned and there are many children now who need your protection."

"Farewell, Mickie and Melkana. You have given us great joy. Our adventures together will long be told in the history of the Zlan."

"Farewell, my friends."

With a small pop of imploding air, the eight spiders vanished. The Sillaron appeared to have recovered their normal capacities and now stood around the two children, three metres high, the smoke swirling in a slow rotation. The sun was setting lower and shadows grew longer.

"So now we can feed on the souls of the last barriers to us," came the hiss of cold hatred in Mickie's mind. The sense of triumph was huge in that coldness.

Mickie drew Melkana a little closer. He could feel the sweat of fear on her palm. He struggled to control his own emotions.

"Give us a little time," he asked. "We have fought each other for three years. Let me have some answers before you take us."

"What would you wish to know before you die?" sneered the Sillaron.

"You're the last? And you're the same entities as were originally created?"

"We are the first and the last and we have lived over a million years. And now we have you."

Mickie tested the teleportation senses and learned that the Sillaron had the suppressor in operation.

"And you began to dominate the ordinary Sillaron?"

"They were weak. They bred us to destroy the Pfafth, but we saw no point in allowing them to take mastery of the universe when we could do it so much better."

"And yet we were able to destroy two of you. Perhaps you're not as powerful as you believe?"

The hiss of rage almost hurt his head it was so violent. "We have no idea how you managed that, but it matters no longer. Your time is over."

"Probably," Mickie agreed. "You've suppressed our powers like you did to the whole Pfafth race once, a million years ago. And yet we still killed two of you."

"Enough! I think we will feed on the female and make you watch!"

From one of the Sillaron, a balloon of black smoke began to grow from its base and spread outward towards Melkana. Mickie used the white crystal device he had hung back around his neck before leaving and cancelled the suppressor. Together, he and Melkana concentrated on the black smoke, fought its power and suddenly the bubble collapsed into black powder on the grass. The afflicted Sillaron screamed in pain. The others retreated several metres in shock.

"That is not possible!" The hiss of fury was mixed with deep panic.

"Ah, but it is!" Mickie felt a surge of joy. The Sillaron had been badly hurt. "Do you think your little suppressor can stop a

Pfafth? And now you will see just how badly you've messed up."

A small shiver hit the ground and vibrated across the lawn. Several trees shook and leaves fell from them. From the house came a rattle of windows.

"What is that?" The Sillaron's panic and confusion rose even higher.

"Look up!" Melkana called, laughter bubbling in her voice. Above, the stars had come out, clear and bright in the clean air. But as Mickie looked, the stars trembled, seemed to shift in position, while at their feet, the ground shook more violently. The disturbance lasted just a few seconds then calm returned.

The Sillaron were in a panic. The pillars rotated faster, a high-pitched humming sound came from the smoke and occasional flashes of white faces could be seen, the eyes wide in terror.

"What has happened?" one called. The fear in the voice covered any traces of rage and hatred.

"This solar system has just moved ahead in time by one second," Mickie said. "After doing it to a whole galaxy, do you think it was a difficult task for the Pfafth agents to accomplish for just one little sun and a few planets?"

He turned round and looked at each of the pillars in turn. "You can't teleport, you can never cross the barrier of that one second of time. Nothing can come and rescue you. You're here for eternity or as long as you survive. There's no other life on this planet for you to rule, except for birds and insects. Enjoy your new empire."

He turned to face Melkana. They were still holding hands. Keeping his senses tuned to the Sillaron, but seeing nothing but increasingly helpless panic, he smiled at her.

"I think we're done here," he said.

"Time to go home," she agreed, also smiling.

"Something we need to do first," he said.

"Probably."

Still smiling, he kissed her lightly on the mouth. It tasted like the first time he had drunk *Sle'Ach*.

He and Melkana leaped away to the edge of the black band of Nothing that had appeared between the solar system and the rest of the Universe. A few moments later they had crossed Time and they were back on the Ship.

Chapter 21 – Finale

"One tiny solar system out of the entire Universe won't affect the balance," Mickie said. "That's what Mister Brown assured us. And the ten Sillaron Masters were manufactured, they weren't really part of the Sillaron species, so there's no imbalance with them gone, either."

"Brandon was back on home world over the last two weeks," Melkana joined in. "The Management Committee seems to have recovered its senses and agreed to start up a University with lecturers from several species to start introducing the Pfafth to the Universe. More schools will follow."

"What about the general state of the people there?" Allie asked.

"Shamefaced, Brandon said," Melkana replied. "They can't understand how they went so nutty."

"Can they remember seeing the Sillaron Masters?" Grant asked curiously.

"Brandon says not. They're all a lot confused and embarrassed."

"Is there any interest in rediscovering their old Pfafth powers?" Fencris asked. "As we Cassoleans have learned, that can be a dangerous process."

"Just a few, Brandon reported," Mickie said. "Some of the agents are going to set up a training school for a couple of hundred. They say that any Pfafth with the old powers could be really useful as messengers, guardians and, I suppose, secret agents for people who still need those sorts of things."

"So is there any opportunity for trading with them?" Grant seemed doubtful, though he grinned at the round of laughter his question received.

"Always the businessman!" Allie chuckled. "But he's right, nonetheless. Is there anything we can trade?"

"Actually, yes!" Fencris was eager. "That quantum mechanics thing we were talking about, the ones in the robots. I had a look at the communications device and it really did work. We could develop it further so it becomes a remote control device for any piece of equipment, or a shuttle, or anything at all, and it works instantaneously, regardless of distance. I'd love to work on that project."

Grant became thoughtful. "Legally, the Pfafth would still own the license to them. If we bought that licence, what would they want in return?"

"Almost everything we sell," Allie said. "They've gone back a long way in many technologies. They could use computers, medicines..."

"And coffee!" Mickie broke in. "That stuff I had there was just *awful*! They'd go crazy for Mayoowani coffee!"

"I'll get onto that immediately," Grant said. He walked through the cabin toward his study. "Speaker 356, will you connect me to the Chairman of the Pfafth Management...." he said before the closing door cut off his words.

There was a short silence in the cabin.

"So what happens from here?" Mickie finally asked.

"A normal life, I hope," Allie replied. "School for you kids, growing up, trading for us, and maybe think about what you want to do in another three or four years."

"And trombone lessons for Mickie!" Melkana said with a grin. "He really, *really* needs them!"

Mickie blew her a gently raspberry. "But yes, what she said," he agreed. "A normal life, please."

"You've no interest, either of you, in going back to help the Pfafth rejoin the Universe?" Allie asked. She looked worried.

"None!" Mickie and Melkana spoke together then laughed.

"No, none," Melkana carried on. "Our home is on the Ship, with all of you. We're Kalamosians, not Pfafth."

"I agree," Mickie said. "Hey, where's Drellion?"

"At Gravity-Ball practice," Fencris replied. "He should be done about now."

"You think he'll still play Loopies with us peasants?"

"I think so!" Fencris laughed and his eyes gleamed bright red.

"Then the last one to Hangar Ten is a dead yurkel!" Mickie yelled and raced for the door before the others could get to their feet.

www.ingramcontent.com/pod-product-compliance
Lightning Source LLC
Chambersburg PA
CBHW062138170626
46813CB00002B/739